Before the *Larkspur Blooms*

Also by Caroline Fyffe

Where the Wind Blows

Before *the* Larkspur Blooms

Caroline Fyffe

Montlake
Romance

Text copyright © 2013 Caroline Fyffe

Published by Montlake Romance
PO Box 400818
Las Vegas, NV 89140

ISBN-13: 9781612187136
ISBN-10: 1612187137

Dedicated to my dear sister, Sherry Harm, with love.

CHAPTER ONE

Logan Meadows, Wyoming Territory, May 1881

A powerful kick of emotion almost dropped Thom Donovan to his knees. *Finally!* After eight long years—he was home.

He stopped for a moment on the side of the deserted country road and stared at the Red Rooster Inn just ahead. The rooster-shaped iron weathervane on the steep-thatched roof and the crudely cut logs separated by a ten-inch white chink made his heart thump against his rib cage. The boardinghouse was more welcome than a spanking-new calf on Christmas Day.

Logan Meadows, the town he'd been raised in and his hope for a new beginning, was just around the next bend. He pictured lifting his ma into his arms and swinging her around. She'd laugh and kiss his cheek. And Pa? Well, he wasn't quite sure what his father's reaction would be. Thom would ask his forgiveness. Tell him how sorry he was for the trouble he'd caused.

Best not to get ahead of himself. Thom gave himself a mental shake and walked on. It wasn't until he passed directly in front of the inn's porch that he noticed the beaten-up old sign he remembered from his youth. The proprietor's name had been struck through and "Violet Hollyhock" written in below. He frowned, and in his perusal, he almost missed the old woman sitting in one of the rockers. Her shawl, tight around her scrawny shoulders, covered a blue-and-brown calico dress buttoned right up under her chin. Her eyes were alight with curiosity.

"You look mighty thirsty, young man," she called in a scratchy voice. "Why not stop a spell and wet your whistle?" She waved a skinny arm at the chair next to hers. "Come sit and I'll pour ya a cool glass of the best lemonade ya ever tasted."

Thom smiled and shook his head. "That's a kind offer, ma'am, but I have an appointment in town I have to keep." At the thought, a boulder wedged in the pit of his stomach. "Thank you all the same, though." When her eyes dimmed in disappointment, he quickly added, "But I may stop back by another time. It's been years since I've tasted lemonade."

Actually, the twenty-four hours since his last meal had his insides completely twisted. He'd walked the entire way from his drop spot in New Meringue, some fifteen miles, with only a drink from a nearby stream. His throat felt no better than sawdust, but he knew better than to deviate from his instructions.

After several minutes, he rounded the corner onto Main Street and stopped on the wide boardwalk. Logan Meadows had grown. Was growing now, it seemed. The hustle and bustle looked inviting—a sense of community, belonging, made him stand there for an entire minute, taking it all in. *Time to pick up the pieces of my life.*

A burly man carrying boards on his shoulder crossed the street from the lumber mill and disappeared into an alley. Horses dozed in the sun. As two wagons passed in the road, the driver of one doffed his hat to the occupants of the other. Several men hammered away on the roof of the saloon. The once-sleepy town of Logan Meadows had come to life and the nail-pounding activity had the town in a stir.

Thom continued on, knowing no one would recognize him. He'd left a boy and returned a man. He glanced across the street at the mercantile. Scents of pine oil, tobacco, and candles being dipped all flitted through his mind. The recollection of molasses brought welcome moisture to his mouth, and sounds of childish laughter reverberated in his head as he recalled the row of thick glass jars filled with all sorts of colorful confections. He blinked, and the images evaporated into the air.

Surprisingly, old Mrs. Miller, the owner of the mercantile and as prune-faced as ever, was still alive and out sweeping the boardwalk. She stopped and stared at him, clearly unmindful of her rudeness, then waved her broom to shoo away two scraggly boys kicking an old can back and forth across the wooden slats.

Thom crossed the alley and stepped back on the boardwalk. He'd taken only a few steps when the dented can shot through his feet, almost tripping him, and slid under the doors of the Bright Nugget Saloon. The dirtier of the two urchins tried to scramble past in pursuit, but Thom caught him by his small shoulders. "Let me, son. A saloon is no place for such a young lad."

"You sure, mister?" the boy said timidly. He kicked at the ground with a well-worn boot and glanced in the direction of the mercantile, probably hoping to avoid Mrs. Miller's broom.

Thom ruffled the kid's thick mass of blond hair. "Sure I'm sure. Us men have got to stick together, right?" He winked. "Now, wait here, and I'll be right back."

Pushing through the swinging doors, Thom let his eyes adjust. The saloon was dark in contrast to the sunny day. Music and carefree laughter careened around the room. Waitresses served drinks to the occupied tables and flirted with the men at the bar. Remembering the reason he was there, he bent and picked up the can. As he turned to leave, he froze. A cowboy with a large bowed nose threw down his poker hand and hooted, collecting the pile of dollar bills and coins from the middle of the table.

Anger flooded Thom's body, and a buzzing hummed in his ears. That nose could belong to only one man: Rome Littleton. A hundred times Thom had dreamed of wrapping his hands around the cur's throat and slowly squeezing the life out of him. What was

Rome doing in Logan Meadows? Whatever the reason, it couldn't be good.

He took a step toward the poker table and stopped. As much as he hated to admit it—he had to leave it go. Reining in his temper, he walked out, handed the can to the boy waiting in the street, and headed toward the sheriff's office next door.

The medium-size jailhouse looked as if it had suffered a fire at one time. Thom yanked open the thick oak door and stepped through. Two men looked up.

The loose-fitting pants, a parting gift from the penitentiary up in Deer Creek, suddenly felt awkward. Thom ran his left palm around the inside of his waistband, making sure his ragged shirt was properly tucked in.

Sheriff Albert Preston, presumably the current sheriff because of the silver star pinned to his vest and the name on the wall, sat at the desk. Across the room in one of the open cells, another fellow was stretched out on a cot, his fingers laced behind his head and his boots propped up on the metal end post.

The sheriff took in Thom's ragged appearance, and his eyes narrowed a bit. His hand stilled from whatever he was writing.

Thinks I'm a beggar looking for a handout.

"May I help you?"

"I was told to check in with you when I got to town."

The sheriff stood. The other fellow sat up and then came out of the cell. *Dwight Hoskins*—Thom immediately recognized him. The sorry excuse of a human being had gone from shifty-eyed youth to full-grown man. He had a silver star, too. *Damn.* Bad luck running into him first thing.

"You have something to say or not, *tramp*?" Dwight asked.

"Be quiet." The sheriff shot his deputy a reproving look. He came around his desk and waited.

"My name is Thom—"

"Donovan!" Dwight blurted. He rocked back on his heels. "I knew you looked familiar. Wait a minute, your twelve years for

4

rustling aren't up yet. Why, it's only been—" He held his hand out and started counting his fingers under his breath.

"Eight," Thom supplied, after Dwight had started over twice. "Got time off." It galled him to tell Dwight anything, but soon the whole town would know, so what difference did it make?

Dwight gawked. "Look at you!" He reached out to touch Thom's tattered shirt, but Thom knocked his hand away.

Dwight's eyes went wide as nervous tension exploded across Thom's back. *You better be scared. I'm no longer the same Irish lad you enjoyed pushing around every chance you got.* Countless times during their youth, Dwight, a year older and many pounds heavier, had knocked Thom into the dirt, laughing and calling him names. He'd stolen food from his lunch pail. Messed up his schoolwork. Worse yet, he'd made up lies about the Donovan family, claiming they were broke and living off loans, and he'd even spread unclean talk about Anne Marie, Thom's baby sister.

Their gazes locked.

A sneer appeared on Dwight's face. "I could lock you up right now, Donovan. For threatening a deputy." He gestured to the vacant cell a few feet away. "Want to head back to the clink?" He laughed, but Thom noticed he'd stepped back, giving him space.

"Dwight, be quiet!" the sheriff barked. He took a deep breath, then turned back to Thom. "You're Loughlan Donovan's youngest boy?"

"Yes, sir." Thom stood straight. The encounter with Dwight had his blood pumping hot. *Dwight. A bottle of ink. The new shirt his mother had made, ruined.*

The sheriff ran a hand through his hair, then returned to his seat. "That's right. I got a letter a few months back from the warden saying you'd be getting out soon." He took a key from his pocket and unlocked a drawer in his desk. He found the letter and skimmed down the sheet. "What're your plans?" he finally asked.

"The mick sure ain't staying in Logan Meadows," Dwight said. "This town is for law-abiding citizens. Not rustlers and thieves."

The sheriff sighed loudly. "Am I going to have to embarrass you in front of this gentleman, Deputy? Go take a walk so Mr. Donovan and I can have a civil conversation."

Dwight's face flamed crimson.

"Go on. And don't be running your mouth off to anyone who'll listen. You understand?" Preston waited until Dwight left, then gestured to a row of vacant chairs. "Pull one up."

Uncomfortably, Thom did. He seated himself and waited to be spoken to, a lesson he had learned well up in Deer Creek. The sheriff seemed fair-minded. He had a good face, kind eyes. Surprising for a man in his line of work. Thom was used to the harsh treatment of guards who were just plain mean. This sheriff seemed different. He was only in his late twenties, a handful of years older than Thom himself, if he were to guess.

"Well? What're your plans? Do you have any?"

"I'm going out to the farm. My family isn't aware I'm coming home—that is, unless you've told them." A pained expression on Sheriff Preston's face made Thom swallow. "There's always work to be done. Pa's getting on in—"

"Mr. Donovan—"

"Please, call me Thom."

"Thom, your pa passed on three years ago. I'm sorry. I should have made sure that you were informed. Your mother about two months ago, right before I got the letter from the warden about your release."

A knifelike pain sliced through his core. *Ma! Pa! Both... dead?* Thom winced and turned away. He struggled to control his composure, blinking away the moisture gathering in his eyes. *It can't be.*

He stood abruptly and moved to the window, gazing out but not seeing anything. His last memory of his father was the ugly shouting match they'd had the day Thom had left home.

He felt the sheriff's gaze on his back and realized he had not responded. "What about the rest of them?" His vocal cords were strangling steel fingers as he struggled to get the words out. "Roland and Anne Marie?"

"Your sister married and went north somewhere. Can't give you a name or a place. Your brother died several months back, before your mother—shot in the saloon. Some sort of dispute. You'll find his grave in the cemetery next to your parents'."

Thom leaned his forehead against the cool glass, not wanting to think. Just like that—the Donovan family all but wiped out. "Eight years is a long time," he said. "But I wasn't expecting this."

"I'm sure you weren't. Do you have any money?"

Thom shook his head, turned to face the sheriff. "I did plenty of carpentry work while I was locked up but never got paid for any of it."

"I didn't think so. That may present a problem."

"What about the farm? Used to be we weren't rich, but the place prospered, at least a little."

"We've had a couple of droughts. Your pa seemed to lose his will for farming. When he died, there wasn't anyone to make the payment. After your mother passed, the title went back to the bank. If a young couple hadn't just bought it, I'm sure the bank manager, Frank Lloyd, would have tried to work something out with you. The land's in bad shape."

So much for starting fresh.

"You're going to need a way to support yourself."

Thom glanced at the vacant cells so close by. The doors gaped open like the smile on some ghoulish clown face…mocking, dingy, damp.

"My brother owns the livery and forge and is in the process of expanding. Just yesterday he mentioned something about needing help. I'll see if he's willing to hire you. If not, there are other opportunities in town with the possibility of the railroad coming through."

"I'm much obliged," Thom said. The ticking of a clock on the wall felt like hammer blows to his heart. "Why are you so willing to help, Sheriff? Me, an ex-convict."

Albert Preston cocked his head. "Maybe it's what the warden said, you being so young when your problems started. And I respected your parents. They were good people. Every man deserves a second chance, if he pays for his crime. You've paid for yours."

It really stuck in Thom's craw. He wasn't guilty, but there was no way to prove it. Still, he felt compelled to defend himself to the sheriff. "I want you to know I'm innocent of the charges. I didn't know the Colorado outfit I signed on with was rustling cattle. By the time I did, it was too late." But Rome Littleton had known. He had hired a scared, fifteen-year-old boy who was trying to outrun his remorse and pain, knowing that they were breaking the law. Littleton had gotten away, while all the others had been strung up immediately. Whether or not they deserved their punishment was between them and God, but for Thom, eight years in the penitentiary was a heck of a price to pay for being in the wrong place at the wrong time.

"The letter from the warden states that you were shot when the gang was apprehended."

"That's right. Before I realized who I was riding with, one of the rustlers drew on the posse that had stopped us. I tried to save one of 'em and took the bullet myself. It was the son of the sheriff I'd saved, and because of that they didn't hang me with the rest. They took me to a doctor, and from there I was tried and sent up to Deer Creek. The bullet still rests in the base of my skull."

The sheriff whistled.

"Doctor said it was the thick sheepskin coat that saved my life."

"It's still there?"

Thom nodded. "Can't do anything about it. I could wake up paralyzed or dead at any time. Or I could go blind." He resisted the urge to reach up and finger the spot he knew so well. "I'd appreciate it if this stayed between you and me. It's no one's business but mine. I don't want anyone's pity." Without warning, his stomach growled loudly.

The sheriff nodded, then replaced the letter and locked the drawer. He stood and reached for his black Stetson hanging on the hat rack. "How about some lunch? I don't know about you, but I have a powerful hunger today. Afterward, we'll go over to the livery and talk with Winthrop, then ride out to the farm. I'm sure you'd like to see it."

"I don't want charity, Sheriff. I'll work—"

The man chuckled, compassion coloring his tone. "I assure you, I can spare twenty-five cents for your meal. If it will make you feel better, consider it a loan until you can pay me back. You need some meat on those bones." He settled his hat firmly on his head. "I have a good mind to write that warden and tell him to be a little more generous with the vittles."

With a heavy heart, Thom followed the sheriff out the door and into the sunlight, amazed again to actually be home, in Logan Meadows. The optimism he had felt at first seeing the Red Rooster was gone. His family, gone. Any hope he may have entertained about his future was all but gone, too. But if the past eight years had taught him anything, it was that he would do whatever it took to survive.

CHAPTER TWO

*H*ere you are." Hannah Hoskins set one bowl of stew before Gabe Garrison and the other in front of his friend Jake. She rolled her weight off the sore pads of her feet to her heels and wiggled her cramped toes. The new boots she had ordered would have to wait—business was dismal. She was just scraping by. All she could do was pray that things would pick up when the railroad— *if* the railroad—came through. Until then, she'd have to cut back on everything that wasn't absolutely essential—like new boots. How she'd rein in her mother's excessive spending, though, gave her pause.

"Thanks, Hannah. That looks delicious." Gabe rubbed his hands together, then put his face over the bowl and took an extended whiff, closing his eyes in appreciation. One thing about Gabe, he always appreciated a good plateful of food.

Jake smiled shyly before looking away. Where Gabe was clean-shaven and combed, Jake was wild. Not unkempt, just his own man, as she liked to think. He stepped to a different drum. Local boys now, they had come to town three years ago with Chase and Jessie Logan, and the Logans' little girl, Sarah. The family had expanded when Shane was born the following year.

Hannah peeked under the napkin in the breadbasket to make sure they had enough biscuits. "Tell Jessie that Markus is over his cold and is full of vim and vigor. Any day she wants to bring Sarah into town to play is fine."

"Will do," Gabe mumbled around a mouthful of stew.

Hannah laughed. "You boys always cheer me up. Let me know if you need anything else."

"We're hardly boys," Jake said softly. "I'm nineteen, almost the same age as you."

Was Jake puffing out his chest? If she didn't know better, she'd think he was flirting. The gaze he leveled at her stopped her in her tracks, and her cheeks actually felt warm. "I may only be one year your elder, Jake, but don't forget I'm a mama, too. Because of Markus I've grown up fast." She smiled to soften her words, but before she could say anything else, the door opened.

"I'll be right with you, Sheriff," she called as Albert entered the restaurant and hung his hat on the rack. A tall fellow dressed in raggedy clothes followed close behind, and something about him caught Hannah's attention. Was it the way he walked? Well, solving that mystery would have to wait. While she refilled the water glass of her one other customer, the men seated themselves at the table by the window.

"Susanna," she called out. "Albert's here." The antique Dutch pendulum clock above the wooden sideboard chimed twelve noon. "Can you believe it? He's right on time."

Walking over to the table, she said, "Good day, Sheriff." Then she looked at the stranger, and deep black eyes met hers. A momentary bolt of confusion rocked her.

"I'm hungry as a horse," Albert replied. "What're the specials?"

She quickly gathered her composure. "Let's see." She looked down at her notepad to break the gaze from those eyes. "Cottage pie topped with breadcrumbs, baked chicken, one order of liver and onions, and the usual beef stew. The latter has lots of meat and potatoes. What sounds good?"

"I'll have stew. I can smell Gabe and Jake's all the way over here. What about you, Thom?"

Hannah snapped up straight. The sharp intake of her breath couldn't have been more obvious.

Thomas Winslow Donovan in the flesh!

Yes, of course, why hadn't she seen it sooner? His silky chestnut locks were cropped short and he was thin—awfully thin. A shadow of a beard had replaced the baby-soft chick fuzz that had once covered his square jaw, but heaven's saints above, Thom was home! She took a good, long, heart-shuddering look, slowly drinking in his every detail. If they had been alone, she would have thrown herself into his arms and hugged him until he got mad, just like old times.

"Up you go," Thom said, lifting her from the dry, sun-scorched July dirt after she'd fallen from her saddle. She was seven and he was ten. He dried her tears with the tail of his shirt. "Are you hurt?" he asked on bended knee, turning her around, checking for scrapes and bruises. "Nope, you're good as new. Takes more than a little fall to hurt you, Hannah-Bobanna." He stood, and his smile sent a strange fluttery feeling rolling around in her heart, making her cheeks heat almost painfully. From that moment on, Thom was more than the brother of her best friend—he was her champion, and she found herself looking for him before school and after, and every moment in between.

A slight quiver took over her hands, so she locked them behind her back as she pushed away the memories. "Hello, Thom," she finally made herself say, trying to act nonchalant but failing miserably. He looked up at her with that haunted black gaze. "It's mighty nice to see you," she said. "When did you get back?"

His eyes roamed her face briefly before he glanced away. "Just today. A few minutes ago, actually."

Sheriff Preston grinned. "You two know each other? Well, fine. Hannah Hoskins owns the Silky Hen, Thom. A big responsibility for such a slip of a girl. But don't let her small stature fool you. She's strong as an ox and twice—no—thrice as cantankerous."

"Sheriff Preston! Being a cantankerous ox is hardly how a woman wants to be thought of." She laughed, but she didn't miss the muscle clenching at the side of Thom's jaw when Albert mentioned her last name.

"You and Dwight?" he asked. "You were Hannah Brown the last time I saw you."

His voice was still honey-warm, slow, and thoughtful. How she used to hang on each and every word that came out of his mouth. Even though his hair was now short, she remembered it ruffling in the breeze as they walked home from school, the warm scents of dry earth and brittle grass filling the air. Their group of friends was always the same: Thom, his older brother, Roland, Anne Marie, and Hannah. Levi Smith walked with them, too, even though he was Dwight's friend and a bit callous. He lived past their farms on the same road. Occasionally Caleb joined them when he was coming out to visit. Caleb and Levi loved to tease. They would snatch one of her books, or slate, tossing it back and forth to keep it from her until Thom stepped in to intervene. It was all done in fun, but she used to fantasize that Thom defended her because he secretly adored her as much as she did him. Other times, she and Anne Marie would lock arms and totally ignore the boys, walking along behind them in quiet conversation.

All those good times. So long ago. She dropped her hands to her hips. "Dwight? You know me better than that. No, not Dwight. His cousin Caleb. We weren't married long, God rest his soul. Four months to the day of our wedding. He caught the flu and passed on." She paused, remembering the day. "It was terrible. That was a little over five years ago."

Thom's expression was unreadable; he glanced down at his hands resting on the tabletop. He and Caleb had been close. Even though Caleb lived in town and Thom on the farm next to hers, the two boys were often together with their heads bent over some book or playing a game of chess. Where Thom was dark, Caleb had been fair, but as opposite as they could be in external things, their hearts seemed to be cut from the same cloth. It was natural Thom would take the news of his friend's passing hard. *Has he been told yet about his own family?*

"I'm sorry. I shouldn't have just blurted the news about Caleb like that." She cleared her throat softly. "The restaurant was his pa's, if you remember. When he passed on, being Caleb was the only child, it went to him. We have a small son, so someday, if things go as they should"—*and I can keep it afloat*—"he'll inherit it, too." She glanced back toward the kitchen, wishing Susanna would come to her rescue. She was babbling on like an idiot and sounded crass, all this talk about money and dying and such, but she didn't know what else to say. As much as she used to dream about Thom and his wide shoulders and dashing smile, she'd eventually convinced herself that he never even knew she existed except as his little sister's pesky best friend. Taking a deep breath, she glanced into his face to see what, if anything, he was thinking.

Before Thom could respond, the kitchen door swung open and Susanna hurried over to join them. Tall and slender, she looked pretty in her dress and apron. Her wavy black hair was piled high on her head. She set a small plate of something that looked like a cross between custard and cobbler in front of Albert. "I need you to taste that." Finally noticing Thom, she smiled and gave him a quick once-over.

"What is it?" Albert took the spoon and scooped out a large bite. He brought it to his nose. "Smells good."

As Albert tried Susanna's new creation, Hannah couldn't stop herself from looking at Thom again. Their eyes met and held. She reminded herself to breathe.

"Susanna," Hannah said, gently tugging her sleeve to get her attention. "This is Thom. Thom Donovan. Do you remember me telling you how he used to be the smartest boy in class? I can't remember a time he ever missed a spelling word or math problem—not even once. He was—"

Thom cleared his throat self-consciously, but he seemed to relax a little. "You're exaggerating, Hannah. If you want to bring up the past, *I* recall going out to spend a leisurely day at the fishing hole. All was fine until a strange sound caught my attention—something of a grunt—and I went to investigate. I was rewarded with a pinecone painfully cutting my scalp open."

Hannah gasped and then laughed. "I've apologized for that more times than I can count. When are you going to forgive me?"

"Did she throw it at you?" Susanna asked incredulously. Her large eyes were riveted on her friend.

A slow smile crept over Thom's face. "No. She was sitting on a branch at the top of a pine tree, spying on me. She hadn't realized just how high she'd climbed until a breeze came up and the branch she was perched on began to sway. She was terrified to come down."

Hannah nodded, willing herself not to blush. "That's right. After Thom found me, he climbed up, bloody head and all. I was so scared and embarrassed I started to cry. It took him hours to coax me down."

"What exactly is this?" Albert interrupted, pointing to the dessert. "The texture is quite different. A bit lumpy."

Susanna whisked it off the table. "It's in the experimentation stage. I'll tell you later." She turned for the kitchen. "Hmmmm, texture. Lumpy..." she mumbled as she walked away.

The brief distraction was enough for Hannah to find her footing and calm her jittery nerves. "Now, what were you saying?" she asked, picking up where they had left off. "Stew for you, Albert. What about you, Thom?"

"The same for me."

She could tell he was happy to see her, too. His expression had softened, and a light had come into his eyes. She'd cried for days, even months, after he'd left. By then, she'd been twelve and him fifteen. He was her first love, her only love, even if he'd never known it. Finally, Anne Marie had had enough and had given her a stern talking-to. Then the horrible news had come about him going to prison. One year grew into two, then three. Thoughts and dreams of Thom ever coming home faded. Now, here he was again, as if the past had never happened. Except it had. So much had changed. She wondered if he even knew the extent of it all.

"Albert, your usual cup of black coffee?" He nodded, and she looked at Thom. But he'd slipped off into his thoughts and seemed a million miles away. "Thom?" she asked. "Would you like coffee, too?"

He blinked. His expression was hard. "Sure." It came out gruffly, and she wondered at the reason. Yes, much had changed. And not just here in Logan Meadows.

CHAPTER THREE

$\mathscr{J}$essie Logan hummed softly as she moved about the large front room of the ranch house, dusting cloth in hand. Shane had finally given up his babbling and fallen asleep, which gave her precious little time to get things in order before Chase showed up hungry as a horse and wanting his noon meal.

At the mantel she paused, set her cloth aside, and picked up the small wooden picture frame that held the infant-size woolen bootie she had knitted for Sarah all those years ago in the New Mexico orphanage. She'd kept it with her since the day she'd left the horrible place, traveled north to Wyoming on the orphan train, married Nathan, met Chase after Nathan's death, and married him—all so she could be reunited with Sarah and adopt her.

She held the framed bootie to her chest and closed her eyes, tamping down the panic that washed through her at the thought of the letter she had received from Mrs. Hobbs, the mistress of the drafty old orphan's house. A mystery of sorts was brewing over a woman who had visited there. Jessie had yet to share the news with Chase. No use both of them fretting.

Bitterness toward Mrs. Hobbs, the woman who had treated Jessie and all the other children so cruelly, bubbled up inside her. The time the old crow sent Sarah to the root cellar to be taught a lesson still had the power to infuriate. She would not be surprised if the letter was some sort of mean-spirited prank just to upset her. She set the keepsake back on the mantel, vowing not to let Mrs.

Hobbs have any more control over her happiness. In all actuality, it was probably nothing at all.

"Mommy, I need help," Sarah called from her spot at the kitchen table. The child's slender legs hung six inches from the floor as she practiced writing the alphabet. "I can't make the tail of Mr. Y go like a fishhook. It's squiggly like a worm. Something's wrong."

When she'd married Chase, he couldn't read a word. Now, after months of Jessie's instruction, he was not only literate, but also an enormous lover of books. He took great interest in learning new words every night. Two years ago, when Sarah had turned five, he had taken on the task of teaching her her letters himself. Every time Jessie witnessed his abiding patience with Sarah, she nearly burst with love. Next year, when Sarah was old enough to go to school in town, the child would already know all her letters and would be reading simple sentences.

"Let me see." Jessie leaned over her daughter's small shoulder, her heart swelling. Sarah's waist-length nut-brown hair was brushed to a high sheen and her little hands worked busily as if her assignment was of the utmost importance. "Why, you've just turned the fishhook in the wrong direction. Try it again the other way."

A horse nickered outside. Going to the window, Jessie saw Chase tying Cody, his bay gelding, to the hitching rail. He stroked the horse once on the neck and headed for the back door. It wasn't but a moment before the door opened. "Anyone home?" he called out playfully.

Jessie rushed to shush him. "Quiet, please," she said, slipping into his arms. "Your son has finally decided to give me a break. I don't want you waking him before I get a few more things accomplished."

"Is that so?"

Jessie ran her hands up the chilly fabric of Chase's vest, admiring the dark flecks of gold in his expressive brown eyes. He pulled

BEFORE THE LARKSPUR BLOOMS

her close as he lowered his face to hers. *Even after three years of marriage, he still makes my heart flutter around like a newly hatched butterfly.*

Chase brushed a soft kiss across her lips. "And just what are those things that need doing?" He chuckled and kissed her neck.

She tried to sound annoyed. "You may think I don't do all that much, but if I ever stopped doing them, you'd be surprised how fast this home fell down around your e-e-ears."

She struggled to get the last word out coherently. He was trailing warm kisses around her earlobe, making it impossible to think of anything but him.

"Oh, I'm sure it would, honey. I don't doubt that for a second. And to tell you the truth, I'd hate to find out." He pulled back and put his nose in the air. "I smell something good. What's cooking?"

She smacked him on the chest. "Is that all you ever think about, Chase Logan, what you'll be eating for your next meal?"

He tented his brows. The look he gave her said she was his next meal.

Instantly, her insides warmed. She couldn't hide the smile that tugged at the corners of her mouth. She turned and preceded him into the kitchen, where Sarah still worked at the table.

Chase hooked his hat on one of the brass wall pegs, then started for Sarah. Before he reached the table, she turned and lifted up the slate she'd been working on. "Look, Pa. I finished the whole alphabet."

He took the slate from her hands and studied every letter. "You sure did, pumpkin. And you did a mighty fine job." He leaned down and kissed the top of her head. Sarah's smile revealed a missing front tooth. There wasn't a man in the world who could love the child more than he did.

"Where're Gabe and Jake?" Jessie asked as Chase got comfortable at the table. "I thought they were coming here for lunch." With thick cotton mitts, she opened the heavy oven door and extracted a plate heaped full of shepherd's pie. Steam wafted up when she set it in front of Chase.

"Actually, no. They went into town, said they wanted to see if there was any new Union Pacific news. I think Jake just wanted to get another moment with Hannah. That boy's acting like a love-sick pup."

Jessie shook her head. "I hope not. I don't think she feels anything more for him than friendship. Not only that, Mrs. Brown doesn't think any man is good enough to wipe her daughter's boots, let alone marry her now that Caleb has passed on." Her spine stiffened at the thought of going up against Hannah's mother for any reason. "I'd hate for Jake to get hurt."

"It's bound to happen sooner or later. Part of growing up."

She poured a tall glass of fresh water and put it on the table beside Chase's meal. "I know. Still, I think he harbors a lot of pain inside that he doesn't share. I just wish both he and Gabe would find nice young women to settle with."

Chase swallowed and then wiped his mouth with his napkin. "They're young yet, sweetheart. Give 'em some time to sow a few wild oats."

"Chase!" She glanced at Sarah, who was still playing with her chalk and slate. When he didn't seem to catch her meaning or pointed look, she aimed the biscuit she was holding and threw it playfully at his head. He snatched it out of the air before it hit him.

He smiled and took an exaggerated bite. "It's true," he went on, not missing a beat. "Why, I found Jake in the saloon the other day talking with Daisy and Philomena."

"You did?" Sadness for the two young women who worked at the Bright Nugget surfaced. She had once faced the possibility of saloon work. Thank goodness Nathan had taken pity all those years ago and married her. Whoring was a bad business—for the girls and for the men who used them. "That worries me, considering the life he left behind in Valley Springs and all he suffered before he moved to Logan Meadows with us. I know his mother had a hard life, but she treated him very badly. I witnessed her screaming from the saloon balcony, half-dressed, calling him every sort of horrible name as he walked down the street. If it weren't for Mrs. Hollyhock..." She stopped and pulled herself together. "Why do you think he was in the saloon?"

Chase swallowed. "It's obvious—and surely not a crime. He wanted to talk to some pretty girls. Don't worry so much, Jessie. It's part of life, and you can't change it—as much as I know you'd like to."

"I hope he doesn't take to drinking and gambling."

Chase took another bite and said while he chewed, "I never said anything about drinking and gambling." He tossed Jessie a look that said he had everything under control and for her to butt out.

A loud knock at the front door reverberated to the kitchen, followed by a cry from Shane's room.

"Oh, no. He won't go back to sleep now."

"I'll see who it is," Chase said as he wiped his mouth and stood.

While he went to the door, Jessie hurried to the baby's room. Two-year-old Shane sat in his pinewood crib rubbing his watery eyes. His soft light-brown hair, sprinkled with Jessie's golden highlights, curled over his forehead and down his neck, moist from his nap. His bottom lip protruded unhappily. When he saw her, he lifted his arms, then released a smile identical to his father's. Jessie laughed and picked him up, patting his back. "Come on, you little charmer," she said, heading toward the kitchen.

Chase was back in his seat finishing his meal. "Who was it?" Jessie asked. She sat, and Chase leaned forward to rub the baby's head.

"One of the hands. Wanted to tell me the new heifers have settled in fine with our herd and that he's going into town after he eats. Talk of the railroad has everyone keyed up."

Shane gurgled and looked around happily. "It's exciting that the train might actually come to Logan Meadows," Jessie said. "It was only last year that we got a daily stage coming through, and now this." She kissed Shane's cheek and bounced him on her knee. *But it will put us so much closer to New Mexico, too. And Mrs. Hobbs. And whoever that person is who's looking for Sarah.* "Do you think it will actually happen?"

Chase chuckled. "It will if Frank Lloyd has anything to say about it. He's dreaming about all the money the newcomers will be depositing into his bank. Plus, he's making loans right and left to business owners fixing up their places in hopes the Union Pacific will pick Logan Meadows."

"What if the railroad decides in favor of New Meringue instead of Logan Meadows?" Jessie sat forward and brushed a few wisps of hair from Sarah's face, not wanting her to feel left out. The child had stopped playing when the conversation had taken on a more serious tone, and she was listening to every word. "Everyone will be so disappointed. I love our small town, Chase. Logan Meadows is the place our children will grow up and raise families of their own. Just doesn't feel right that the railroad is pitting us into competition with our neighbors. One thing is for sure...one of us is going to lose."

Chase pushed his plate away and sat back, a sated grin on his face. "But—one town is going to win. I'm in favor of the railroad and all the life it's brought to our town already. The demand for our beef and horses has doubled in the last three months and has been a boon for this ranch. New immigrants could double or even triple that number. And, let's not forget, our hefty investment on the herd we've contracted for next year *depends* on Logan Meadows winning."

Jessie nodded. "I know, I know—I'm not complaining. I hope it comes, too." But did she? It was getting harder by the day to pretend nothing was worrying her. As it was, Logan Meadows was cocooned away from the rest of the world. If this all turned out to be Mrs. Hobbs's idea of a prank, Sarah's real parents could still be out there looking for her, regretting their decision to give her away. Jessie forced herself to relax the frown pulling at her brows. She should be counting her many blessings and not looking for trouble behind every rock. "Well, I'm sure the meeting tomorrow will tell us more," she said, purposely using a cheery tone.

At the excitement in Jessie's voice, Sarah scooted over to Chase and climbed into his lap. She smoothed back his hair, a tender action she often did, then patted his shoulder. "I hope it comes, too, Pa," she said. "I've never been on a train before. Gabe said he'd make sure I rode on the eggnog ride!"

Chase chuckled softly. "You mean the inaugural ride, sugarfoot?" He glanced at Jessie, an expression of love and amusement on his face. "Although eggnog sounds pretty darn good right about now."

Sarah shivered with anticipation. "I'm going to take Patches with me. She'll be the first cat to ride the train."

Jessie gave Chase another knowing look. "See what I mean? Everyone is counting on the Union Pacific. Even little children!"

CHAPTER FOUR

*T*hom rode beside Sheriff Preston on the way from town to his family's old farm. As he surveyed the land, awe at actually being there filled his soul. All those years locked behind grimy walls, crushed in with dirty, filthy men—himself one of them—washed away. He took a deep breath of fresh country air and held it. Such a simple thing and yet so dear. The feel of the saddle and motion of the horse fed his hopeful mood. "It was kind of your brother to lend me this horse," he said, unable to pull his gaze away from the country he had missed so much. "He didn't have to do it."

A noisy cloud of sparrows raced from one tree to the next, following the men's progress.

Sheriff Preston laughed. "Well, if it's one thing Winthrop has a lot of, it's horses. You're most likely doing him a favor relieving a small portion of his responsibility." He glanced over and smiled. "You'll like working for Win. He's a good man."

The smell of the land was exactly as Thom remembered, as was the blueness of the sky. He'd missed the sky—and its sapphire shade that seemed to reach into eternity. All those hours staring up at the ceiling of his cell, he'd imagined he was right here, on this very road, going home.

They stopped on the crest overlooking the land that had once been the Donovan farm. The sheriff rested his palms, one on top of the other, on his saddle horn and stretched up to get a good look.

"There she is."

It was hard for Thom to look. The farm, one of the finest pieces of land in all of the Wyoming Territory, sat dry and fallow. The front field, which had once produced an abundance of wheat, corn, and barley, was overrun in a blanket of weeds. The dirt blew on the breeze and seemed to cry out to him with a haunted voice, admonishing him for the poor treatment it had suffered. Thom knew its potential, and the sight rocked him to his core.

"I was the son that inherited the love of the land," he said. "Roland and Anne Marie had no interest at all. They did only the chores they had to. Strange that I was the one to run off and leave it behind." The house looked small now. Run-down. Lonely.

A dog barked. Thom watched as a German shepherd crawled from beneath the front porch and glanced about.

"Ivan! He's still alive." The desperate loneliness that had enveloped him since being released dissolved at the sight of his dog.

Ivan looked to the barn and then to the corral that held two horses, not yet catching the humans' scent. He took the stairs stiffly, gave a halfhearted woof, then lay down on the porch.

"He's old," Thom said under his breath. He nudged his mount down the road.

This time, Ivan spotted them and began barking in earnest. His glossy black-and-tan coat was dull, and his muzzle sported white hair, like an old man's beard.

"Ivan. Here, boy," Thom called, dismounting. The dog tipped his head and his barking stopped. "Ivan, come."

The dog hurried down the steps as best he could, and Thom met him halfway. Bending to one knee, he wrapped his arms around the old dog's neck as Ivan whined happily, his warm tongue licking Thom's face.

"Well, I'll be. I think he remembers me," Thom said, barely getting the words past the stiffness of his throat. He hugged Ivan close to his heart and then buried his face in the thick fur, wishing it were possible to be transported back in time eight years and one day.

Time ticked by. Albert cleared his throat. "He wouldn't leave the place when your mother passed on. Hannah tried to take him to her house in town so she could care for him, but he kept running away and coming back here. Soon after, the new owners moved in and they have been seeing to his needs."

Thom nodded, the only response he could manage.

Ivan's dark eyes gazed lovingly into his. It was good to know that someone was glad he was home; someone had missed him. He thought about his mother and father and Roland, buried in the graveyard. About Anne Marie, somewhere far up north. Tears prickled behind his eyes. Taking a firm hold of his emotions, he rocked back on his heels and stared across Ivan's back in the direction of Hannah's old farm. He assumed Hannah's mother had sold it at some point, maybe when Hannah married Caleb, and they'd all moved into the house in town.

Eight years felt like a lifetime. He'd left for the shame he'd caused his family, but only later, when he was traveling alone on the road, did he realize how much more he'd lost. He'd taken with him a handkerchief Hannah had left behind on one of her visits—Hannah, who had held his happiness in the palm of her hand for as long as he could remember. Seeing her again today had brought all those feelings rushing back with force. For several fleeting seconds, time had melted away and he felt fifteen again, in love, lost in her eyes. Somewhere along the way he'd misplaced the handkerchief, maybe during the arrest or the time he'd spent recuperating, he didn't know. But he'd pictured it many times over the years, drawing from it strength to go on. He used to think prison was the worst thing in the world that could happen to him; now he knew better.

Thom stood and took one last gut-wrenching look at his childhood home. "Come on, Ivan," he said without taking his gaze off the place. "I'm not leaving you behind again."

"Markus, I'm home." Hannah stopped in the entry of the two-story, gingerbread-trimmed Victorian home and untied the sashes under her chin. She was tired. Thank goodness the restaurant wasn't far from her home on the west side of town—just over the small bridge that crossed Shady Creek and down Main Street. She hung her bonnet over the banister as she crossed the room, a drawn-out sigh escaping her lips. She collapsed into a chair. When she closed her eyes, Thom popped into her mind.

"Mommy!" Markus's voice rang out from somewhere upstairs. A door slammed. Footfalls raced across the floor.

Hannah sat up and quickly unlaced her boots. She pulled them off one by one and, as unladylike as usual, pulled her left foot into her lap, massaging out the kinks.

"I thought I heard you come in." Her mother descended the long staircase with a firm grip on Markus's little hand. His face shone with excitement as he struggled to get free.

"Hi, Mommy!" His high-pitched voice practically echoed around the room.

"My goodness." Hannah laughed. "You do have a healthy set of lungs. Come here and give your tired ole ma a hug."

He tried, but his grandmother kept a tight hold on him. "He mustn't run in the house, Hannah. When will you teach him some manners?"

"You are not old, Mommy." Markus glanced up innocently into Roberta Brown's face. "Grammy is old." Hannah had to bite the inside of her cheek to keep from laughing. Her mother, thirty-eight and a widow for six years, hardly considered herself past her prime.

Hannah set her left foot down, picked up her right, and began massaging its aches and pains.

Her mother wrinkled her nose. "Really, Hannah. Must you?"

"Yes, Mother, I must. I'm sorry if it offends your delicate sensibilities, but my old boots are ready to be thrown out. They're paper-thin, and I feel the tiniest of pebbles each time I take a step."

Almost down the staircase, Markus pulled free and leaped down the last step. He ran the last few feet to Hannah, wriggling into her lap. Shiny brown hair tickled her face, and she had to draw back quickly and rub her nose to squelch a sneeze. "So what did you do today, little man? Did you get into any trouble?"

He shook his head. "No, ma'am. I was a very good boy."

"Of course you were." She kissed one cheek and then the other, relishing the feel of her son in her arms. Markus was the center of her universe. Her reason for living.

"Young man? Are you telling a fib?" Roberta asked sternly.

Hannah kissed him again and rubbed his small back, holding back her sharp retort. *A five-year-old does not intentionally lie.* Hannah had already had that conversation with her mother several times. She hated to get off on the wrong foot again tonight. She was worn out.

Her mother seated herself opposite Hannah, her expression pulled tight like a drum. "I can see you've been told."

"Told what?"

"Don't play games with me, Hannah. News travels fast in a town this size. Your face is all rosy because of it. That *Irishman* is out of prison. I sincerely hope you're not considering picking up where you left off."

Hannah set Markus on the floor and touched the end of his nose, making him smile despite the crinkle of worry between his expressive eyebrows. Even at his tender age, he was quite astute at picking up on the unsettling undertones of a conversation.

"Where's your toy puppy?" she asked Markus. "Go find him for me, will you? I'd like to give him a pat on the head."

After Markus had gone, Hannah turned, looking her mother square in the eye. "If you remember, I was twelve when Thom left town. Hardly old enough to have something to pick up, don't you think? His sister, Anne Marie, was my best friend and our neighbor. So, yes, it's true. I did see Thom often when I visited her. Avoiding him would have been impossible."

Roberta's brows arched in disbelief, and her eyes glittered dangerously. "If that's what you want to believe, go right ahead—but I know better. All those nights weeping in your room after he left just confirmed my suspicions. You were always a-blush whenever he was around. A mother can see these things easily. You fancied yourself in love."

Hannah flushed. "Mother! I was just a girl."

"Remember, you have your son to consider. And your standing in this community. Not to mention my brother's. Frank has worked very hard to make something of this town, and his bank has played a big part in doing so. I don't want you casting any undesirable light on him by associating with trash."

Hannah stood, hardly holding her temper in check, but her mother, oblivious, continued. "You should be thankful Caleb left you with a means of support for yourself when he died."

At the mention of the restaurant, Hannah deflated. Now would be a good time to tell her mother about their lack of customers so that Roberta could consider tightening her spending habits. Her mother had run through the money from the sale of the farm long ago, to Hannah's dismay. But bringing that up would create a bigger fight, and Hannah didn't want Markus to come into the room while angry words were being exchanged. She'd save the money talk for another time soon.

Roberta sniffed and pulled her handkerchief from her sleeve. "Think good and hard before you throw away your future on someone like Mr. Donovan. You could be a prize for some gentleman. Just look at what that hooligan did when he was only a boy—he was a criminal even before he was arrested for rustling. Believe you me—that Irish thug is no gentleman!"

"Mother!"

"Don't 'Mother' me." Roberta dabbed her cheeks and neck. "Why won't you consider Dwight?" Her tone had turned pleading. "He's handsome and has a good name and—"

"Because I don't even *like* Dwight. I've told you that before." Hannah picked up her boots and walked over to place them on the bottom stair to later take up to her room.

Her mother looked down her nose knowingly. "Markus wet his bed again today during his nap. He needs the strong hand of a father or you'll turn him into a sissy. Who better than his loving uncle Dwight?" Roberta rose and headed for the door. "And that's the last word I'll say on the matter." She took her shawl from a peg. "Now that you're home, I think I'll go for a walk," she said. "Do you need anything at the mercantile?"

You're not going for a walk, but out to gossip. And it's not hard for me to guess just who you'll be talking about. "No," she said and watched Roberta leave.

Her mother's narrow-mindedness against Thom's heritage was still alive and well. It was enough to make Hannah sick. Thom's mother, Katherine Donovan, had been the most giving person Hannah had ever met. Charitable to a fault. And yet some of the townsfolk had still looked down on her until her dying day. Especially Hannah's own mother—who for years had lived right next door and had been the recipient of countless kind deeds and a Christmas Eve pie each December.

Hannah padded quickly to the door, opened it, and leaned out. "Don't be gossiping about Thom!" she called. "I mean it. He'll have a hard enough time making his way in this town as it is."

Her mother shrugged without turning. "He should have thought about that before he let that Irish temper get the best of him, don't you think?"

CHAPTER FIVE

evi turned. A knife that hadn't been there a moment before glistened in his hand. He lunged. Thom jumped back, already bloody from the fight that had started with a few taunts, and now had gone on far too long. His nose stung, and blood flowed freely down his face. Excited voices carried through the trees, shouting, getting closer. Thom ducked, then jabbed with his left, connecting with Levi's chin, knocking him off balance. Someone screamed, "Stop!" Thom leaped forward and both boys fell to the ground—

Thom jerked up in bed, sending his blanket sliding around his waist. Sweat trickled down his temples, between his shoulder blades, and along his bare chest, quickly turning cool in the morning air. Blinking, he brushed a shaky hand over his face and glanced around expecting to see bars, iron doors, dull gray walls.

Where am I?

The room felt strange, unfamiliar. Floral curtains bemused him as he grasped at consciousness. Outside a rooster crowed, followed by the long, low moo of a cow. He was somewhere in the country.

Logan Meadows.

The recognition brought an instant flood of happiness—followed by a crushing wave of guilt. And grief. *Ma. Pa. Roland.*

He lay back on his pillow and let his heart rate slow down. It had been months since he'd had the nightmare. That day Dwight and Levi had been whispering about Anne Marie just loud enough for Thom to hear. Ugly things. Untrue things. Fed up, Thom vowed to teach them once and for all they couldn't go around ruining people's names. Irish or not.

The dream always ended as he and Levi fell to the ground. Before they wrestled. Before Levi weakened and stopped, the ebony hilt of Levi's own knife protruding from the boy's side as blood gushed onto the dusty earth.

Regret made him shake his head. First Levi's death, then his arrest for rustling, when all his ma and pa ever raised him to be was honest and hardworking. Somehow, he'd clear the Donovan name of rustling. He didn't know how yet, but for his family's sake, he had to try.

A clanking noise from another room stirred him from his thoughts. A woodsy aroma that mingled with the deep, rich scent of coffee made his mouth water.

Ivan lay on the floor by his bed, gazing at him adoringly. The dog let out a low, plaintive sound as he stood and placed his head on the mattress.

"Hello, boy." Thom swallowed back the pain of the past. He raised himself onto his elbow and rubbed his dog between the ears.

Pa had brought the pup home one day, a happy, long-haired ball of energy, all feet and lapping tongue. A smile pulled at Thom's lips as he remembered Ma's none-too-pleased expression. She already had her hands full with three children, a barnyard of animals, and household chores.

A soft knock came at the door, and Ivan's head turned.

"Yes?"

The door creaked open slowly. "I thought I heard ya stirrin'. How'd ya sleep?"

Self-conscious, Thom discreetly pulled up the blanket. "I think it's the first time I've slept through the night in many years."

Mrs. Hollyhock, owner of the Red Rooster Inn, had been delighted when Thom had reappeared on her doorstep beside

Sheriff Preston last night. She'd immediately poured him the lemonade she'd offered earlier, and, in return for woodcutting and help around the inn, she'd generously offered him room and board—just until he could get on his feet, so to speak. She'd also accepted Ivan, albeit a bit grudgingly and with the warning that things might have to change if he started scaring off her would-be customers with his big teeth and wolflike appearance.

"Well, go on and get yourself dressed," she said, her eyes straying to Ivan. Thom almost chuckled when the dog seemed to duck his head. "I have your breakfast cooked and the day's a-wastin'."

When she'd left, Thom stood and pulled on his pants, shrugged into his shirt, and then washed his face at the porcelain bowl on the cabinet in the corner. The cool water was refreshing—and welcome. He ran handfuls of it over his short hair and dried his head with the clean towel, enjoying the luxury of fresh water in the privacy of his own space.

In the main room, a newly lit fire snapped and popped as it chased away the chilly air. Several hanging lamps glowed warmly, reminding Thom of his boyhood home. They showcased a lengthy couch he hadn't noticed the night before. A blue-and-yellow quilt stretched across the back, and several more hung around, decorating the walls. Several chairs and two crudely made side tables competed for space on the braided round rug, the grouping as ruggedly made as the inn itself.

So welcome was the homey sight after the years spent in prison, all Thom could do was stand there and stare. Outside, a few birds chirped, followed by the sound of wheels moving past the inn toward town.

"Best get that wolf outside before he does something he shouldn't on my floor," Mrs. Hollyhock said, marching to the heavy front door. "Afterward, you can tie him to the rope I put out back by the woodshed. I don't want the beast messin' up my place while you're at work. You understand? No whinin' from you later on sayin' you didn't get my meanin'."

Thom, still standing in the same spot, nodded. "Yes, ma'am."

"No need for formality either. You can call me Violet and I'll call you Thom, and we'll get along jist fine. There's also a few house rules I forgot to tell ya last night. No drinking spirits in your room. No cussin' or bein' belligerent. Absolutely no muddy boots. Keep your bed made and don't leave any of your personal belongings out here." Her arm swept the room. "I'll feed ya and house ya and wash your beddin'. Your clothes are your own responsibility. You can use my kettle, or if you're feeling wealthy, take 'em to the laundry in town." Finished, she pulled open the large door with both hands.

Ivan looked up at Thom questioningly. His tail moved slowly back and forth.

"Understood—Violet." As he exited, Ivan stayed close to his side. The guards at Deer Creek had nothing on the undersize, no-nonsense sentry that was Mrs. Hollyhock.

With Ivan tied up outside, Thom seated himself at the table, set with two place settings. He hadn't seen another guest, and he wondered if someone new was coming. Maybe Violet herself hadn't eaten yet? Dang, she was making him nervous—ironic, given he'd just been released from a prison filled with killers and thieves and guards with guns. He stared at the napkin folded on his plate.

She poured his coffee. "Take milk?"

"No, ma'am."

"Violet."

"Yes, ma'am, er—Violet."

A moment passed and then she laughed, a sound resembling a rattling cackle, and placed a gentle hand on his shoulder.

When he looked up into her face, she winked. "I ain't been known to bite, Thom. At least not too hard."

He let go the breath he was holding and smiled. "That's a relief. I was starting to wonder."

"I've jist been testing ya a little. Having fun at your expense, you might say. I wanted to see if you'd sass me or tell me to go to the devil. I heard you had a mean Irish temper but wanted to see for myself if it were true before believing it."

That didn't take long, Thom thought. *Dwight up to his old business?*

She went to the stove and returned with a bowl filled with cinnamon-and-butter-covered mush, four slices of bacon, and a thick piece of bread on a side plate. The mouthwatering sight played havoc on his empty stomach. Since coming home, seemed like the more he ate the hungrier he got.

"But," she added as she placed his breakfast in front of him, "I twern't joshing about the hairy beast outside." Her eyes were stern. "Now, before you run off, I'd like a day's supply of firewood chopped, enough to do some laundry. Then if you'd please fill both kettles out back with water, I'll be set for my day. I'm sure you noticed the well kitty-corner the left wall."

Thom nodded his understanding and picked up his spoon. She went back to the stove. "While you were out, I put some clothes in your room. A pair of britches, a shirt, and a fairly new hat. A shifty feller, sneaking out without paying, left 'em behind." A loud clatter filled the air as she muscled the heavy pan into a tin bucket. "If ya change into 'em after your chores, I'll give the ones you're wearing a good washing—they can use it." She held up her finger. "But jist this once, mind you. I ain't no maid."

No one ever did join them for breakfast, but with so many chores to do Thom didn't give it another thought.

A bit tired, but thoroughly satisfied with his first day of unchaperoned work in years, Thom surveyed Main Street from the front door of the livery, taking in the busy inhabitants as they went about their lives. Directly across the street, the Bright Nugget, and to its right, the sheriff's office, seemed quiet. The boy he'd met his first day smiled and waved, then kicked his can with a *thwack* and ran off in pursuit.

The sun felt good. His eyes drooped as a languid bliss seeped into his muscles after the day of hay sheering, cleaning stalls, and grooming horses. There was much to be said about working with animals. Even more to be said about being free and master of one's own ship. A bud of hopefulness sprouted in his chest.

Thom's exhaustion vanished the moment he noticed Hannah step out the door from the Silky Hen a block away and start down the boardwalk toward the livery. On her way, she paused at the mercantile window and looked inside.

His gaze ran the length of her, from her face to the boots that poked from beneath her ankle-length dress, back up to the bright-yellow bonnet that covered most of her hair. A few wayward wisps shimmered like golden sassafras in the late afternoon sun. Longing warmed his belly as he acknowledged she'd transformed from a skinny little lass into a beautiful young woman. He took a moment to admire her loveliness.

Spotting him, she waved. As she got closer her cheeks blossomed into a pretty show of pink.

"Hannah," he said, tipping the hat Violet had given him.

A bashful little grin moved her lips upward. "I was hoping I'd run into you today, Thom."

He felt suddenly shy. "Were you?" Lovesick was an understatement for what he'd felt for Hannah Brown as a kid all those years ago, although he'd never told anyone—most certainly not *her*. He was poor Irish. The Browns were quite well-off. A mountain, three prairies, and a desert lay between them, something Dwight never let him forget.

He gestured to her feet. "Did I just see you limping?"

"No," she responded too quickly. Her cheeks darkened further, reminding him of his ma's cherry-topped buttermilk cake. "You must have imagined it."

"Where're you off to?"

Her smile broadened and her eyes twinkled, giving him the impression she was up to no good. He remembered that well. She had been almost as mischievous as he had been, way back then. In the summer, just the mention of wading had her stripping off her stockings to follow the boys into the stream. *Are you still a free spirit, Hannah?*

"I'm delivering a few loaves of bread to the mercantile. We make them, put them in the store, and split the profit with Maude. She has a standing order for three loaves on Monday and another three on Thursday." Hannah pulled back the blue-checkered cloth on the basket she carried. "After that, I'm going to the town meeting."

"But the mercantile is back there, next to the restaurant."

She sputtered, embarrassed. "Well, I'm going there next. Maude was busy when I looked in the window."

"You mean ole prune face?" he teased.

"Thom, stop!" she admonished, and then softly laughed. She glanced about. "I'm too old for that kind of tomfoolery anymore. Maude is my business partner, of sorts. And I've grown up. All that silly talk is behind me."

"As it should be, I guess. But you're still the Hannah I remember." It was true. Just not the skinny little wisp of a girl part. Hannah Brown—*Hoskins*, he corrected himself—was a beautiful, desirable woman, capable, he was sure, of breaking his heart all over again.

"Irish flattery will get you nowhere, Mr. Donovan," she teased. "Before we know it we'll both have lines on our faces and our bellies will protrude out to here." She stuck out her arms, basket and all. "Life goes by in a blink of the eye."

He grinned, enjoying this not-so-chance meeting even more than a hearty lamb stew and colcannon, his favorite mashed potatoes and cabbage dish.

"How are you making out at the Red Rooster? Is Violet treating you well?" she asked, her gaze lowering briefly to his lips.

"I can't complain. The bed is soft, and she's keeping me fed."
He patted his stomach.

Hannah's smile fell away. "It's such a shame about her chickens. She was very upset when coyotes got into her henhouse last week and killed them all. She loved those birds like family."

"I didn't know."

Hannah nodded. "Day after tomorrow is her birthday. She'll be eighty-five. Can you imagine?"

Thom whistled. "I didn't realize she was that old by the way she gets around." He glanced about, remembering that he had something he wanted to tell her. "Listen, Hannah, I want to thank you for looking after my mother after my pa died," he said. They'd been talking for a few minutes, and he knew it wouldn't be long before they drew the attention of the upstanding citizens of Logan Meadows, who wouldn't want Hannah fraternizing with the likes of *him*. Word was out. People were curious. Scared. This morning, a woman with a small child in tow had ducked into a doorway when she'd seen him coming. His stomach clenched and the sunny mood he'd been feeling dissolved.

"The sheriff told me that you, as well as several others from the community, saw to it that she had enough to eat and wood for her stove. You also cared for Ivan. That was kind. I'd like to repay you for your time and expenses when I can."

Hannah took a surprised step back. "Repay me?" Her expression darkened as her brows dropped down over her snapping sapphire eyes. "You don't owe me anything. Katherine was my friend. Friends take care of each other, especially in this community. Since Anne Marie had married and moved away, I was happy to do what I could. I have a serious mind to be mad at you, Thomas Donovan. I felt closer to her than even my—" She shut her mouth and glared. Rising up on tiptoe, she pointed a finger in his face. "You should be ashamed!" She straightened her skirt as if she needed a moment to corral her temper. "You certainly know how to ruin a nice conversation."

"Thom," Win called from inside the livery. "Mr. Cooper is around back and needs to stable his horse. I'd do it but I'm right in the middle of shoeing. Thom? You out there?"

"Yes, sir," he called back, the title slipping out before he could stop it. Win had insisted he use his given name, but addressing everyone as sir was a hard habit to break. He felt his face warm.

"Go on, Thom. We'll talk another time." She took a step past him and stopped, her clean floral scent wafting around him like a wreath of spring flowers. She turned back. A soft smile had replaced her frown, her anger all but gone. "Perhaps you'd like to come to supper this Sunday? It's been way too long—"

Thom was touched—and tempted. But between Dwight, who he was certain would be itching for any reason to start trouble, and the blasted bullet in the back of his skull, waiting to drop him when he least expected it, he was the last person Hannah needed in her life to complicate things. Now wasn't the time to get involved with anyone.

"Sorry, Hannah, but I'm busy." Even as he said it, he winced at the hardness in his tone. It was easy to see his words had hurt. He felt bad, but there was no help for it. He and Hannah had been from two different worlds back then, and that hadn't changed a bit. *Want to head back to the clink?* Dwight's words rumbled around in his head, giving him another reason to stay away.

Never one to run from a fight, she just stared. Her nostrils flared just a tad as she held his gaze. "Just like that? You won't even think about it?"

"Said I have a previous engagement."

"You do not and you know it."

The wounded glimmer in her eyes almost made him change his mind. But even if he wanted to, he couldn't. Sticking to his guns, he slowly shook his head.

"Well, that's clear enough for a turkey on a rainy day. Please forgive me for extending my hospitality. God forbid you get the wrong idea about my wanting to welcome you back to town." Her back was rigid as a fence post and her dark lashes shuttered her eyes, making it impossible for him to gauge her feelings. She'd come for him. Sought him out. He knew it. She knew it. Her heart was right there on her sleeve for the entire world to see, just like it had always been. He longed to explain himself, so it wouldn't hurt so much, but if he did that, her tenacity would kick in and she'd be back at him working to change his mind. The Hannah who'd been his champion for as long as his memory stretched back, even from her spindly childhood, as if she'd understood small-mindedness even then—that Hannah deserved so much better than an ex-convict whose days may be numbered.

CHAPTER SIX

$\mathcal{C}$ hase reined up at the old two-story barn Logan Meadows used as a hall whenever its residents had to talk about something important. Looking around, he finally found a spot and tied Cody to the hitching rail between the other horses. The barn, with its missing boards and open roof, sat in a clearing a good distance behind the hotel and appraiser's office. From the sound of the commotion inside, he was late. Entering, he scanned the faces for Gabe and Jake.

Spotting them against the left wall, he picked his way through the crowd to stand by their side. The room resounded with heated talk. Frank Lloyd and another man stood at the front of the room, deep in discussion with Albert Preston and a few others seated on the first row of benches.

Gabe leaned over. "You're late," he whispered.

"Couldn't be helped. What's going on?"

"That's the new spokesman for the railroad next to Frank," Jake said angrily. "Seems Mr. Peabody has come up with a few more requirements for Logan Meadows if we want the railroad coming through our town. Who's to say the railroad don't keep on upping the stakes on us every chance they get?"

"Gentlemen, *please*," the dandy said. "I assure you, every town from the East Coast to the West Coast has gone through these same growing pains." He pulled a handkerchief from the breast pocket of his finely tailored jacket and swabbed his forehead. "I'm not asking for the moon. Please just hear me out, and then I'll take questions."

Frank held up a hand. "Give Mr. Peabody your attention so he can speak."

The railroad man smiled his appreciation. "Thank you, Mr. Lloyd. As my colleague already informed you three months ago February, the Union Pacific plans to lay track through your town. Logan Meadows will—"

"Will it be here or New Meringue? That's all we want to know!" someone yelled out. "There's a lot of money being spent in hopes—"

"As I stated earlier, *that* decision has yet to be determined and depends solely on you townsfolk. The Union Pacific is bent on making traveling as enjoyable as possible for its customers. Every stop must count. No one wants to pull up to a broken-down ramshackle of a place with nowhere to eat and nothing to see. Tourists want to be entertained. Experience something they don't have back home. You, on the other hand, want to seduce them to stay on, buy property, help Logan Meadows grow into a thriving community."

Chase leaned forward, nudging Gabe. "Has he said yet what any of the new requirements are?"

"Yeah," Gabe grumbled. "Larger schoolhouse. Several more eateries, a town hall."

Chase folded his arms over his chest. "Pretty tall order when you consider the overall general repairs of the town they held over our heads before."

"Don't forget about the park and festival grounds we built last month," Jake added. "Don't feel right."

"Sir!" A female voice rang out from the back of the room. Several men moved aside to let Hannah Hoskins through, followed by Maude Miller. "Have you given any thought to what will happen if we do all the things you ask and the train does not come to Logan Meadows? Without it, this town is not large enough to support three or four restaurants. I, for one, don't want to lose my livelihood."

Jake straightened. "Hannah sure is a firecracker."

"Agreed," Gabe responded, the admiration in his voice hard to miss.

Chase eyed the two young cowboys he and Jessie had taken under their roof three years ago. They had grown into fine men right before his eyes. He could not be prouder if he was their father. Still, he wondered if Jessie was right—he should be encouraging them to find good women and settle down, start families of their own.

"My niece is right, Mr. Peabody," Frank said, affirming Hannah's statement. "Many of the townsfolk have already taken out loans with the bank."

Mr. Peabody looked annoyed. He lifted his chin and leveled an accusing stare on the crowd before turning to Frank. "Well, that should make you a happy man, Mr. Lloyd. Business must be good." His gaze bounced around the room, and then his eyes narrowed. "The forward-thinking citizens of New Meringue do not seem to have the concerns that many of you are voicing here. They comprehend that their property values will increase more than four- or fivefold as people migrate from the east and their town grows in population. Merchants will get rich selling supplies to a flood of newcomers. Perhaps the good people of Logan Meadows like their lifestyle just the way it is now. Mayhap they don't want progress at all. Would you rather remain small, uncivilized?" He coughed into his hand. "I never intended to imply that the railroad *had* to come through Logan Meadows."

Anger slammed Chase. He removed his hat and ran his fingers through his hair. *Why, the little vermin.* He stepped forward, feeling Gabe and Jake at his back. These boys would both need a ranch of their own in the years to come, and he intended to help them get started. Yes, the railroad would be a vast boon for the Broken Horn. And it was also true the extra cattle next year would be an enormous strain if plans didn't work out. But they would figure something out. They had prospered in the past, and would again in the future, by the sweat of their brows and strength of their backs. No one was going to bully them! "That almost sounds like a threat, Mr. Peabody," he said, his hat still dangling in his fingers. "I don't think that's how you meant it to come out." Chase looked around at all the nodding heads. "Or did you?"

"A threat? Of course not. I was only pointing out that without progress your town will eventually die out. What does not go forward sooner or later stalls and then backslides. Nothing stays the same."

Chase could have heard a fly hiccup as everyone mulled over the man's words.

"A real snake in the woods," Jake whispered close to Chase's ear. "He sure knows how to work a crowd."

"I'd like to smash him with my boot heel," Gabe whispered.

The racket of stagecoach wheels, jangling steel chains to leather trace, and thundering hooves made everyone look out the open double doors. "Whoa, there," a deep voice called out. Dust swirled as the stage horses were pulled to a halt in front of the alley next to the El Dorado Hotel.

"That would be the twelve o'clock from Denver," Chase said. "Right on time like clockwork. Amazing how they can do that."

"That's all I have for today," Mr. Peabody said, as if thankful for the distraction. "I'll return in two weeks to address any new concerns you may have. Just keep one thing in mind while I've gone back to the conveniences of New York City, where new gadgets and gismos are imported daily from far-reaching countries, where crystal and silk are things of the ordinary." He pointed out to the stagecoach. "Consider what your poor, threadbare lives were like before you got the daily stage." He sniffed loudly and swatted at a fly on his arm. "That little forward step has greatly improved your livelihoods and connected you to the rest of the world. Just think what the railroad could do."

As the crowd dispersed, Hannah kept her gaze on the dumpy man from the Union Pacific, angry he would not commit with a straight answer. The stances and faces of her fellow townsfolk said they shared her frustration.

Maude took her by the elbow. "Come on, girl. It won't do any good to hang around here. You best get back to your restaurant and me to my store."

Hannah harrumphed. "I'm not ready to leave yet, Maude. I need to get a close look at that railroad man. See what Mr. Peabody is *really* thinking." She pushed forward, and Maude dutifully followed. She was almost to the front of the room when Dwight stepped in her path, fingering his deputy's badge the way he always did, as if to reinforce his own importance.

"Just what are you up to, Hannah?" Dwight asked. Taller than Caleb had been, he towered over the two women. "I can see in your expression you have something planned." He tilted his head toward the spot where Mr. Peabody was trying to escape the crowd that had surrounded him. "This is men's work. Leave it to us."

Hannah arched a brow. "What I'm planning is none of your concern, Dwight. I'm a business owner. I have as much at stake as the rest of the townspeople." She didn't miss the tightening of his mouth or the displeasure in his eyes, but that didn't stop her. "Just because your cousin was my late husband, you've no right sticking your nose in my life every chance you get. You've got no claim on me."

Dwight cleared his throat and glanced at Maude; to his credit, he looked sheepish. "I wish you'd stop being so prickly toward me, Hannah. I'm a deputy sheriff with a good income. You'd be hard-pressed to do better." He lowered his voice. "Besides, who better to be a father to Markus than his uncle?"

Hannah couldn't help laughing. Dwight's conceit and stubborn hardheadedness were unbelievable. Problem was, her mother kept encouraging him as much as Hannah was discouraging him. "Dwight, please. I've already made it as clear as I can. Now, let me by before I lose my chance to speak with Mr. Peabody."

Too late. The railroad representative pushed his way through the men and hurried away.

Dwight cleared his throat again, but this time it sounded more like a deep growl. Hannah turned, surprised. "Don't you try to intimidate me, Dwight. I'm no frightened field mouse you can send scurrying for cover!" Even standing as tall as she could, her eyes came only to his badge. A tiny seed of uncertainty planted in her belly at the livid glint in his gaze.

Maude took her arm, eyes rounded in warning. "This crowd is closing in on me. I need some air."

"Yes, let's go. Good day, Mr. Hoskins," she said, nodding politely.

"I'll see you for dinner Sunday evening. Your mother invited me over to visit Markus. She thinks he's getting unruly and needs a man's influence." It was impossible to miss his gloating expression.

Hannah bit the inside of her cheek and kept her face carefully blank as she helped Maude through the crowd to the back of the dusty gathering area. Once they were blessedly outside, she sucked in a lungful of fresh, cool air. A few feet away, Chase Logan, along with Gabe, Jake, and one of his ranch hands, Blake Hansen, stood beneath some alders in deep conversation. Blake was flanked by Rome Littleton, one of her least favorite people. He'd made an attempt last year to catch her attention, coming into the restaurant and making a pest of himself. When she let him know she wasn't interested, he'd never come in again. She was glad. There was something very disturbing about the ranch owner from New Meringue besides his prominent nose—she couldn't help but feel something dark lurked behind his eyes.

"Hannah," a woman's voice called.

Brenna Lane, a widow who had three children of her own and had recently taken in another parentless child, hurried in her direction. Brenna's ragged appearance, as well as her thinness, made Hannah's heart ache. It was apparent the young mother gave all the leftovers Hannah sent her to the children, keeping little for herself.

Maude patted Hannah's arm. "I'll see you back at the restaurant." The older woman's gaze darted back toward Dwight, who was now talking with someone else. "You take care."

Hannah laughed carelessly, although she didn't feel it. "Him? Oh, he's just a big nincompoop."

"Still." Maude gave her a significant look before she walked away.

"I don't want to intrude on your day," Brenna said nervously, worry etched in her brow. "But may I speak with you a moment?"

"Of course," Hannah replied, smiling. She adored this woman—everything about her was sweet and caring. She only wished she could do more for her. "Where are the children?"

"Penny is watching them." Brenna's voice lightened a smidge. "What I'd do without that girl, I don't know."

Hannah was sure Brenna had something on her mind but didn't want to rush her. She had her pride, albeit a bit tattered. "That's good," she said kindly. "Gives you a moment to get out."

"So true. A few minutes a day is all I need to deliver my sewing. And with the growing town, I'm seeing a real need for stitching repairs and even some special projects." She glanced around. "Hannah?"

"Yes?"

"I hate to tell you this, but a nasty raccoon broke into our pantry three nights ago. I guess Stevie forgot to close the door all the way. Pretty much cleaned it out." Her hesitant voice and downcast eyes almost undid Hannah. She knew what it must cost her friend to come to her for more help.

"Brenna, you should have told me right away. Three days? Surely the children are famished."

"We're making do." It was barely a whisper. "I'm sorry. I appreciate what you're already doing for me and my brood each week. Do you need any extra cleaning done in your house? Something I might do in trade for—"

"Hush now." When Brenna's face clouded up, Hannah put her arm around the woman's small shoulder. "Nothing I can think of at the moment."

Brenna sniffed. "I hate asking like this."

"I know you do. However, youngsters have to eat. I have a loaf of bread and some stew I can spare, and probably more after I take stock. I'll get it to you within the hour."

A burst of masculine laughter made Hannah look up. Chase and his men were headed their way. Thankfully, Rome was not with them.

Brenna gave her a quick hug and then turned to leave.

"Don't go on our account, Mrs. Lane," Chase called, warming Hannah with his attractive smile. Jessie was a lucky woman to have such a fine, upstanding husband, who was also a pleasing sight to look at. "How is that houseful you have?"

"Just fine, Mr. Logan," Brenna said, cheeks flushing slightly. "Thank you for asking." She glanced once at Hannah, then hurried away.

Chase gestured to the group. "I'm sorry. We didn't mean to barge in and run Mrs. Lane off. Just wanted to say hello and invite you out to the ranch. Jessie sends a message that she needs a dose of female company. Shane keeps her running."

"What about Sarah?" Gabe said, always protective over the child he'd helped deliver from the orphanage in New Mexico. "She's a girl."

"She don't count for conversation." Jake laughed. "'Less you want to sing songs and count." He laughed again and inched a step closer. His shirt was clean and buttoned to the collar. "I could pick you up later today in the buggy and bring you out, Hannah."

Hannah smiled, appreciating Jake's offer. "As much as I'd like to, Jake, I can't today. I have a few things to take care of." She glanced between the men and saw that Brenna was now out to the street. As soon as she could get back to her restaurant, she'd pack up any leftovers and take them over to the young mother. It must be a horrible feeling to see the hunger in your young 'uns' eyes. Would she run into Thom again when she passed by the livery? She bristled. Some people were just too stubborn for their own good. "Tell Jessie I'll stop by on Monday sometime in the late morning. Tell her too that I'm really looking forward to seeing her."

Chase cleared his throat and clamped a hand on Jake's shoulder. He'd watched the way Jake stood taller in Hannah's presence. The boy had clearly taken special care with his appearance, too. "Jessie will be pleased to see you Monday, Hannah. Jake here forgot all about the ranch and things he needs to get done today. A place that size can't run itself."

Jake jerked away almost angrily, startling Chase. Something was going on in Jake's head, and that *something* had him worried. He remembered Jessie's fretting and wondered if he needed to have a conversation with the boy about Hannah. Was it that or something else entirely?

Blake's cool gaze assessed the men. "I could give you a list if you want, Jake. Starting with mending fences and ending with digging out the water hole."

Jake scowled.

Chase hadn't meant to embarrass Jake, but he could feel the boy's resentment as sure as if a wet blanket had dropped over the group. "Let's go, men, time to let Mrs. Hoskins get back to her day." He tipped his hat as Jake strode off toward his horse. Gabe and Blake followed.

Hannah stopped Chase as he turned to leave. "What's bothering Jake?" Her eyes searched his with genuine concern, and he wondered if he should tell her what he and Jessie suspected.

In loyalty to Jake, he quickly decided against it. He shrugged. "I'm not sure, but no need to worry, Hannah. Jake's a big boy. He can take care of himself."

She let go a small sigh. "I just hate to see him miserable."

The last thing Jake needed was for Hannah to get closer to him, trying to help. The boy was sure to misconstrue her intentions. "He'll work it out, whatever it is." Chase turned to leave, but Hannah stopped him short.

"I'm glad I remembered before you rode off. There's a little something I want to talk to you about."

He rubbed the back of his neck, wondering what Hannah Hoskins might need from him.

She came close and kept her voice low. "An old friend of mine has come home to Logan Meadows. I was wondering if you would introduce yourself to him. Befriend…"

"Thomas Donovan?"

"You've heard."

He nodded. Most everyone was now gone from the meeting area, leaving the two of them alone. "Who hasn't? An ex-convict moving into the community is more gossip worthy than who's sparking who each spring."

"Logan Meadows is his home, Chase. Where else should he go?"

He held out his hands. "I'm not judging. I was friends with his mother before she passed on. I never knew him, since he was gone by the time Jessie and I moved to town."

Her smile wobbled, and she looked away. "Albert has helped set him up in a job with Win at the livery, and he's living over at the Red Rooster."

He couldn't stop a half-teasing groan. "With Violet Hollyhock? Oh, the poor man."

Hannah gave him a stern look. "She's not so bad, and you know it. Jessie would feed you cold supper for a week if she heard you talking that way. That woman is the only grandmother she's ever known."

Chase wedged his hat onto his head, barely able to keep the grin from his face. His wife loved that ancient woman. "Don't I know it. I promise to look Thom up as soon as I can, Hannah. Even if it means enduring teatime over at the Red Rooster."

CHAPTER SEVEN

*I*t was almost six in the evening as Thom, a bit doggedly, climbed the ladder to the loft and hoisted himself onto the platform where hay was piled ceiling high. He was worn out from a long day of stall cleaning and wheel mending, but even after only two days, it was amazing how one's body kept working without one's mind even having to think about the tasks. He began tossing armfuls of hay down into each stall.

"Thom, I'm leaving," Win called up. "After you bring the horses inside and lock up, would you mind stopping by the Silky Hen on your way home? Mrs. Hoskins has a problem with her water pump."

Thom straightened and ran his arm across his sweaty forehead. Win was looking up at him, the reins of the horse already in his hand.

"I don't mind." *That's a barefaced lie.* He'd be lucky if God didn't strike him dead right there in the loft. After their conversation yesterday it would be awkward seeking Hannah out, even if it was to help.

"Thanks. I meant to do it earlier and forgot," Win said, smiling up at him. He was younger than Albert by two years and shorter by three inches. They both had brown hair and thick eyebrows. Today Win hadn't shaved, leaving a thick stubble covering his square jaw. "I'm usually called upon to fix things around town, you know, pumps, windmills, and such. Her pump is pretty straightforward. You know where the tools are in the storage shed?"

Thom nodded.

"Good. It's free of charge given that she's a widow. In exchange, she usually sends me home with a nice meat pie or something else just as tasty. It's yours, of course. I'm late or I'd do it myself."

The muscles in Thom's jaw tightened. "No problem. I'll take care of it just as soon as I'm finished here."

Win nodded. "Tell her I'm sorry I forgot about it," he called as he left. "I expect she's plenty annoyed with me."

The clip-clop of hooves finally faded. Thom climbed down and stabled the six horses, running a brush quickly over each. Mentally he ticked off the list of chores Win expected him to complete before leaving. As he rushed to finish, Maximus, Win's orphaned bison calf, followed him around, hungry for attention. Thom constantly had to sidestep to keep from being tripped. With a handful of hay, he persuaded the bison into his outdoor pen, then fastened the gate. Lastly, in the grain room, he found the barn cat asleep on top of three sacks of oats.

"Out you go." He picked her up and set her in the aisle outside the door. "Time for you to go to work." He snapped the padlock closed as she blinked up at him sleepily.

Thom glanced down at his clothes and curled his lip at the grime that stuck to him like a magnet. He swiped at his hair, divesting it of bits of hay and cobwebs he'd collected in the loft, but he knew it did little to improve his appearance. Lifting his arm, he gave a sniff. He was due a bath, but he'd not be able to accomplish that until tonight, after supper. Well, there was no help for that now. Collecting a wrench and a handful of silver washers from the shed, he took his horse's reins and headed up the street.

Up to her elbows in bubbles, Hannah attacked a dirty pot with her scrub brush, anxious to get home to Markus. Thank goodness she'd had a busy turnout today—twenty-four meals, seven with dessert. Just like old times. If only more days could be like this one.

It wasn't hard to figure out that the two new restaurants were hurting business. Charley's had opened on the north end of town seven months ago, causing a pinch. Then when an older couple new to town had heard about the railroad, they'd opened Nana's Place. That was three months ago, and half of her regular clientele had gone missing the first week. Still, it was hard to begrudge them trying something new.

Someone rapped on the back door. *Thank goodness Win's finally here.* With her hands still in the water, she glanced around for the dish towel, and in the process gave the temperamental water pump a withering stare. Another day like today, hauling water from the hotel, would be the end of her.

The knock sounded again. Normally she would have called for Susanna to get it, but today her helper had a headache and Hannah had sent her home.

"Come in, Win," she finally called in exasperation as she caught sight of the dish towel beneath a pile of soiled dishes. What a day for the pump to slow to a trickle. The sink was overflowing with dishes, and pots and pans all but hid the drain board. Thom stepped in, and she pulled up short.

"Thom." She yanked her hands from the bubbles and dried them on her apron. Hair drooped in her eyes, and her face was moist. Even in her wet dress, the room felt several degrees warmer as she struggled for something to say.

He held a wrench in his hand. "Win sent me over to have a look at your water pump."

His gaze roamed around her kitchen in every direction except hers. If her eyes weren't playing a trick on her, there was a blush creeping up his neck. A kernel of pleasure budded inside her—she felt it sprout, blossom, and ripen as he took a deep breath and shifted his weight from side to side. With his hot and cold moods he might say he didn't want to come to dinner on Sunday, but here, now, alone with her in the restaurant, he was unable to hide the softening of his eyes, the slight curve of his lips.

A replica expression of a day long ago but not forgotten. She'd baked a cherry pie for his fourteenth birthday. Excitedly, with only the light from one candle, she'd gotten up at midnight so her mother wouldn't know what she was about, then hidden the sweet away until after school. Late in the afternoon after chores were done, she'd run across the expanse of her father's field and then the Donovans', with the covered pie held firmly in her hands. She'd found Thom in the barn. He'd been surprised at first, but soon the expression he was trying so hard to hide now had crept over his face, warming her adolescent heart to overflowing. Despite Thom's gruffness yesterday and now, he *was* pleased to see her—and he couldn't tell her otherwise.

Thom closed the few feet between them and looked the pump over a moment before turning to her. "This pump?"

She bit the inside of her cheek. "Yes."

"A ragtag group of children were at your back door. Took off as soon as they saw me. Looks like they were carrying something."

"That would be Brenna's brood. If I have any leftovers to spare, or an extra this or that, I hang it out my back door. Maude at the store does the same. My friend Jessie Logan also helps out. It's a group effort." She gave him a caring look. "Times are tough for a lot of people these days."

His eyes softened. "Guess they are." They were staring at each other in silence. She glanced away, and he reached for the pump handle, working it up and down. "Sorry about my condition. You may want to step back a couple of feet."

"It's no worse than mine." She ran her hands down the front of her dress. "It's been a madhouse all day. I haven't had a second to even look in the mirror."

Thom glanced at her over his shoulder. "You don't show it."

Hannah warmed further at the compliment and shrugged. She tried to distract herself by folding some clean towels left on the small table they used for a break. Despite what she thought she knew of Thom's expressions, he'd been clear about his feelings for her when they'd talked in the restaurant, and she'd best remember that. Though it hadn't stopped her from lying awake last night, thinking about him.

"Logan Meadows suits you," she said, watching him bend back to his chore.

Her statement drew him around to look at her questioningly.

"I can't help notice how tan you are. You—" She closed her mouth. Even in the short time he'd been home, it seemed he'd gained weight and his face had been kissed gently by the sun. "You must be spending a lot of time outside with the livestock."

He looked amused. "Spend most my time chasing Win's bison calf around. Maximus can be a nuisance."

"Oh." That was the best she could come up with with him gazing at her like that. "Can—can I get you anything? A cold glass of chokecherry juice?" Without waiting for his answer, she snatched a tall glass off the shelf and hurried into the storeroom, where they kept a few chunks of ice in a pail as often as possible to try and keep the room cool. From a pitcher, she filled the glass to the top, added a heaping teaspoon of sugar, and stirred.

Thom was taking the contraption apart with his wrench. She set his drink on the counter next to him. "Here you go. I think you'll like it. It's fresh."

He straightened and picked up the glass, his biceps flexing as he held the drink to his mouth. He drained it to the bottom, and his eyes opened wide as he handed it back to her. "That was sweet!"

She laughed, and he smiled ear to ear. "That's the way you used to like it," she replied. "With lots of sugar. Remember? Your mother always made it best."

His smile ebbed. Before he could glance away, hurt, dark as a moonless sky, shadowed his eyes.

"Thom, I'm so sorry about your family. It must be very difficult to hear about your parents like you did. I wrote to you after your mother passed on, but my letter was returned unopened. It was the hardest letter I have ever written. I know it was the same for her when she wrote to tell you about your pa. It also came back unopened. She grieved over that a lot. That you didn't know."

He stood silent.

"I have her things. There aren't very many. Let me know when you're ready."

He nodded.

"Anne Marie finally wrote to me a few weeks ago. She lives up in Montana. Until now, nobody knew where she was. She's expecting a baby," she said, wanting to cheer him up. "I can give you her address."

He looked down at her, his eyes unreadable. "Thank you."

Unable to stop herself, she slipped into his arms and laid her head against his chest. His arms came around her.

"Hannah, please. I smell like a week-old stall. I can notice it myself, and that's saying something."

He hadn't yet set her away. "You smell fine to me. I've been dreaming about giving you this hug since the moment I saw you sitting in the restaurant with Albert." She squeezed, but it wasn't returned.

"I think I know where you're going with this, Hannah." His husky whisper sent a tingle up her back. His heart beat slowly against her ear. "It just can't be. Too much has happened. We're different. It'd be nothing but heartache for you, and you'd be a problem for me, too. It would be a whole lot easier if you didn't keep this up."

She leaned back so she could see into his face, search his coffee-brown eyes. "Keep what up?"

"You know. I see it in your eyes." It might have been her imagination, but she thought he pulled her closer. "You don't have to say a word for me to know what's going on in your head."

All the years yearning for him fell away. Now, it was just the two of them, and she didn't want to regret not taking a chance. "Thom, I have something to tell you," she started slowly.

CHAPTER EIGHT

*H*annah." He stepped back, putting space between them. "I can tell by your tone it's nothing I want to hear."

Hurt blossomed in her chest, but she knew Thom, knew he couldn't mean it. He'd been through a lot, and it was his own hurt talking. She reconsidered her actions, but only for a moment. Too much time had already been lost, and truths that should have been said a long time ago needed saying now. She folded her arms across her chest and stepped in front of the water pump, making it impossible for him to get to the contraption without going over the top of her.

Thom's eyebrow arched. "Go on, then. Spit it out." He also crossed his arms over his chest and stared down at her, giving as good as he got. "I've yet to be able to stop you from doing something that you've set your mind to. Go on, or I'll never get home." There was irritation in his voice, but she didn't miss the smile tugging again at the corner of his lips. "The time you wanted to come with Caleb and me to deliver a plow to New Meringue and we said no because you were just a girl, you squirreled away in the back of our wagon until it was too late for us to turn around. I was so blaming mad at you! We had a hard time explaining that one away."

"I remember. That was just a few weeks before you ran off."

He nodded.

"Well, if you haven't noticed, I'm not a girl anymore. If your leaving has taught me anything, it's that every day is precious." She stopped. Worried her bottom lip with her teeth. "I know I never told you," she began uncertainly. "But…" She searched for the right words to show him how much he meant to her. How devastated she'd been when he'd left town. How overcome with pain when they'd heard he'd been sent to prison. The look on his face said he'd not make this easy.

"After you left, I waited for you to come back. I prayed you would. Night after night I begged God to bring you home. Your sister got fed up with me, and my mother was beside herself thinking I'd lost my mind."

"You had a schoolgirl crush."

Hannah sucked in a breath. "You knew?"

He chuckled. "Kinda hard not to."

Hannah swallowed. He'd known—all those years. Yes, they'd been young, but lots of couples met in school, got married, loved each other till their dying day. *He'd known and still didn't return my feelings.* She felt compelled to continue even though the ground where she stood seemed to rock. "It wasn't until three years after you left that we got news you'd been in prison the whole time. I never believed you were guilty, Thom. You'd never do something illegal like rustling cattle. Caleb, you know how much he loved you, well—he saw I was pining away for you, saw my anguish—he tried to make up for it. He invited me to supper almost every Sunday. Once I turned fifteen he asked me to every social that year. Gave me his coat when I was cold. I couldn't help but respond to his kindness."

Thom's stalwart expression made her wish she hadn't launched into this at all. "Finally," she continued, although her bravado was waning, "he started talking about marriage. After my father passed away, my mother was fearful of everything. Afraid I'd end up a spinster. Afraid we would lose everything without a way to support ourselves. Afraid to stay on the farm unprotected."

Thom reached out and smoothed a wisp of hair from her face, his eyes softening. "I appreciate what you're doing, but all this has nothing to do with who we are now, Hannah. No one can turn back the hands of time. Not even you. Don't you think I would if I could?"

Why couldn't he bend just a little? Meet her halfway. In exasperation, she stamped her foot and the old plank boards gave, causing a slight sway in the floor. A second later, a decorative plate slipped from a narrow display shelf above the door. It fell and shattered with a loud crash.

Thom ached to pull Hannah into his arms, kiss the sweet lips that had just confessed her devotion. But he couldn't. All the hurt and disappointment he'd already caused those who loved him... Hannah deserved so much better. Especially since she'd already suffered through Caleb's death, and at such a young age. She needed someone who could care for her and her son for years to come. Someone she could lean on. He had no idea what his future held, not with a bullet ready to drop him. He was damaged goods.

He had to keep a clear head, do what was best for her. While he tried to think of what he could say to make her understand, he stared at the remnants of the broken plate.

A quick rap on the back door startled both of them.

"Is everything all right in here, Hannah?" Dwight came in without invitation. He glanced at the plate and then back at Hannah. "I heard something shatter. Are you hurt?"

The deputy's posture all but snapped straight when he saw Thom. His wide-eyed concern vanished as his hand lowered to the handle of the Colt 45 strapped to his leg.

Thom swore under his breath. *Exactly what I have been trying to avoid.* It wouldn't take much to get himself shot or sent back to

Deer Lodge. Not much at all, especially with Dwight's predatory temperament watching his every move with wolflike precision. The warden had warned Thom. People were afraid of ex-convicts. He had to be twenty times more observant of the law than most.

"What the devil is going on in here?" The white bone china crackled and popped underneath Dwight's boots as he strode possessively toward Hannah.

Thom gritted his teeth and looked down at the floor. Surely Dwight would notice her flushed face. The tears glistening in her eyes.

"He try to hurt you, Hannah? In any way at all? Did he put his hands on you?" Dwight's fingers curled around the handle of his gun. "You can tell me. Did he make improper advances?"

"Of course not!" Hannah said firmly. Sparks fairly sprang from her eyes. "That is outrageous. Win sent him over to fix my water pump. He's been a perfect gentleman in every way."

"I don't know if I believe you, Hannah. Why didn't Win come himself, like he always does? Mayhap this jailbird just wanted a moment alone with you. Do a little sweet-talking." He jerked his gaze toward Thom. "Perhaps he's hungry from all those years locked away."

Thom dug deeper for his quiet. He'd learned how to play the game, but it rankled more with Dwight than it had with any prison guard. He uncurled his fingers in an attempt to relax and took deep breaths through his nose. "I came to fix the pump, Dwight," he said, counting backward from five. "Just doing my job. Nothing more."

Dwight jammed a finger into Thom's chest, trying to push him back, but Thom held his ground. They both knew Dwight had him where he wanted him. Without Sheriff Preston here, Dwight could claim anything. "You're to call me sir whenever you address me. You understand, mick jailbird?"

Hannah threw up her hands. "Be serious! No one calls you sir. Why should Thom?"

A line of crimson started on Dwight's neck and slowly crept over his face toward the unkempt hair hanging down into his eyes. Thom didn't like what he saw before Dwight's small eyes darted over to Hannah. "Because I said so. That's all the reason I need." He looked back at Thom. "Understand?"

"Yes, sir," Thom said clearly, this time locking his gaze on the pink-and-green wallpaper. "Now, *sir*—can I get back to work? I have chores waiting for me back at the inn. It's getting late."

"Maybe you should have thought about that before you killed Levi Smith and then ran off with your tail between your legs. You're nothing more than a cold-blooded killer."

"Stop it!" Hannah shoved Dwight in the chest with both hands. "That was an accident. A boyhood fight. Levi pulled the knife to use on Thom. He stumbled and fell. Thom was cleared of any wrongdoing, and you know it! He didn't kill Levi. Levi killed himself."

"Innocent men don't run."

Dwight was enjoying this all too much. But he was right. Innocent men didn't run, and Thom hadn't. He'd just packed up one night and took off, unable to stay in Logan Meadows another day. Unable to stand the look on his father's face every time he thought about the shame he'd brought down on the Donovan name by accidently killing a friend. But leaving Logan Meadows had only led him to Rome Littleton and prison.

"I don't care if you are my cousin-in-law, Dwight Hoskins. You're mean and crude. I don't understand what makes you that way. I'm going for Albert if you don't stop this foolishness this instant." She glared up at Dwight. "Thom has served his time. Don't you dare threaten him!"

"I don't need you fighting my fights, Hannah," Thom said evenly. "I don't want you to either." He reached for the wrench, and Dwight drew on him.

"I could kill you right now."

If it weren't for Hannah standing so close, Thom might have taken Dwight on. But there she stood, like a beautiful goddess carved from marble.

"You could, Dwight—but you won't," Thom said softly. "You know why? Because you don't have the guts." He took a tiny step in Dwight's direction. "You were a spineless fool back when we were boys, and you still are."

Dwight's laugh was a bit too forced to be real.

Thom picked up the wrench and turned to the pump. He withdrew two worn-out washers from the contraption's core, then replaced them with the ones in his pocket. He refastened the spout, then the pump handle. Screwing them down tight, he gave one last muscle-popping yank, just because it felt good.

CHAPTER NINE

*J*ake lounged an arm on the walnut bar top inside the Bright Nugget Saloon and lazily placed one boot on the footrest. Irritation gripped his insides. All he wanted was for Kendall to get over here and pour him a drink. Was that too much to ask?

Through the gold-plated mirror, he watched the lean, middle-aged bartender give Daisy a stiff dressing-down at the back of the room. The girl must be in some sort of trouble. She kept her mouth shut and eyes cast at the sawdust-covered floor.

"You best remember that, missy," Kendall threw over his shoulder as he turned and started Jake's way. "That is, if you want to stay employed here!" He stopped behind the bar. Taking the draped towel from his shoulder, he wiped his hands. "Now, Jake, what can I do you for?"

Annoyed with everyone and everything, Jake had decided to skip supper at the bunkhouse and distract himself with a game of cards. Problem was, he was the only customer in the saloon.

"Whiskey." He pulled a quarter from his pocket and placed it on the glossy wood.

Kendall gave him a long look, then took a bottle off the shelf. He pulled the cork and poured a shot. The amber liquid swirled invitingly around the smooth glass. As the tumbler filled, the memory of bleary eyes looked back from its depths. Jake almost gagged as the stink of his mother's liquor-coated breath wafted over him, more real than if she were standing by his side. Fury ripped through him, and before he could lose his nerve, he reached for the glass. Kendall stopped him with a hand to his arm.

"I never known you to be a drinker, Jake."

"A lot of things you don't know about me. Now, do I need your permission to drink the whiskey I just bought?"

They stood eye to eye. "Guess not." Kendall stepped back.

"Good." Jake tossed the shot down his throat, ignoring the burn that scalded his insides. He'd not give Kendall the satisfaction of knowing that his eyes felt as if they were about to pop from their sockets. He'd had whiskey before, of course, but never in such a large quantity. He breathed out, then smacked his lips. "That's better. Give me another."

Kendall poured in silence.

Jake turned and leaned against the bar, feeling the warmth in his chest and belly. He could see why men liked it. As Daisy made her way over, Kendall wrestled up the trash barrel and started for the back door.

"Evening, Jake." She smiled a bit sadly, and a hundred memories from his youth tried to intrude on him, threatened to wreck his good time. No doing. He kicked them out of his mind.

"Evening, Daisy. Where is everyone? Town is sure quiet for a Friday night." Light-chestnut-colored hair neatly swept to the top of her head in some sort of fancy style, and her full lips were painted soft pink. Her tight dress emphasized her tiny waist and petite, delicately powdered breasts pushing up to entice him. He was duly enticed. But when he dragged his gaze back up to her face, it was her emerald eyes, looking as though they'd seen a world of hurt and then some, that caught and kept his attention.

"I don't know. I was wondering the same thing. It'll be a long night if I don't have *something* to help pass the time." She batted her eyelashes. When he didn't say anything, she dipped a slender finger in his glass, then placed it on her tongue.

Darn, she was young. Too young to be doing this. He wondered if she was even sixteen. He turned quickly and picked up the shot and tossed it back, now enjoying the scorched trail to his gut.

"You in some sort of trouble with Kendall?" he said low, changing the direction of the conversation.

She lifted her shoulder, and her eyes hardened. "He don't think I'm earning my keep. Said I'm not working the men." Her lips trembled before they flattened into a hard line. Lacing her arm through the crook of his elbow, she leaned into him with her lithe body, and every nerve ending he had ignited.

His heart lurched, as well as other parts of him. As a young boy he'd watched from the dark shadows as his mother and the other saloon girls sold their wares. Night after night. Day after day.

When her invitation went unanswered, she pulled back, hurt.

"Daisy," he said, wishing he could be someone else and take what she offered. She wouldn't look at him.

"I really need you, Jake." It was a whispered plea. The sound of her voice gave him pause.

Before he could answer, the swinging doors swooshed open, and Gabe stepped inside. He looked around the room and then headed Jake's way.

"Thought I might find you here," he said, his tone instantly grating on Jake's nerves.

"Well, you found me. So what?"

"What the devil is your problem?" Gabe shot back, sliding onto a stool. Daisy stepped away and started straightening up the already-straightened room. "You've been acting sorry for yourself for a whole month. I wouldn't care except Jessie is worried about you."

Anger had been simmering in Jake too long. It bubbled up and spilled over. He took hold of the bar to keep from bashing Gabe in the face. They'd been like brothers for the last three years, and yet now it felt like he didn't have a friend in the world. "Go meddle in someone else's business and leave me alone," he snarled, liking the surprise that registered on Gabe's face. "I have a right to go wherever I please."

Gabe swung his arm wide. "So this is how you're going to repay Chase and Jessie for taking you in? Putting a roof over your head and giving you a job? Darn good of you, Jake!"

Before Jake knew what he was about, he grasped Gabe by the shirtfront and shoved him against the bar. "You're always so Sunday-going good, aren't you, Gabe? So attentive, so polite." Their faces were only an inch apart, and Jake knew the exact moment his advantage of surprise was up.

They were fairly matched in height and weight. Gabe shoved, and Jake stumbled back. He caught his balance, then swung with his left fist, connecting with Gabe's jaw and almost knocking him down.

Gabe took a step back, hands clenched at his side. "You sorry bas—" He clamped his mouth shut.

"Go on and say it, Gabe. You've been thinking it since the day we met."

Gabe's eyes glittered with anger. "No. I'll not fight you. You can stay in this bar feeling sorry for yourself for as long as you want."

"You're damn right I'm feeling sorry for myself. You would, too, if you didn't know who your father was because your mother was a whore."

Behind him, he heard Daisy gasp. She made a swift exit up the stairs.

Gabe watched her go for a moment. He rubbed his jaw. Finally he said, "I didn't realize you were so upset, Jake. Thought you'd left all that behind you in Valley Springs." He reached out for Jake's shoulder, but Jake pulled back, not ready to give up the fight.

Always the peacemaker, Gabe added, "I'm sorry. I just thought you were nursing your wounds over Hannah. Her not, well..." He was rubbing salt in the wound of Jake's pride, and it riled his ire even more.

Jake swung back to the bar and poured himself a third glass from the whiskey bottle Kendall had left. He couldn't stop a bitter laugh. "Hannah? What could I offer someone like her? No. I knew I had no chance with her. But it just reinforced who I'm *not* and where I'm *not* going."

"Jake, be reasonable. Lots of men don't know who their fathers are. Why—"

"Save it for someone who cares, because I don't."

The bar doors swung open then, and Rome Littleton strode into the room. After a quick glance around and a silent nod to Jake and Gabe, he approached the bar. He pulled a quarter out of his pocket and placed it on the bar. "Where's Kendall?"

"Emptying the trash," Jake said, wrestling with his anger.

Gabe leaned in close, keeping his voice low. "Look at Chase and the good life he's built for himself. He told me he took his name from this town, when he got tired of not having a last name. He never knew either of his parents."

"I know that." And he did. The story had helped him three years ago, but it couldn't stop the thing deep inside that was eating him up. A longing for things that could never be. Things like respect. That was something Jake was going to have to earn for himself. "You about finished?"

Gabe stepped back. The spot on his jaw had turned red. "Yeah." He walked out.

Rome gave Jake a quizzical look. "Buy you a drink?"

Jake nodded. Slid closer, anger rolling around inside.

Rome chuckled. "Shrug it off, Jake. Whatever the problem is can't be that bad."

Kendall was back, and he pulled an expensive bottle off a lower shelf under the bar. "Your usual, Rome?" He set a glass on the bar and poured, then filled Jake's at Rome's direction. Rome's clothes were new; his boots looked expensive. The other men seemed to respect the loner from New Meringue.

"Like I said, shake it off. As you get older, you'll find friendship is overrated. Doesn't mean squat. It's what someone can do for you; now that's important. Figure out how you can work your disagreement with Gabe to your advantage."

Jake glanced over to find Rome smiling at him, as if gauging his reaction to what he had just said. Suddenly the quiet saloon was suffocating. Jake glanced at his glass as an eerie feeling snaked down his spine. Without saying a word, he tossed it back and walked out.

CHAPTER TEN

*T*hom circled around to the hitching post and his sleeping horse. The street was quiet. In his hands he carried the rectangular dish Hannah had offered as he'd exited the back door of the restaurant after fixing the water pump. Dwight had hovered the whole time and had even tried to interfere when Hannah approached him with it, but she'd turned on him like a she-wolf protecting her pups. Thom stifled a smile at the image.

Next door, the mercantile was dark, save for one lantern that illuminated Maude Miller inside sweeping up. He hesitated for a moment at the closed sign, then advanced and knocked on the glass. It took the old woman a moment to realize she wasn't alone.

"Yes? Who is it?" she called as she leaned the broom on the long wooden counter. She looked out and took a step back when she recognized him.

"Hello, Mrs. Miller?" he said through the glass. "It's Thomas Donovan." He smiled, trying to put her at ease, but he could tell she was frightened. Probably thought he wanted to rob her or something. "I don't know if you remember me. My mother was Katherine Donovan." His family used to have an account at the store, but Hannah had said his mother had closed it after his father had died. "I'm sorry to intrude, but I was kept late at work. Do you think I might impose on you for a moment? It won't take long."

Her hand went to the white collar of her blue-and-tan dress, and her fingers moved nervously as the moments ticked by. It was no use. He gave a little wave. "Thanks, anyway." Feeling low, he turned to go.

He was almost to his horse when he heard the door open. "Mr. Donovan." She widened the door a few inches but kept her foot behind it—just in case. "What was it you needed?"

He stayed where he was on the boardwalk. "I noticed today that you had a crate of pullets out back. And another of cockerels."

"That's correct."

"I'd like to purchase three females and one male."

She looked at him for a long minute, as if weighing the risk. "How would you pay for them?"

"Win Preston said he was going to come by and set up an account that would allow me to charge a few things until I got my first month's pay. Did he do that?"

Her eyes widened, and her shoulders seemed to relax a little. "Why, yes. He did in fact do that yesterday, now that you mention it." He thought she gave a little laugh, but he wasn't sure. "I'm getting on in age, you know. If you stay put, I'll catch up what you're after and be right back."

Thom waited next to his horse, cradling the ceramic pot from Hannah in one arm like a baby. It was slightly warm and smelled tempting, the rich aroma torturing his empty stomach. The door to the mercantile opened, and Mrs. Miller emerged with a gunnysack. The gray bag writhed as if alive, and fearful clucking filled the air. She handed it to him.

"Thank you, ma'am."

"You're welcome."

She held out a small white bag. "A little surprise for you. No fair peeking."

Warmth seeped through Thom's chest.

"Go on now," she prompted. "You don't want to keep them in the bag for too long. Poultry traumatize easily."

Thom hurried around to the left side of his horse. "Thank you, Mrs. Miller," he said, slipping into the stirrup and mounting awkwardly with all the things he had to carry. "You have a good evening."

Thom stabled his mount in the small shed behind the inn and tossed the horse an armload of hay. He glanced about, looking for Ivan. Had the dog chewed through the rope and run back to the farm? With trepidation, he covered the ground to the porch and gently set the gunnysack in one of the rocking chairs. The chirping stopped, as if the young poultry sensed they were in new surroundings.

Kicking his boots clean, he opened the front door and stepped inside, instantly seduced by the scent of freshly baked bread. Mrs. Hollyhock turned from the stove, and Ivan, lying next to the fire, jumped up and ran to his side. It wasn't a moment before the dog smelled the poultry on the porch and dashed to the door, barking.

Thom set the dish down and grabbed for his collar.

"Was Ivan a problem today?" he asked as Mrs. Hollyhock made her way over.

"I went out to check on his water, and he gave me the most sorrowful face." Her tone was gruff, but her eyes crinkled at the corners and her lips tipped up. "I felt guilty leaving him out."

"You needn't worry about him."

"I know. Now come eat."

He picked up Hannah's dish and gave it to Mrs. Hollyhock. "From Mrs. Hoskins for fixing her water pump."

Violet removed the lid. "Bless that child." She looked up at him with twinkling eyes. "Cottage pie. The whole county wants to know how they make it. There's something just a mite different in the flavor—and for the life of me, I can't figure it out."

Thom led Ivan back to his spot by the hearth and told him to lie down and stay. The table was set for three, and a little flame danced on top of a candle between their plates. There was an extra place set at every meal, and Thom had grown so used to it that he no longer gave it a second thought. Everyone was entitled to their secrets. "I hope you went ahead and ate your supper."

She stirred something in a pot. "No. We'll eat together. It's potato soup and a fresh loaf of bread. Now, cottage pie, too."

"I'm pretty rank." He gestured to his clothes as he washed his hands at the sink. "I can take a quick splash in the creek. I promise to be fast."

She waved off his concern. "You're fine. Later, I'll heat some water for a proper bath."

Thom slipped the small bag from Mrs. Miller onto an empty chair as the rich aroma wafting from the stove made his mouth water. He thought of Hannah, her arms up to her elbows in bubbles, and it made him smile. Her flushed face had brightened seeing him instead of Win coming to fix her pump.

Ivan whined and looked to the door. Without getting up, the dog slowly inched closer, like a sneaky child.

"*Ivan*," Thom said, sternly. "You stay."

"That beast has been jist fine since I brought him in. Been lying by the fire as quiet as a mole. Wonder what has his dander up? Maybe he needs ta go out." She raised an eyebrow knowingly.

Thom quickly sat at the table. He didn't want the dog to spoil the surprise. If Ivan got the chance to get to the chickens, all heck would break loose. "I'll take him out as soon as we eat. He can wait a few moments. My stomach is about to wear a hole right through." She gave him a funny look. Thom flipped his napkin open and put it in his lap. With a slight turn of his body, he shot the dog a surreptitious glare. The shepherd dropped his head between his paws but didn't take his eyes off the door.

Thom picked up Hannah's dish and passed it. "Ladies first."

Mrs. Hollyhock smiled and opened her mouth to respond, but before she could Ivan jumped up, bounded to the door, and began digging energetically at the base. He let go a long, pleading whine followed by a bark.

The old woman stood and set her napkin beside her plate, a lifetime of worry scrunching her brow. "Trouble must be out there, Thom. I'll get my shotgun."

Thom knew the surprise was up. He stood. "It's not trouble. It's your birthday present."

Violet's eyes widened. "My, my—what?"

"Your birthday present. Surely you haven't forgotten," he teased.

Violet looked away for a moment. "Why, I guess you're right. I did forget."

"I have a small gift for you out on the porch. I guess Ivan knows what I'm about." For the first time since meeting Mrs. Hollyhock, the old woman was speechless. "Come on, I'll show you."

He opened the door, and Ivan lunged out. Thom had to hurry to reach the poultry before the dog. He placed the squirming bag into Mrs. Hollyhock's arms, and her eyes popped open.

Carefully, she opened the sack. "Chicks! I can't believe it. I've missed having my little friends." She smiled shyly and her eyes filled. "I keep forgettin' and goin' out to collect eggs." For a moment, Thom was afraid she'd dissolve into a ball of tears. "In no time we'll have newly laid eggs every day!"

The shepherd circled them excitedly, trying to get a good sniff of the interesting bag.

"I'd like ta put them in the coop right away," Mrs. Hollyhock said. "Poor little things must be mighty scared." She handed the sack back to him. "I'll be right back with the lantern. Don't let that beast get too close." She pointed a crooked finger at Ivan. "Sit!"

Thom clamped his mouth shut when Ivan's haunches dropped immediately, as if the dog knew he'd better watch his p's and q's. Ivan gazed longingly at the poultry bag, and a soft whine resonated from his throat.

"But what about supper?" Thom asked. "Won't it get cold?"

Her nostrils flared. "Chicks come first."

Later, with the chicks securely housed, they sat back down at the table. "You were right, Violet. Hannah's concoction is tasty. And so is your soup and bread."

"I'll bake something ta send with you tomorrow. Hannah and Susanna are always on the giving end. I'd like ta do a little something for them."

Thom knew better than to object, even though the last thing he wanted to do was search out Hannah—*again*. Dwight wouldn't waste a moment spreading around what had happened earlier today, exaggerating every detail. Another visit would only add fuel to the fire. Win usually did errands in the mornings. Perhaps he wouldn't mind dropping Mrs. Hollyhock's gift by the restaurant for him. He pushed his chair back and rubbed his belly. "I'm gaining weight."

"I noticed it, too. You'll be as big as an ox when I get through with ya." Her crooked smile turned her face into a vast prairie of wrinkles.

He retrieved the bag off the chair and slid it over to her.

"What's this?"

"I'm not sure. I haven't looked inside yet. Something Mrs. Miller sent along. She told me not to peek, so I didn't."

Mrs. Hollyhock regarded the little cloth bag dubiously, so Thom pushed it closer. "Go on. Take it. It's your birthday, you know."

"She meant it for you, Thom—not me, I'm sure," Mrs. Hollyhock said. She withdrew a big chuck of fudge and eyeballed it for several moments. "You'll soon learn that Maude and me jist can't seem to get along. She thinks I'm a busybody, and has told me so more times than I care to count. All I'm trying ta do is help the poor, addle-brained woman turn a profit."

Thom stretched out his legs, getting comfortable as he took a bite of the fudge and chewed. He hid his smile as he watched the old woman's face grow pinker, thankful Hannah had told him about her birthday. He might actually be able to build a life here again in Logan Meadows. Be a part of the community. He'd been doubtful, but now optimism filled his chest, pushing away the ghosts of his past, the bullet, Levi. "What chores do you need done before I bathe tonight, Violet? Don't hold back on me."

CHAPTER ELEVEN

$\mathscr{H}$annah stood in front of the dining room window, polishing the salt and pepper shakers on table number two. The cheerful tune she hummed felt hypocritical. Her usual Saturday lunch crowd was nowhere to be found. Did the one and only diner, a guest from the El Dorado, notice her discomfort? Muted voices floated in from the lobby.

Down the boardwalk, Dwight stood in the doorway of the saloon, a satisfied smile plastered on his face. Hannah scowled. She'd never speak to the deputy again if she could help it, after the way he'd treated her in her own kitchen last night. She had the right to associate with Thom or anyone else she pleased.

Somewhere outside, a shot went up, startling her, and the saltshaker slipped through her fingers, bounced off the table, and shattered into pieces as it hit the floor. Salt spilled everywhere.

The man stood, concerned. He started around his table. "Are you all right, ma'am?"

She groaned, eyeing the mess she'd created. "Yes. Just clumsy. I'll get the whisk broom and dustpan and be right back."

Back at the mess, Hannah squatted, her lavender dress billowing out around her like a giant umbrella.

The man wiped his mouth on his napkin. "Guess your luck's gonna go bad now." He grinned, and she resisted a prick of anger pooling in her belly. "You better throw some over your shoulder." He took a long drink from his glass of water.

"I'm not superstitious," Hannah replied. She forced a smile. "A mess of spilled salt isn't going to control my destiny." That was a fact. She'd worked too hard to think her success or her failure was due to anything other than backbreaking labor and God's blessings.

A round of laughter erupted outside. Hannah turned hastily, hands still full, and searched out the window, an uneasy feeling growing in the pit of her stomach as she remembered the shot. It soon exploded into full-fledged dismay. A handful of young men blocked the street, their arms locked at the elbows. Behind them was Thom on his horse. They wouldn't let him pass. Hannah couldn't hear what the men were saying, but by their expressions and gestures, she was sure they were stewing for a fight. *Dwight*, she thought.

"It's the jailbird. I wonder what he's gone and done."

She spun around. "He hasn't done anything," she replied defensively. "He has a right to live in Logan Meadows as much as any of us. He served his time." She felt desperate to get outside. "If you're finished, *sir*, your meal comes to thirty-five cents." She held out her hand as he fished around in his pocket.

He placed a few coins into her palm. "Keep the change."

As soon as he left, Hannah dashed into the kitchen and discarded everything, tossing the money on the drain board. Then she ran out the front door and down the boardwalk, trying to hear what was happening.

Without turning, Thom knew the moment Hannah came out of her restaurant behind his horse. Of course she would hear the commotion from the crowd. He removed his hat and dug his hand through his hair as he took stock of the men—if you could call them that—blocking his way. Anger roiled through his belly, hot and acrid. Truth be told, most of them were gangly kids, and he could whip all eight without much trouble. But that's what Dwight wanted. *An excuse to lock me up.*

A fight would be more dangerous than that, though. The doctor's words came back to him: any jostling could move the bullet. Then again, it might never move at all.

"Step aside!" Thom demanded, replacing his hat. He pressed his horse forward with a firm nudge of his heel, and the reluctant gelding tried to step forward. But the line held, causing the horse to snort and throw his head, confused. Thom squeezed forcefully, and the horse lunged, opening a path and spurring a round of taunts and shouts from the agitators. A husky youth clad in overalls reached up. Thom slipped his foot from his stirrup and kicked out, aiming for his shoulder but nicking his face in the process. The young man yelped. Blood gushed from his nose. His friends closed in around Thom's horse.

From the corner of his eye, Thom saw a flash of lavender and knew Hannah was on her way. Anger surged. Didn't she know she was likely to get hurt? She needed to back off. Let him fight his own battles. He'd tried to make that clear to her last night. The more she got involved, the worse it would be for her. *And him.*

From the corner of his eye, he saw Dwight catch hold of her as she rushed by, swinging her around to an arm-twirling halt.

Rage exploded inside him. He reined his horse around, intending to go back, but someone encircled his waist and yanked him from the saddle. The warm loaf of bread Mrs. Hollyhock had made for Hannah and Susanna that morning fell from its cloth bag and tumbled into the dirt.

Surrounded and on his back, Thom took one blow to his face. Amid shouting and taunts, he drew up his knees and catapulted his attacker into the others, successfully knocking several down in the process. He scrambled to his feet, ducked a punch, then slammed his fist into another assailant's belly. Circling, he guarded his face with his fists, but he never had a chance to throw another punch.

A gun blast brought them all up short.

CHAPTER TWELVE

*S*kedaddle!" Maude Miller shouted from the porch of the mercantile. Her smoking shotgun rested in her arms. "Go on. Get! Don't you have work to do somewhere?" The men gathered took a step back, surprised. "None of you are to show your face in my store for a full week, you hear? It won't matter to me if you're starving to death. You won't be getting anything here!" She looked down the walk toward Dwight. "Includes you, too, Deputy. Disgraceful. That's what it is. I'm thankful your pa's not still around to see the likes of this."

With his hat, Thom brushed the dirt from his pants and picked up the flattened loaf that the frightened horse had smashed. He gathered up his reins, trying to calm his fury. He'd like nothing better than to teach them all a lesson. If this was what he had to look forward to for the rest of his life, he didn't need it. He took a step toward the livery.

"Mr. Donovan," the old woman called.

Thom stopped and turned, the pain in his jaw still pulsating.

"After your shift today, will you please come by the store? There's something I'd like to speak with you about."

He nodded. Hannah was still in his line of sight, and he saw her stomp down on Dwight's instep. Dwight let go with an angry curse. She started his way, but Thom stopped her with a look.

"I will, Mrs. Miller. Thank you." He tipped his hat.

"I'll look forward to talking with you." She shot the remaining roughnecks an angry glare.

Squaring his shoulders, Thom led his horse down the street. He kept his gaze riveted on the big double doors of the stable, feeling self-conscious and out of sorts. Hannah's mother was among the growing number of curious spectators. By her side stood a wide-eyed boy, barely reaching to his grandma's middle. His shaggy brown hair was windswept, his body wiry and strong. But it was his eyes that grabbed Thom. They were a startling color of blue that matched Hannah's exactly. Mrs. Brown saw him looking. She frowned and stepped around the boy, shielding him from Thom's view.

This was the first time he'd seen Mrs. Brown since his return. There had never been any love lost between them. She'd been indifferent to Anne Marie, which his sister didn't seem to mind, but whenever he'd come around to pick her up or drop her off, Roberta had made sure he knew exactly where he stood with her. Snide little remarks about his appearance or the way he spoke, with the slightest hint of an Irish brogue, were her specialties. Thom felt the cold chill of her eyes even now. He tipped his hat, making her already-ruddy cheeks deepen in shade.

No one said coming home would be easy. He reached up and stroked the horse's warm neck, thankful when he reached the livery. Stepping into the cool sanctuary of the barn, he called, "Win, I'm here," in a voice that surprised him with his steadiness.

Win poked his head out the door of the smithy. His easy smile helped smooth Thom's ragged nerves. "Good to see you, Thom. You're just in time to help me shoe a horse. He's a kicker and you—" Win's smile fell. He took in Thom's rumpled appearance. "What happened?"

It would be so easy to tell Win what Dwight was up to. *So darn easy.* In turn, Win would report it to Sheriff Preston, and the game would be up. But then he'd still have to prove himself to Dwight and the rest of the town—at least to those Dwight had poisoned against him. There was no getting around that. No, it was better he make it through this one day at a time—on his own.

Win was still waiting on his answer. "Just had a little upset on the way in, nothing much."

"You sure about that?"

"Yeah." Thom would take care of Dwight himself, or he'd never have a moment of peace in his life. He'd find a way of stopping him. He just didn't know how yet.

Between horse grooming and stall cleaning, the day passed quickly. Before Thom knew it, it was time to go home. He wiped his hands and face the best he could. He'd wondered all day why Mrs. Miller would want to speak with him, and he was about to find out. He closed up shop, saddled his horse, and started down the quiet street. At the mercantile, he looped his reins around the hitching rail and went inside.

"There you are," Maude said, swooping out of the back room. "I was starting to think you'd forgotten."

He doffed his hat and remained in the entry.

He was at a loss. It had been years since he'd had to make polite conversation with anyone, never mind the fact that she was an older woman he hardly knew. "Er, we enjoyed the fudge you sent out. We both would like to thank you again for that."

"Both?" She waved him off. "That was nothing. A little welcome home gift—*for you.*"

Welcome home? He glanced away, and a tiny portion of his rejected heart warmed up.

"Mr. Donovan, I have something I'd like to discuss with you."

His curiosity multiplied with each tick of the big grandfather clock in the back of the store. "Thom's fine, ma'am. Just call me Thom."

"Fine," she said as she came closer. "I'll get right to the point. Once the rainy season sets in, this place is no better than my kitchen colander with rivulets running this way and that. My inventory gets damp and moldy. If I don't have enough receptacles to catch all the drips, I have to borrow from Hannah at the restaurant, then spend the rest of the day running to and fro dumping them out." She paused and took a breath. "I'm so exhausted by closing time I can hardly fall into bed. Then I worry the whole night long."

She peered up at him through her scant lashes, a small smile playing around her lips. Was she batting her eyelashes? "If you haven't already noticed, Thomas, I'm a mature woman."

"Ma'am?"

She seemed to be measuring her thoughts. "Well, the sheriff said you have quite a lot of experience with carpentry. What I'm leading up to is this—would you be willing to put a new roof on my store? For pay, of course."

He'd done his share of carpentry in prison. He was good. Reflex made him rub his palms together. "I appreciate the offer, Mrs. Miller, but I'm not sure I'd have the time to do it with my job at the livery." Carpentry paid so much better than the work he was doing now. He hated to turn it down.

"Yes, I realize that. I thought you could work for me in your spare time, perhaps. All the shingles you'd need are in my back room. I have a small rental house on Oak Street that is also due for a new roof. I'd pay you ten dollars for the mercantile and five for the house."

He had no idea why she'd hire him over anyone else. "That's a lot of money, Mrs. Miller."

She ran her wrinkled hands down her apron. "That it is, young man. Are you saying you don't want the job?"

He was silent for a moment. "I don't know how fast I can have it finished for you, but I'll do my best."

"That's all I'm asking. Just start when you can."

Again, thankfulness mixed with a large dose of humility rumbled around in his chest. He nodded and replaced his hat. "Yes, ma'am. Thank you." He turned and reached for the porcelain doorknob.

"Wait. I almost forgot." She hurried over to the mail counter and took a tattered envelope from a covey of small boxes fixed to the wall.

Returning, she held it out to him. "All the way from the bonny green hills of Ireland. It arrived yesterday."

She was trying so hard to make up for the fray that had happened in the street on his way into work today. "Thank you for this." He put the letter into his front pocket and gave it a pat. "I better get going."

CHAPTER THIRTEEN

*H*annah held tight to the reins as the buggy jiggled down the road. She did her best to avoid the ruts caused from the winter runoff, but that proved nearly impossible. Markus, worn out from the morning he'd spent playing with Sarah out at Chase and Jessie's ranch, snuggled next to her side. His flushed face and his half-mast eyes said he'd soon be sound asleep.

She tried not to think about Thom, but that was as difficult as avoiding the ruts. Two days had come and gone without exchanging a word. She'd wanted to talk to him after that horrible fight Saturday, but the look on his face told her to keep her distance. She missed him. She missed his smile and his voice. She missed how she felt when he walked into the room. She missed the way he looked deep into her eyes, even when he didn't mean to. Warmth coiled around inside, stealing her breath.

A sharp bump in the road brought her out of her musings. *What am I doing?* Thom had made his position perfectly clear. A burst of pain pushed away the warm feeling as she remembered him standing in her kitchen, arms crossed and eyes flinty. The fact that he'd known all along that she was sweet on him made the rejection all the worse. *I'm done with him,* she thought. Dwight popped into her mind, and she grunted. *As a matter of fact, I'm finished with men in general.*

Agitated, she straightened in her seat. "Look, Markus," she said, nudging him. She pointed to the rolling meadow halved by the narrow but fast-flowing Shady Creek. A doe and two fawns stood knee-deep in the wild grass, watching their approach.

"A mommy deer," he said in awe. "And two babies."

The doe bobbed her head twice before bounding for the cover of trees, followed by her speckle-backed twins.

She patted his leg. "It's such a pretty day. They must be enjoying it as much as we are."

He nodded agreement, and her good mood returned. She loved Mondays. It was the day Susanna and Hannah's mother minded the restaurant and she had the entire day with Markus.

"Did you and Sarah have fun? After you ran up to her room, I never saw you again. What were you two doing for all that time?"

Sarah, two years older, liked playing the role of big sister. "We played with her dolls until I stuck one in her pa's boot and made her cry. Then she wrote numbers and letters and I had to guess." He slapped his hand on his thigh in an expression of exasperation, the way she'd seen Dwight do many times before. "*Then* she taught me how to make a braid." His face squished in disgust.

Hannah couldn't contain her smile. "Oh, my. She did, did she?"

As he nodded, one of his brows launched into a sharp peak. "Yep. Want me to show you?" He reached up and took a chunk of her hair in his hand, climbing to one knee.

"*Markus*. Sit down before you fall." Grasping his elbow, she settled him back on the seat. "The buggy is no place for shenanigans. You know that," she said more softly and kissed the top of his head. *This little guy can find trouble anywhere.* "Well, did you have any fun at all?"

He shrugged as he let go a long-suffering sigh. "I guess. I wanted to go out to the corral and see the horses. Or find Jake or Gabe." His tone was heavy.

As much as I hate to admit it, Mother is right. Markus needs more male companionship. Last night's dinner with Dwight had been tolerable. Markus seemed to like him. They'd talked for quite a while about fishing and what kind of bait to use. Was that what she should be focusing on—someone who'd make a good father for Markus, regardless of her own feelings?

Entering Logan Meadows proper, the gelding trotted smartly across the short bridge that crossed over Shady Creek and Hannah guided him left, onto Oak Street, on their way to Brenna Lane's house. She had a basket filled with food from the restaurant and fixings Jessie had sent along. Her friend was so blessed with the life she had, her husband…

Life with Thom? A small smile tickled her lips. *What would that be like?* The rhythm of the horses' hooves and the warmth of the summer air drew Hannah back to her daydreaming. She imagined him coming home after a long day of work. Pulling her into his arms first thing and kissing her until she dissolved into a pool of desire. Working around the kitchen, bumping elbows. Lying in front of a crackling fire as the snow outside piled high. She'd known him as her childhood crush, her adolescent first love—even if her feelings *weren't* returned—and now in adulthood, *her friend?* Is that what he was to her? *No!* It would never be enough, she realized. She wanted Thom as her man.

She sighed and gave herself a shake. Daydreaming wouldn't change Thom's mind.

Brenna's was the last home on the street before it turned and connected with the road that led into Logan Meadows. As Hannah drew near, the rhythmic pounding noise of someone at work reverberated above the spinning wheels of the buggy. She glanced about, looking for the source. Then she saw him. If she hadn't had such a firm grip on the reins, they might have dropped from her hands.

Directly across the street from her destination, someone—a large, formidable, and *very handsome* someone—was hammering away on top of Maude Miller's tiny rental house.

Jessie set her clean, carefully folded camisole on top of her shawl, trying desperately to ignore the two letters tucked out of sight at the bottom of the drawer. What was she going to do? She wanted to tell Chase but feared he'd want to take this on like everything else he did—directly. That would mean contacting Mrs. Hobbs. Jessie was not ready to take that step yet. "Stay still," she said gently over her shoulder to Shane. She'd set him on the bed for the moment to free up her hands. As she slid the drawer closed, voices on the front porch of the ranch house drew her attention. Collecting Shane, she hurried through the kitchen to the front room, not wanting who-ever it was to wake Sarah. Totally worn out from her play day with Markus, Sarah had finally agreed to lie down for a few minutes. That was a half hour ago. Opening the heavy pine door, she found Chase, Gabe, and their ranch hand, Blake, in an intense conversation.

"What's wrong?" she asked as she stepped out. Patches the cat darted out and leaped onto the porch rail just as Jessie closed the door. "Has something happened?" Shane brightened at seeing his father, and a smile stretched across his face.

Chase greeted her with a slight nod. His smile looked strained as he gently tousled Shane's hair. "Rustlers. They get bolder by the week. A month ago it was Jeb Swanson's place, then the Triple T in New Meringue. Last night they got us."

Jessie stayed her reaction. Rustlers not only stole cattle; they injured or killed anyone who got in their way. "How bad?"

Chase paced to the porch rail and slammed his open palm against the support post, a hiss escaping through his teeth. When he turned back to face her, his expression was dark. "Eighteen head. Not so bad, but over time…"

"They'll bleed us dry like a nail-poked snake," Gabe drawled. "What can we do? We're not going to just sit around and take it, are we?"

Chase shook his head slowly. "No, we're not. We've worked too hard just to hand it over to rustlers. But with so many new faces showing up in Logan Meadows because of the railroad, it won't be easy to smoke them out."

Lines of strain showed around the corners of Chase's eyes, and he'd yet to shave. His soft-as-whipped-butter chaps rippled when he shifted his weight from one hip to the other. If anyone could catch the rustlers, it was Chase.

"Used to be," he went on, calmer now, more resigned, "we more or less knew everyone in town. We knew if someone was sick, birthing a baby, or spoiling for a fight. Now, not so much."

Blake looked between the men. "What do you want me to do, boss?"

"Double the night shifts."

Blake gave a long whistle. "The men are already pulling extended hours." He plucked the toothpick that dangled between his teeth and tossed it into the flower bed. "They ain't going to like it."

Jessie averted her eyes, but not before she noticed Chase stiffen.

"They'll like it less if they're out of a job." He looked pointedly at Gabe, who nodded his agreement.

Shane wriggled in Jessie's arms, and she bounced him up and down to calm him.

"And tell every man to keep a sharper eye," Chase said. "If things get any worse, we'll have to hire on a few more hands." He glanced down to the bunkhouse. "Where's Jake? I haven't seen him all day."

"In the north pasture mending fence," Gabe said. He looked in that direction with a perplexed expression, and Jessie reminded herself to ask him about it later. Jake had been so quiet for the past few weeks. Had hardly visited up at the house at all. She knew Sarah was missing him as much as she was.

"What about that Irishman, Donovan?" Blake asked. "He served time for rustlin'. Maybe his gang has been waitin' for him to get out of prison."

Jessie sat Shane in the rocking chair, staying close so he couldn't fall out. "I don't think he has anything to do with it," she said. "He was little more than a boy when that happened."

Chase cocked an eyebrow. "So?"

"Well, for one, it would be too obvious. Hannah was just here and had only complimentary things to say about him. He's working at the livery and trying his best to get his life back in order. From what she says, folks aren't making it easy for him to come home."

Chase rubbed his chin. "I've been thinking about him, actually. The day of the town meeting, Hannah asked me to stop by the Red Rooster and introduce myself. You know, befriend him. Things just keep getting in the way. I haven't done it yet."

"Chase, that's not like you," Jessie said. She kept a firm grip on Shane's shirt as he tried to rock the big chair forward and back. "I think you should ride over there this evening and invite him to supper this week sometime. Invite Mrs. Hollyhock, too."

Chase looked at her for a long moment, raising his eyebrows wryly.

"Pa!" the two-year-old said. "Ride Cody!"

Chase smiled, the tension dissipated. He lifted Shane from the rocking chair and bounced him around roughly, extracting a delighted gurgle-laugh. "Cody," Shane called. "Ride Cody."

"That's a fine idea, Jessie," he said, leaning over Shane to kiss her on the cheek. "I'll do it. It's about time we met Thom Donovan."

Jessie shook her head. "Never you mind. You had your chance. I'm going into town on Tuesday afternoon to do some errands and visit Mrs. Hollyhock. I'll take care of the matter myself." *And check to see if any more letters have arrived.*

Hannah took the opportunity to drink in the sight of Thom as he worked on the roof. He'd stripped naked to the waist and had a bandanna tied around his head to keep the sweat from dripping into his eyes. He was beautiful. Imposing. His skin fairly glistened, a result of the sun and hard work. Her heart took off at a gallop, and she once again felt twelve. She smiled, remembering how she and Anne Marie used to hide in the bushes and watch Thom and Caleb skinny-dipping in the creek. Of course, they'd always covered their eyes when the boys entered or exited the water.

Thom dragged his arm across his brow, spotting the approaching buggy. His brows shot up in surprise, and Hannah pulled up on the reins.

"Hello," she called quickly and waved. She tried to act startled, like she'd just seen him, too, and she willed the blush on her face not to give away the fact that she'd been gawking.

She followed his gaze down to his shirt draped across the porch rail. He set the hammer down and started for the ladder. "Guess it's time for a break." He looked from her to Markus, and she remembered the two had yet to be introduced.

"Fancy meeting you here today," she said, standing in the buggy to straighten her dress. She wanted to keep things light. The vivid memory of his angry, battered face, the result of his last meeting with Dwight and the others, was one she couldn't shake. She'd wanted to visit him at the inn afterward, to make sure he was OK, but she knew he wouldn't like it.

He climbed down the ladder and went straight to the three-foot-high rain barrel at the edge of the porch. Taking a bucket, he doused himself, letting the water splash over his body and flood the ground. "God bless the man who invented barrels," he said and smiled. He shook the water from his hair, then ran a small towel over his upper body. He pulled his shirt over his still-damp chest and arms, buttoning up from the bottom as he crossed the street toward them.

Lands above! She tried to look anywhere but at him. Her cheeks scorched hot, and she was sure he saw her embarrassment because his eyes fairly twinkled.

"Something wrong, Hannah?"

"Of course not!" Needing a distraction, she looked down at Markus.

"You have an uncanny talent for seeing me at my worst." His smile was warm. "I think you do it on purpose."

The cotton fabric of his shirt stretched across his chest and forearms. He stood tall, bracing his hands on his lean hips, boots planted a foot apart. He looked dashing. Almost roguish. There was still a shadow of a bruise on his left cheek from the fight Saturday afternoon, which made him look even more dangerous. His eyes narrowed an infinitesimal amount as if wondering what she was doing there. "H-how come," she stuttered, "you're not working at the livery today?"

"Win, good man that he is, gave me the day off so I could get this job done for Maude. He knows she's paying me plenty." He braced one of his boots on the buggy step. "And because the place is small, I'll have it done in a day."

Hannah nodded. The home was tiny but cute. The new shingles stood out easily next to the old, showing his progress.

"Actually, I'm almost finished now. Another couple of hours is all."

"Oh, I almost forgot." Hannah quickly went through her cloth handbag and handed Thom a small piece of paper. "Anne Marie's address. I wrote it down so I'd have it handy the next time we met."

"Thank you." He glanced at it and put it in his pocket. "I appreciate it very much."

Markus stood quietly beside her, but he quickly ducked behind the yards of her pink-flowered dress when Thom looked his way.

"Markus, come here." She reached around and pulled him into view. His eyes were wide. "What is it? Don't be afraid. This is Thom, Nana Katherine's boy," she added in a soft tone. "We've been waiting for him to come home for a very long time." She couldn't stop a quick sideward glance. Their gazes touched. "You've heard us talk about him, right?"

She was proud of her little man. When Markus started to make a fuss, rocking the buggy, she turned back to Thom. "I'm sorry. He's being shy. Let's do proper introductions on the ground, where I won't lose my balance and fall on my head."

She reached out and placed her hands on Thom's wide shoulders, and he easily swung her to the ground. His hands branded her waist, making her insides do a soft flip-flop, and a breathless sensation filled her. Before he had a chance to let go, she went up on tiptoe and kissed his cheek. She was tired of wasting time. She could tell herself she was done with him until she was blue in the face, but it wasn't true. Only one person made her feel this way, and that was Thom. He was in such a good mood, she didn't want to throw away this chance of opening his eyes to what they could have together.

"Hope you don't mind," she said playfully, trying to gauge his reaction.

"You're as light as a feather, why would I?" His face was unreadable, but she thought she saw pleasure in his gaze.

She laughed. "I meant the kiss."

"Oh, *that*." He blushed, then stepped back, out of her reach, and tucked in the tails of his shirt with a sweep of his hand. "What brings you to this side of town?"

"I come almost every week. Brenna Lane's my friend." She motioned to the modest little house that stood a few yards away. "Doesn't look like anyone is home, though." She took the basket of food from behind the buggy seat. "I'll lock this safely away in her kitchen."

Markus hopped down and stood by her side.

"So you must be Markus," Thom said softly, looking at the boy, a sweet yearning written on his face.

"I've wanted to introduce the two of you for the longest time. Since your first day home, actually. You'll see so much of Caleb in his eyes and expressions."

Markus just stood there, his eyes downcast.

"Markus? What's wrong? Have you forgotten your manners?"
Markus heaved a big sigh and shook his head. "No, ma'am."

Thom was struck by how much, up close, Markus looked like Caleb had at that age. The boy had Hannah's eyes, but his mouth and the way it tilted in a cross of contemplation and doubt reminded him so much of his childhood friend that his heart ached. The expression was all Caleb.

It didn't take a genius to see that Markus was upset about something, though, and that *something*, Thom was sure, had to do with him. He grasped the back of his neck, working out the kinks that had been building all morning to a dull ache. He'd wanted to meet Hannah's son, but when she knelt down in front of Markus, a heap of worry on her face, he wasn't so sure it was a good idea.

"Markus?" she said in a soft voice, rubbing his small back.

"Leave the boy. We can meet another time, after I've bathed." He flicked a damp clump of something from his pants. "I'm not fit company at the moment. He's probably scared." Thom laughed, and even to his own ears it sounded strained, harsh.

Hannah glanced over her shoulder and tried to smile. "You're not that dirty, Thom. Something else is wrong. He's never acted like this before. I'd like to get to the bottom of it now." She turned back to Markus. "Son, is there a reason for your behavior? Come on—you can tell me."

Markus kept his gaze trained at his feet. He scuffed them for a moment, and then all was quiet. Thom's pulse pumped in his ears.

"Grammy said not to talk to him." He pointed but didn't look up. "He killed a boy wif a knife. He might hurt me."

Hannah's sharp intake of breath echoed in the silence of the day.

Heat scorched Thom's neck and worked up into his face, hotter than the noontime sun in July. He took a step back. Hannah must have been at a loss for words because she just looked at Markus, not saying anything. What could she say?

"I need to get back to work, Hannah," Thom said gently. "We'll get acquainted another time."

A farm wagon rounded the corner of the dirt road just then, headed for Main Street. Even from this distance, Thom recognized Win driving Bertie and Ned, the draft horse team he took care of. He shook his head and a bit of his humor returned. *I can't believe those horses are my business partners, so to speak. I know their habits and moods better than anyone else I've met in town.* His frame of mind improved even more when Albert gave a friendly wave from the passenger seat. A loud cry of some sort resonated from deep inside the wagon bed.

Thom walked out to meet them as they pulled up in the street. The mournful cries of whatever they were carrying never let up. Hannah and Markus followed.

"What do you have back there?" Thom asked, ignoring the fact that both men were covered in dirt and grime. Looking over the slats he saw a tiny baby buffalo, all ribs and eyes.

Thom's brows shot up in surprise. "Another?" On reflex, Thom reached down, lifted Markus, and set him in the front of the tall wagon so he could see. The boy had been searching for a toehold on the worn steel wheel, trying to climb up. Markus sucked in a breath at the sight of the tiny creature.

"I know what you're thinking, Thom, but I couldn't help it," Win replied. "Last night in the saloon I heard a man talking about a small herd getting decimated. I knew the place he mentioned and recruited my brother's help. It's more than a shame how the United States government, and General Philip Sheridan in particular, is ordering the slaughter just to bring the few Indian buck resisters to their knees. It's downright disgusting."

Albert nodded in agreement. "Just not right."

The nervous calf quivered in the corner, eyeing them fearfully. A half smile warmed Win's face. "It was only a matter of time before some wolf came along."

"Well," Thom said, smiling at Hannah, who stood by his side alight with excitement as she looked at the tiny creature. "I guess Max will have some company now besides me. He follows me around like a lovesick puppy. Bull calf or heifer?" he asked, looking back up at the Preston brothers.

Win beamed. "Heifer. And a real nice one."

Thom cocked a brow. "Oh, boy. I can see where this is going."

Win put up a hand to stop him. "It'd only be natural if—"

Despite her small size, the calf let out an earsplitting bellow, cutting Win off. Win rubbed his ear, and Markus laughed.

"She's hungry," Albert said. "From the look of the carcasses, I'd guess it's been about three days since her last meal."

Markus climbed between the big men and plopped down on the seat. "Can I ride back to town with them, Ma? I'll help wif the calf. She'll need a dummy bottle like we gave Max."

With the newborn bleating for milk and her son dwarfed between the two large men, Hannah's face was awash with love. Her beauty almost stole Thom's breath, and he forced himself to look away.

"What do you think, Thom? " she asked, glancing in his direction. "Do you think the men need Markus's help? Perhaps he could hold the gate for Win and Albert. They're going to have their hands full with this young beauty."

Is she asking to help me win Markus over? Warmth filled him. "You know, I think you're right, Hannah. If it's OK with Albert and Win. A good hand is always welcome."

"You know it's fine with us," Albert said. "Don't worry. We'll keep a close watch on him."

Thom nodded. "Markus, can you be sure to see that Max gets some attention, too? He's usually the main attraction around the livery and might get a little confused. Just a little pat or hug should do it."

Hannah's approving gaze met his, and he suddenly felt like a father, part of a family unit. Somewhere where he belonged. His insides twisted with regret. It would be so easy to give in to his feelings for Hannah. If he was truthful with himself, he'd admit she'd owned his heart forever. And she always would.

Markus, unmindful to what was going on, nodded excitedly. "I'll gib him a scratch on his big furry forehead, just where he likes it."

CHAPTER FOURTEEN

*J*ake hefted the roll of barbed wire into the back of the buckboard, placing it next to several wooden fence posts, and then collected his tools. This was the only part of the Broken Horn's vast
acreage that was fenced. They wouldn't have even had to string
wire here if it weren't for the Cotton Ranch that butted up to their
land. Nell Page was a widow and a cranky one at that—nineteen
and pretty, but set in her ways. Her husband had been full partner
with her brother, Seth Cotton, in the good-size ranch. When he'd
been killed, Nell had stepped into her husband's boots and ran the
ranch alongside her brother.

Chase's cattle had ruined Nell's vegetable garden last year.
When they got into it a second time that spring, Jessie had insisted
Chase do something. It wasn't right to destroy others' property,
especially something as dear as a garden. Chase understood com-
pletely, but he was hesitant. Fencing the land was progress; the
Logan Meadows Herald was printing articles about it all the time.
Still, once that happened and all the outfits in the territories fol-
lowed suit, the range would never be the same.

He leaned against the wagon and removed his hat, swiping his
arm across his moist brow. He was tired. His muscles ached. But
this was exactly what he'd needed to be to get his thinking back on
track. He cussed under his breath, remembering how he'd treated
Gabe in the saloon. He'd acted like the backside of a mule, for sure.

The piercing call of a red-tailed hawk shattered the quiet. Jake drew his gaze from the rippling green grass to the billowing clouds above him. He watched it for several moments, purposely not thinking of anything or anyone. The bird stopped, or seemed to, floating on the wind. It dipped a wing, then soared westward and disappeared behind the jagged rim of the Big Horn Mountains.

What about me? What's my future hold? Whatever it was, surely he couldn't change it. Couldn't change who and what he was. Couldn't change the ache growing in his belly. If he had an ounce of sense, he'd best put aside this anger for the lot he'd drawn, as he'd done for most of his life. Just hunker down and get on with it. He liked it here, but something inside kept whispering to him to find his own destiny. Chase and Jessie cared for him as their own; he knew that. He owed them for taking him out of the bars and teaching him about ranching, cattle, and all the rest. Still he wanted more. A name. His *real* name.

He shrugged into his shirt. That was something he'd never know. He needed to accept that fact and get on with living. Leave it where he had three years ago, back in Valley Springs where his prostitute of a mother had whelped him and all but thrown him away.

Jake turned at the sound of hoofbeats. There was no mistaking that wild mass of golden hair as Nell Page galloped toward him. She was hatless as usual, and rode a chestnut-and-white paint he'd never seen before. She reined up, swung her leg over the back of the saddle, and hopped down.

Jake hastily buttoned up his shirt. "Morning, Nell," he said in greeting. She wore pants better than anyone he'd ever seen.

"Jake." As usual, her tone was all business as she fastened her reins to one of the posts he'd just replaced. The gelding snorted, then pawed the ground. Did she ever smile? If so, he'd never seen it in the years he'd lived in Logan Meadows.

The animal, tethered on the opposite side of the fence, had good straight legs and nice conformation. He was well groomed, and his coat glistened in the sun. He turned and pulled on the reins, looking back the way they'd come. "I like your new horse," Jake said. "Had him long?"

She rubbed her hip. "Long enough to get thrown twice." She lifted her shoulder as if it was of no consequence at all. "Has a temper. Doesn't like me telling him what to do. He'll be a real prize when he's full broke."

Jake nodded, believing every word she said. One thing about Nell Page, she was smart. Just about smarter than anyone he knew. Behind that pretty face and lithe, tomboyish figure was an intellect not to be trifled with. Most everyone in Logan Meadows knew it, too.

Nell bent and slipped through the wire before he knew what she was up to. "Glad to see you've fixed the fence," she said. "I've been keeping an eye on it for over two weeks."

Jake's face warmed even more than it already was from missing the gentlemanly opportunity to help her. "We were in the middle of branding. This is the first time I've had a chance."

She gave a disbelieving look. "You're the only hand at the Broken Horn?"

Damn it. She knew he wasn't. Why did she always insist on picking a fight?

"We had a good number of cows drop several weeks late or we would've been finished on time and I could've fixed it sooner. Chase don't like to traumatize the babies too soon, you know." He smiled warmly, causing her eyes to narrow. "How'd your calving go this year? Get anything unusual?"

She walked around the wagon slowly, running her hand just above the top of the sideboard, as if thinking of her response. *Or trying to make me nervous*, Jake thought.

She glanced at him over her shoulder. *Yep, she sure knows how to make a man squirm.*

"Actually, Jake, we did," she finally said. "Five of our most well-bred cows birthed twins. We've never had more than one set. Seth was pleased."

Jake tipped up his hat, amazed. Not at what she'd just said about five sets of twins, although that was quite astounding. But more, the sudden change in her demeanor was shocking. Her eyes were soft and inviting, her mouth almost tipped up in a smile. She'd stopped and wrapped her arms around herself as she looked off over the prairie.

Why, it must be because she was thinking about those babies being born. There was absolutely nothing cuter than a tiny white-faced bovine with a pink, slippery nose. When they first stood up, their wobbly legs looked like noodles as they stumbled around, wagging their tails and mooing for their mama. The sight could melt the most frozen, jaded heart. Perhaps Nell had just gone through spring thaw.

"Five sets of twins?" he repeated, wanting to stay on the promising subject. "That's amazing. Chase just might want to rent out your bull—for a fee, that is. Those are better-than-average odds. It can't hurt to infuse a bloodline like that, at least into a few of his stock."

She stiffened. Dropped her arms. "We don't let out our bulls, either one of 'em. Can't chance 'em getting hurt."

He shrugged. "Well, it was just a thought."

Right then a big cloud drifted in front of the sun, causing a shadow to fall across the prairie. A sudden gust of wind caught Jake's tipped hat and it flew off, tumbling across the grass right in front of Nell's gelding. As if the hat were some big scary monster, the paint pulled back until his reins gave way, spun a half circle, and galloped off. He disappeared across the range before either of them could say a word.

Jake stood there with his mouth open, while Nell turned and planted her hands on her hips. "Now look what you've gone and done! Didn't you feel your hat lifting?"

"No. Wind caught me by surprise." He went to retrieve it where it had landed by a post some fifteen feet away. He couldn't help chuckling to himself. She was in a pickle, all right. Her ranch was a good hour's walk from here. A raindrop splashed on his forehead at the exact moment he heard a colorful expression behind him.

He grabbed his hat and screwed it down tight, then jogged to the bed of the buckboard and pulled out a tarp from behind the seat. A light rain wet his shoulders and caused his thin cotton shirt to stick to his body. He kept his eyes trained on Nell's face when he gestured to the wagon seat.

She just stared at him for several seconds, her hair clinging to her face. "Why—" She shook her head angrily and climbed up on the buckboard seat. She took the tarp he held out.

Jake ran around to the other side of the wagon and climbed aboard, holding the tarp over their heads. That done, he picked up the reins in one hand and popped them over the mare's back, turning the wagon back toward the ranch. But he pulled up short as two riders crested the hill.

Jake relaxed a bit when he recognized Rome. The other fellow he didn't know. Just to be safe, Jake leaned down and pulled out his rifle from under the wooden seat and laid it across his lap.

"Jake," Littleton drawled as he came closer. He looked down his long, bowed nose. "Mending fences?"

Jake didn't like the look of the other rider. He had shifty eyes, going everywhere they shouldn't. His horse was in poor condition, too. That was a sure way to tell which side of the fence a man walked.

"That's right," Jake said, feeling a bit protective over Nell. "What brings you out this way? In case you didn't know it, this is Broken Horn land. You take a wrong turn somewhere?"

"No need to take offense. Just scouting. I lost cattle to the rustlers myself."

"Yes, I can see how you'd want to be out riding. It's such lovely weather and all," Nell said, sticking out her hand and catching a palmful of rain. Jake was surprised she'd stayed quiet this long.

Rome laughed and nodded. Raindrops spotted his brown felt hat. "Actually, it was, ma'am, until the cloud let loose. It'll stop in a moment. We best get going." They spurred their horses forward and galloped off toward town.

"Well, what do you think that was all about?" she asked, watching them go.

"Not sure." The buckboard rolled along slowly, bouncing over the occasional rock and dipping into an even rarer gopher hole. Jake was too distracted to appreciate the fact he had a beautiful woman, even if she was encased in denim and crankier than all get out, all to himself on the wagon seat. "Felt to me like they were checking things out more than scouting, if you know what I mean."

CHAPTER FIFTEEN

$\mathscr{H}$annah was worried sick. For the fourth day in a row, she'd had so few customers she'd be forced to dip into her savings to pay Susanna her wages at the end of the week—again. That left absolutely nothing to pay her household expenses. Much more of this and she'd have to close her doors.

That thought made her stomach squeeze. The Silky Hen had been in Caleb's family a long time. Even though it had never been her dream to own a restaurant, she'd taken pride in inheriting it so she could pass it on to Markus. It hurt to think she would be the one to bring it to its demise.

Her one ace and blessing was the Wells Fargo stage. And it was overdue by ten minutes. Reaching in the oven, she carefully withdrew three loaves of bread, setting them on a wire cooling rack by the window. The room filled with a crispy wheat aroma. As soon as lunch was over, she'd deliver them to Maude at the store. She leaned against the drainboard with a sigh and pushed her hair off her forehead using the back of her wrist. As usual, her eyes strayed to the livery down the street. *He's made his choice. It doesn't include me.*

Susanna came breezing in, two dirty dishes and a cup and saucer in her hands. She placed them in the sink with a splash. "Pump sure works well."

"I guess."

Susanna arched a brow. "What do you mean, you guess? Your handsome Irish champion did a fine job, best ever. You said so yourself just two days ago."

"Win could have done the same." She sighed. "And Thomas Donovan is *not* mine."

"Hannah, what's got you so down?" Susanna's eyes searched Hannah's face.

She knew if she didn't change the topic of discussion before long, her friend would wheedle everything out of her. "Nothing. The stage is late."

Susanna glanced at the clock. "Not too. It'll be pulling in soon. And I'm praying it's filled with hungry passengers."

"Me, too. We have a passel of roast beef to get rid of." She opened the oven and peeked inside. "It's not bad covered in gravy."

Susanna gave her a sideward glance. Her brows pulled together in question. "You sure nothing's upset you? I've never found you in here just looking out the window before. Are you warm?" She placed her palm on Hannah's forehead. "Coming down with something, maybe?"

I should tell her—her job is at stake. I should, but I can't. Not yet. Hannah forced herself to laugh.

One day last year, Hannah's cook had run out, leaving her holding the bag with a full dining room. As if sent from God, Susanna had stepped through her door, looked around at the frustrated customers, and asked what she could do to help. The two women had been together ever since. Susanna knew a kitchen better than most men knew a saloon. A blessing, to be sure. "No. Just wishing I could be at Shady Creek fishing with Markus. That boy has been excited all week."

"He with Dwight?" Susanna asked in surprise, as she retied the bow of her apron. She took the scrub brush and began washing the dishes.

"Yes. Mother gave him permission. I packed them a picnic lunch with our leftover chicken."

At the sound of hooves, harness, and a shout of "Logan Meadows!" Hannah gave Susanna a smile of relief. "Here's the stage. At last."

Susanna drew her hands from the water and quickly dried them as Hannah went out to greet and seat. She stopped in her tracks, causing Susanna to bump into her backside. Only Ralph, the stagecoach driver, and one old man wobbled through the door. Heat pressed at the back of Hannah's eyes. It was apparent this was the extent of her lunch rush.

Ralph slapped his dusty hat against his leather-clad leg, sending up a plume of dust. At Susanna's cocked eyebrow and cleared throat, he blushed.

"I'm sorry, Mrs. Hoskins, Susanna," he said sheepishly, looking back and forth between the two women. "I guess that best be done outside next time." He hung the hat on a peg.

Two customers, two tables.

"Er, what was that?" the elderly passenger shouted, looking around. "Did you say something?" He dug through a carpetbag, drew out an ear horn, and held it to his head.

"That's all right, Ralph," Hannah said, happy to have at least the two men. "We're delighted you're here. Take any seat you'd like," she said more loudly.

"Drat," Susanna whispered into Hannah's ear. "Looks like another slow day. If you'd rather deliver the bread to Maude now instead of later, I can handle this easily on my own."

"You sure?"

"Are you serious? If I can't cook and serve two meals on my own, I better start looking for another job. Oh, let's not forget Albert will be in shortly. That'll make three."

Susanna did not know it yet, but she might be looking for other employment soon anyway. Hannah hated the thought and vowed not to let that happen. Susanna'd never said anything about family or the details of her past life, but Hannah got the feeling that her friend wanted to keep the past where it was. "Fine. It won't take me but a minute to run the bread next door."

Albert was coming in just as she stepped through the door to leave. "Going so soon?" he asked with a smile.

She shrugged. "I surely won't be missed," she whispered behind her hand.

"That slow?"

"A turtle could walk to Ft. Kearny and back and not lose his seat. I swear…"

"You're not envious over that new eatery, Nana's Place, are you, Hannah? Your customers are loyal—they'll be back. You can't blame them for trying it out once or twice. Why, today the place looked packed."

"Gee, thanks for sharing that, Sheriff," she huffed. "Besides, you don't count. You come to see Susanna, not for the food. And if you must know, yes, I am envious as all get-out!"

Albert patted her shoulder and smiled as Susanna approached. "Curiosity will die down soon enough. Things will get back to normal. You'll see." He strode away, meeting Susanna in the middle of the room. Hannah barely heard their murmured greeting. Susanna laughed softly when the lawman bachelor whispered something into her ear, making her eyes light up and her cheeks blossom.

Stepping through the mercantile door, she let her eyes adjust to the dim interior for a moment. All was quiet. She set her basket on the counter next to the shiny cash register. A new rocker by the window caught her eye, as well as a nice new selection of lantern globes. A basket of brown eggs.

"Maude, you here?" She rang the bell. A murmur of voices came from behind the partition in the middle of the store, where the textiles department was located.

Maude poked her head around the wall and smiled. "Oh, Hannah, so glad you're here. Come see the fabric your mother has chosen for her new Christmas gown. It is just lovely. Imported all the way from England." She waved a beckoning hand. "She'll look stunning when it's all made up. Come see, girl."

Hannah almost stumbled on her way over. *Christmas gown!*

Stepping around the partition, Hannah blinked. She couldn't believe her eyes. On the counter in front of her, dark-blue taffeta rippled like a carpet of spring flowers bending in the breeze and then cascaded to a bolt in a basket on the hardwood floor. Its staggering cost was obvious, even for the wealthiest shopper. She had to find some way to stop her mother before she bankrupted them.

"Isn't it gorgeous, Hannah?" her mother asked, running her hand over the length. "Just the feel of it makes me light-headed. I can see it in my mind's eye now. Oh, it's simply perfect."

Could things get any worse? Then, as Hannah opened her mouth to respond, they did. The door squeaked and someone came in. "Mrs. Miller, I'm here to start on your roof."

CHAPTER SIXTEEN

*W*ere her eyes playing tricks on her? Hannah wondered. If not, Maude Miller had blushed scarlet at the sound of Thom's deep voice.

"I'll be right there, Thomas," Maude said. "Just give me a minute or two."

"Sure," he called back. "Take your time. I'm in no hurry."

Hannah looked back and forth between the women, wondering how best to dissuade her mother. Once Roberta had her mind set on something, it was next to impossible to change it.

"Hannah, you haven't said anything. Don't you like it?"

"Of course I do. It's like Maude said, very pretty."

"Pretty? It's more than that. I cannot wait to see it made up. It will be the most beautiful gown I've ever owned."

The sound of Thom moving about in the front of the store waylaid Hannah's thoughts, and she struggled to focus on the task at hand. "B-but we should wait until Christmas is a little closer, don't you think? It's only May. Certainly too soon to be thinking about parties and such. You might change your mind." She kept her voice low so Thom wouldn't hear.

"Nonsense. It's never too soon to plan for the Christmas season. A stitch in time saves nine. Don't you remember me saying that?" The superior look on her mother's face made Hannah want to scream.

Maude placed a finger against her lips, thinking. "By the way, Hannah, your new boots arrived yesterday on the stage. I'd planned on delivering them later today, but now that you're here I'll get them out of the back room." Before Hannah could stop her, Maude hurried away.

Hannah groaned inside. She could not look at that fabric a moment longer. In anguish, she turned, coming face-to-face with Thom.

He tipped his head in greeting since his hat already dangled loosely in his fingers. "Hannah. Mrs. Brown."

"Thom, it—it's nice to see you," she stammered. It seemed each time she saw him he had put on weight and filled out more. With just the slightest growth of a beard, he looked devilishly handsome.

Her mother stared. Her chin edged up just enough to make it possible to look down her nose at him.

"I can see you're busy," he said, pointing with his hat toward the fabric. He began to back away.

"That we are, *Mr.* Donovan," Roberta said, the tiny lines around her mouth and eyes deepening.

He turned. "I'll just be looking around."

"Here we are," Maude announced as she came through the back room door, holding out a brown pair of women's boots, connected with a length of twine. "Size six, just like you ordered. Why don't you sit right there and try them on? Make sure they aren't too tight. Nothing worse than standing all day in uncomfortable shoes."

"Maude—" Hannah started.

"Go on now." She gave Hannah a little nudge toward the chair. "Roberta, shall I cut the fabric? Are you sure eight yards will be enough?"

Hannah twirled. "Mother, no!" Material of that quality would cost a small fortune. A fortune she did not have. "You're going to have to wait on the fabric."

"What are you talking about, Hannah? Of course I'm getting it now. If I don't, Lorna Brinkley is going to buy it tomorr—" She snapped her mouth closed and quickly looked away.

Hannah's heart sank. Her mother was buying the material out from under her best friend? Of course the two women couldn't have matching dresses. It was too hard to believe. Too horrible. Her mother would not do a thing like that, would she? The enormity of the unkind action and the answer to her own question sapped Hannah of her strength.

"I'm sorry, Mother," she said. "We just can't afford this"— *unbelievable waste of money*—"at this time. You'll have to wait. And I'll have to wait on these, too," she added, handing the boots back to a very confused-looking Maude. "I apologize, Maude. Can you put them out on the shelf? Perhaps they'll fit someone else."

Maude blinked several times before saying, "I won't mind holding them in the back until you're ready to purchase them, dear." She glanced down at Hannah's feet. "Your old ones are paper-thin and worn clean through in some places."

Oh, she wanted to shrink into a little ball and roll into the mouse hole behind the pickle barrel. Thank goodness Thom had his back to them as he inspected a saddle in the leather section. Surely, he couldn't hear their conversation.

Roberta blinked at Hannah in disbelief. "What's this all about, young lady? I want to know this instant. I have *never* been so embarrassed in all my life." At the same time Maude added, "Of course, you can take them on credit if you want, Hannah."

Hannah held up her hand, at a loss for words, and composed herself. After a long moment, she turned toward the door and said over her shoulder, "The bread's on the counter, Maude. I'll talk with you tonight, Mother. Good day."

As Hannah marched away down the boardwalk, Thom longed to go after her. Comfort her. Find out what was going on. Why would she leave the boots she'd ordered behind? He had seen her limping. She needed those. His heart ached for her as he thought of how just yesterday she had tried to make it good between him and Markus. Wasn't she financially set? He had been in the home she now lived in many times back when he and Caleb were boys, and it was nice. Large compared to most of the homes in Logan Meadows. But, as he knew better than almost anyone, appearances could be deceiving.

The back of Thom's neck prickled. He turned to find Roberta Brown drilling him with hate-filled eyes. Maybe she was the problem, spending without contributing back. That wasn't hard to believe. Everything she ever wore looked new, in style. Most likely she'd gone through her own savings and was now working on Hannah's.

"Do you have something to say, Mr. Donovan?" Her tone stretched his already-thinning temper to its limit.

Thom smiled and held her gaze until she had to look away. "You know I do, *Mrs. Brown.* Would you like my opinion on the Christmas gown? Or something else?" He took a step toward the women. Seemed the shopkeeper was stunned speechless over what had just transpired in her mercantile. She just stood there fanning herself with a piece of paper. "Because I'm more than happy to oblige you."

Roberta gave a loud sniff and then looked to Maude. "I better be going. I want to see what this nonsense with Hannah is all about. Silly girl. Probably making a mountain out of a robin's egg. Can you please put this bolt in the back, at least for a day or two?"

Thom swore under his breath.

Maude looked at the expensive fabric for a long time. "I don't know, Roberta. I can't be carrying lavish inventory. First rule of business is sell what you've got."

Mrs. Brown squirmed in humiliation. Thom knew she hated him to be witnessing such an embarrassing moment. "It's only until tomorrow, Maude. *Please*," she hissed softly. "That's only a few more hours. I promise to let you know by morning if I'm taking it."

"Well, all right. But only if you think that you will indeed be buying it."

Thom gave Roberta a secretive nod of triumph, and her face flamed red.

The shop door opened and Deputy Dwight Hoskins came in. He held the door for Markus, who followed behind, struggling with two long fishing poles and a canvas bag.

Dwight went behind the counter, took down the peppermint jar, and lifted the lid. He took a handful and handed some to Markus, who struggled to take them and not drop what he was carrying.

"I thought I told you not to come into my store for a week, Deputy Hoskins," Maude said. "You forget already?"

He laughed and shrugged. "Put these on my tab." He nodded to Roberta, who looked fortified with the arrival of reinforcements. The instant Dwight saw Thom, his expression hardened.

Silence encompassed the room. Thom smiled at Markus, ignoring everyone else. "Markus, did you catch anything?"

Markus opened his mouth to respond, but his eyes darted over to his grandmother standing a few feet away and then back to him. His little shoulders straightened. "Yeah," he said softly.

"Markus. What did I tell you?"

At his grandmother's domineering voice, everything fell from the boy's arms and clattered to the floor. The canvas bag opened and two fish, some live wriggling worms caked in mud, and a chicken leg wrapped in a cloth napkin all rolled in different directions across Maude's clean floor. Markus took a small step back. His eyes grew round in fear as if he knew he was in big trouble now.

"Here, lad," Thom said, stepping forward. He picked up the poles and set them against the counter before going for the mess.

Roberta hurried to the door, using the distraction to escape. "I'll be going now, Maude. Deputy."

"Don't you want to take Markus with you, Roberta?" Dwight asked. "We're finished for the day."

She stopped only for a moment, glancing back. "You said you'd have him until three today, Dwight. I still have some things to do." The door closed to an uncomfortable hush in the room.

Maude went behind the counter and replaced the lid on the candy jar Dwight had left tottering on the edge of the shelf. "Don't worry about the mess, Markus. Three sweeps of my broom will fix it up fine."

Dwight just watched, too lazy to help and not concerned in the least that Markus looked like he was going to cry. "Come on," he finally said when Thom had most of the disarray put back in the bag. "We have fish to clean."

Dwight took the poles in one hand and Markus's hand in the other. Thom didn't miss the look of interest Markus gave him as the door closed.

"Sorry to have kept you waiting, Thomas," Maude said, turning to him. "Never a dull moment in Miller's Mercantile." She laughed. "You're here to work, I presume?"

He nodded. "Just for the hour over my lunch break. The extra shingles arrive?"

"They did. They're in the back. You know the way?"

CHAPTER SEVENTEEN

$\mathcal{A}$s the buggy rolled into town, Sarah, squished between Gabe and Jessie, chatted away like a chipmunk. She oohed and aahed over every little thing she saw. Shane, overcome with all the wonderful sights, sat quietly on Jessie's lap, his head resting against her breast.

"First, we'll go to the mercantile. I'll say hello to Maude and pick up a few things." *And check the mail.* Jessie pushed away her anxiety, refusing to let anything spoil the day. "Then we need to run by Dr. Thorn and have him take a look at Sarah's throat, just to be sure she's totally healed. From time to time, she tells me it still hurts. I want to know if that's common for a three-month-old tonsillectomy. From there, we'll peek in on Hannah at the restaurant, and if the children aren't totally worn out by then, stay and have a cup of tea. The last stop will be the Red Rooster to invite Thom Donovan and Violet out to the ranch."

Gabe nodded. "That's a full day of visiting."

"Oh, I almost forgot. I also need to go by the bank. Chase has some papers he wants me to drop off." Chase, dreaming about expanding the ranch, had written a business proposal he hoped Frank would consider financing, contingent on the railroad coming through Logan Meadows. She worried he was wearing himself too thin. The rustlers were always in the back of her mind, a threat to everyone.

To change her train of thought, Jessie glanced behind the seat, checking on the baked goods she was bringing along as gifts. "I haven't been to town for two weeks, and I'm seeing so many new faces." They passed a wagon with an unknown man at the reins. He smiled and politely doffed his hat. "See what I mean?" she said, glancing at Gabe. "Where did our sleepy little settlement go?"

"It's growing, Jess. It sure is. Whoa." At the mercantile Gabe hopped out and tied the lead to the hitching rail, then went around to help Jessie and the children.

Maude rushed forward, leaving two ladies to their own devices. "About time you came to town, Jessie," she exclaimed. "And you've brought Sarah and Shane with you. It's been a month of Sundays since I've seen either." She chucked Shane under the chin after giving Sarah a hug.

Bang, bang, bang.

At the sudden noise overhead, Sarah latched on to Jessie's skirt and Shane wrapped his arms around his mother, burying his face in her neck. "What's that?" Jessie asked, alarmed.

Maude chuckled. "Don't be scared, honey," the older woman said to Sarah, and then to Jessie, "That's just my old leaky roof getting dressed up a bit."

The other ladies rushed out the door, holding their hands over their ears. "We'll be back another time!" one called over her shoulder.

"You do that. Thank you for coming in." Maude shouted to be heard over more pounding. She gave a friendly wave. She turned back to Jessie. "I'll be so happy when the rain doesn't come gushing in anymore."

"Gushing?"

Maude seemed to be in an exceptionally good mood.

Bang, bang, bang.

"Well, maybe not gushing, it's more like drip, drip, drip. Still." She laughed and then went on, "It'll be a sight better when everything stays dry. Thom Donovan is doing the repairs."

Jessie filed that fact away. "I haven't yet had the pleasure of meeting our newest citizen."

Maude sidled up close. "He's as handsome as they come—and then some." She glanced down as if to make sure Sarah wasn't listening. "It's his Irish blood, to be sure."

"Maude?" Jessie giggled.

The shopkeeper shrugged. "I may be old, Jessie, but I'm not dead."

Remembering the bread she still held in her arms, Jessie thought it a good diversion. "I've brought you some buffalo berry nut bread."

Maude's eyes went wide. "Oh, you needn't go to all that trouble for me, honey. I have all this at my fingertips." She swept her arm to the side.

"That may be true, but you deserve some home baking, too, now and then. I know how hard you work." She gave Sarah a little nudge on her back. "Why don't you go look through the fabric in the snippets bin? We'll make that new nightgown for Dolly McFolly we've been thinking about."

Sarah ran off, and Maude gave her a knowing look. "You need to talk in private?"

Jessie nodded, bouncing Shane in her arms. "Sarah's birthday is coming up in three weeks and I'd like to order something special. Maybe a play tea set. I hope I didn't wait too long."

Bang, bang, bang, bang, bang.

Every time the banging sounded, Shane clapped his hands.

Smiling, Maude leaned in close, keeping her voice at a whisper. "Not at all. I know of just the one. Made of real china but not expensive. I should be able to get it in by next week if I send a telegram."

"That's wonderful. She'll be turning seven this year, and Chase and I want it to be special. She's growing up so fast."

Bang, bang, bang.

"Mommy, I found the perfect one. It'll even match her other dress." Sarah ran back, emerald material with little yellow flowers clutched in her hand. "See," she cried, holding up her prize. Shane reached out and tried to snag it, but Sarah danced out of his reach, laughing.

"Sweetie, that's perfect. We'll take this, Maude," Jessie said, smiling at the conspiratorial look in Maude's eyes.

Bang, bang, bang, bang, bang.

Jessie squashed the urge to cover her ears and pointed up to the ceiling. "How long is that going to go on?"

Maude shrugged as if it was of no consequence and moved to the counter. She jotted down the purchase in a ledger and then quickly wrapped the small square of fabric in brown paper. She handed it to Sarah. "Here you go."

Jessie waited by the door. Had the mail arrived today? Was there anything new for them? She glanced at the mail counter, but from this distance it was impossible to tell. *That's one of the reasons you're here*, she chided herself.

Bang, bang, bang, bang, bang.

Ask!

"Well, we best be going." She glanced out the window. Gabe leaned against a post, people watching. "Come on, silly girl."

Maude gave her a hug. "Thanks for the nice gift. I'll enjoy it."

"You're welcome." She glanced again to the back of the store. "Er, Maude, have we gotten anything in the mail lately? Chase wanted me to check."

Her face lit up. "I'm glad you asked. Yesterday. I meant to tell you when you first walked in, but we got to talking." She went and retrieved the envelope. "From the orphanage in New Mexico again. This is the third post this year."

A rocklike ball of dread dropped in Jessie's stomach. A quick glance at Sarah showed her darling girl clutching her prize to her chest and smiling sweetly up at Maude. Jessie wouldn't let *anything* break up her family. Sarah belonged to her and Chase. The child had brought them together. They were a family. Jessie pushed away her panic and put the post into her satchel. "Thank you, Maude," she said and smiled. She stepped out into the sunlight. "I just hope you still have some clientele by the time Mr. Donovan is finished."

On the boardwalk, Sarah unwrapped her purchase and held it out to show Gabe. When he saw Jessie, he went over and took Shane from her arms.

"Thank you. He's getting so big, sometimes I forget how heavy he is."

"Why don't I keep him while you take Sarah to the doctor's, the bank, and then to the restaurant?" Gabe said. "Shane and I will meander around town and pet the horses."

"Oh, Gabe, that would be a blessing. Are you sure you don't mind?"

"I got the day off to help you. I'm enjoying some time away from the cattle and flies."

She rubbed Shane on the head. "I can't pass up such a generous offer. You be a good boy for Gabe, you hear?" Shane was already smiling from ear to ear. "In case he needs anything, his duffel is in the buggy."

Gabe took a step back, shaking his head. "I'll find you if he needs a change."

Jessie laughed. "Oh, all right. But you can't blame a girl for trying."

CHAPTER EIGHTEEN

*T*hom rolled his shoulders and stretched his worn muscles as he wandered slowly through the small cemetery. He'd finished at Maude's, his lunch hour gone, then headed back to the livery, only to ask Win if he could have a few more minutes. Setting Maude's shingles had brought on a storm of memories. Working side by side with his pa and Roland, swinging fast on their slippery barn roof, trying to beat the coming rain. They'd just set the last row as a bolt of lightning lit the sky. Scrambling off, they'd found a big stew ready and his ma waiting for them all.

It was time. He needed to do this today. He'd been avoiding the truth for too long.

First things first. Second row, three graves down. He moved slowly. Stopped. Levi Smith. The grave was old. Thom stood there, the sun warming his back. Born 1857. Died 1873. He'd been here before. The day they'd buried Levi and again on the day he had left town.

Thom turned, headed to the back of the cemetery, knowing that was the Irish section, as well as the Polish and German. His steps, muted by the grass-covered earth, took him between the gravestones and alongside a tree where small birds hopped between the branches. Plain wooden crosses, as well as large stone markers, filled his view. Some with stories of the deceased chiseled carefully to commemorate the memory of the loved one. He came upon Caleb's grave next to Caleb's father and mother. No weeds grew around the headstones. Hannah and Markus must tend to them often. *Caleb dead, too.* It was still so unbelievable.

Moving on, he crossed the wooden bridge spanning the dry creek bed, remembering how it would fill as soon as the fall rains hit. On the other side, a small marker noted he was on the hallowed ground of the immigrants of Logan Meadows.

Only a handful of graves. He stopped, unsure he was ready to face the reality of what Sheriff Preston had told him only six days ago. Six days that felt like an eternity.

Katherine Abby Murphy Donovan.

A fistful of wilted flowers adorned the base of her headstone, and the grave was tended just as lovingly as was Caleb's family. *Hannah.* A burning sensation pressed on the back of his eyes. He looked away.

On the left side of his mother's grave was *Roland Aeary Donovan*, and on the other, *Loughlan Donal Donovan*.

He removed his hat. "I'm sorry," he said softly. "I never should have left. Never should have gotten into that fight with Levi. You told me, Pa, nothing was worth fighting over. You taught me to use my brains and not my fists."

He closed his mouth. There was nothing he could say. There were no words deep enough to express his sorrow. If only he could go back. Do everything over.

"Thom?"

His heart lurched. The sound of Hannah's soft whisper caressing his name pulled him from this nightmare, promising love, laughter—life. Oh, how he wished things were different, that he'd never run from his pain, setting the course of his life. If only he and Hannah could find each other now. Pick up where they'd left off. Become the couple they were meant to be. He wiped his eyes again, reining in his emotions before he turned to see her waiting on the bridge. He waved her over.

"I saw you walking across the hill," she said softly as she approached. "I knew it would be difficult for you to see the graves. Do you want me to leave?"

He shook his head.

"If you're sure you don't mind my—"

He pulled her into his arms, burying his face in the crook of her neck. Her body melded to his. Warm, comforting. Her arms went around him, a lifeline, keeping him safe. She turned her head and kissed his cheek, his jaw. To know that she was here, that she loved him and wanted to be part of his life, meant a lot. Warring emotions jumbled up inside. He longed to rage against the injustice of all the lost years. The small orb of metal at the base of his skull dictating his actions. His parents and brother planted here in the ground like a gruesome new crop.

Unable to hold it off, a burning-hot sob fought its way from a grief so deep, it frightened him. Another followed. Then another. And another.

Hannah's calming touch moved up and down his back. She did not have to voice a word for him to know exactly what her touch was saying. Several minutes passed. He stilled. They parted, and he wiped his eyes with the back of his hand.

She reached up and brushed his hair off his forehead, studying his eyes. "I'm sorry you had to come home to this."

"I keep thinking about what they went through," he said, glancing at the graves. "It's difficult for me to believe. The last conversation was a fight with Pa the night I left. He couldn't understand. Why I was leaving, I mean."

She put her hand on his arm, and he studied her delicate fingers for several long moments.

"Why *did* you leave, Thom? The judge ruled Levi's death an accident. You weren't in trouble with the law."

Thom looked at the town, trying to make the jumbled mess make sense. People were moving about on the street, going about their day. He could see the side of the Red Rooster from his vantage point on the hill. "It's hard to explain, Hannah. I couldn't bear the pain on my father's face another minute. I was responsible. I'd killed a boy. Taken a life recklessly. I'd disappointed my pa and let him down. Hell, I'd crushed his soul, if I'm being honest with myself. And what about Levi?"

"What about Levi?" Anger laced her voice and her eyes were hard. "*He* was the one who drew the knife. Just what did you think he was going to do with it? Whittle you a present?"

"What happened to his family?" Thom remembered Levi's mother, totally crushed, weeping by his grave.

"They moved away."

"Hannah."

"No, Thom, listen to me. You were only a boy. I'm sorry Levi died that day—I'll be the first one to say it. But you're not to blame. You did not kill him. He *fell* onto his *own* knife." She grasped his arm and gave it a listen-to-me shake. "I can't say that I understand why your pa didn't stand by you more, if you say he didn't. We don't know what shapes others into who they are. You have to let this go."

All he could do was listen. He'd run out of words.

"Life happens, Thom. As bad as it was for Levi to die, there are more tragic things, I think. A life wasted. Walking through each day trying to pay back something that wasn't your fault. The day Caleb died, I promised myself I'd never spend a day in regret over anything. Never put off something that's important to me. Never leave a good word unsaid." She hesitated. "I'll tell you something I've never shared with anyone. The day Caleb died, I went over to the restaurant when the cook we had summoned me for some problem, I can't even remember what it was now. I hadn't realized Caleb was that sick. None of us did. He died alone. I didn't even get a chance to tell him good-bye. Or that I was carrying his child. I'd had suspicions, but I planned to wait until he felt better. Thom, don't waste a moment of your life. That moment could be your last."

It would be so easy to pull her back into his arms. To taste her lips, feel her warmth, all the things he'd dreamed about so often in his prison cell. It had been the memory of Hannah Brown that had pulled him through day and night. It was Hannah with her laughing eyes and charming smile.

She tipped her head. "What're you thinking?"

"Just trying to figure you out." She didn't know how close she was to the truth of the matter. That bullet could put him down now, right here, this instant. If only he didn't have that piece of metal controlling his life. There were so many *if onlys* he didn't want to think about them anymore. Still, he'd not set Hannah up for more hurt and misery. She had Markus to consider, as well as herself.

She shrugged and walked toward a rustic bench at the edge of the cemetery, where grassland met graves. She sat, then gave him a smile knowing full well he'd follow.

"I need to get back to the livery," he said, now standing in front of her like a dolt. "I told Win I'd only be gone for a little while."

She patted the spot next to her. "Sit for just a moment."

He shook his head. "I really need to get back."

A flicker of hurt crossed her eyes before she looked away. She stood and straightened her dress. "All those years locked up in a cell couldn't have been easy. Then to come home and find your family dead or gone is the most heartbreaking thing in the world. I just want you to know that I'll always be here for you, Thom. And I'll keep being here for you until you see just how much happiness there can still be in your life and just how much you still have to lose." Then, without another word, Hannah turned and started down the path toward town.

Jessie was waiting in front of the El Dorado Hotel when she saw Hannah coming down the hill. She waved. "Perfect timing," she called, holding Sarah by the hand. Dr. Thorn had checked Sarah's throat and said everything looked completely normal. Phantom pains. *Fit as a fiddle,* he'd said, much to Jessie's relief. "I was just coming in for a quick visit and a cup of tea. Do you have a moment? I want to invite you and Markus to a picnic I'm planning."

Hannah smiled warmly, contradicting the shadow of sadness in her eyes. "Sarah, where have you left that little brother of yours?" She squatted, getting eye to eye with Sarah.

Sarah blushed. "Gabe is showing him the horses." She pointed to several tied in front of the bank. "So Ma and me can get things done."

Hannah looked up at Jessie and winked. "I see. Sometimes little hands and feet make that difficult, don't they?"

Sarah nodded, agreeing emphatically. "'Specially when he cries and throws a fit."

Jessie couldn't stop her giggle. "So true. Shane is very good at making his needs known. He's not shy at all." She glanced around. "Markus doesn't happen to be here, does he? Sarah would like to say hello."

"He's not. His uncle Dwight took him fishing today. They're spending fella time together." Sarah scrunched her face, and Hannah laughed. "We can have fun, too. Come on. Let's find something delectable to go along with our tea."

Jessie stepped into the near-vacant dining room. "Where is everyone? Feels pretty quiet in here."

"Oh, it's just one of those turtle days. Every restaurant has them now and then. Follow me. We'll visit in here." Hannah preceded them into the kitchen, where Susanna was mixing up some sort of batter.

Jessie pulled out a chair at the small break table and seated Sarah, hoping beyond hope that Hannah's teasing words were true. They watched as Hannah set about warming water and opening a very interesting-looking crock. Sarah's eyes lit up when she began arranging delicious-looking cookies onto a plate.

"There now," Hannah said, setting cups filled with hot tea onto the table along with the cookies.

Sarah quickly picked one up. "Thank you, Mrs. Hoskins."

"You're very welcome. Such nice manners on this young lady."

The letter in Jessie's bag made it hard to return Hannah's smile. She'd been in a fog since leaving the mercantile. She only nodded.

"I'll bet she's anxious to start school in the fall."

Jessie cup rattled. "She's not ready for school!" Could she bear to let Sarah out of her sight for a whole day? What if someone were to find her, take her, when Jessie wasn't there to stop them?

Hannah's head whipped around. "What are you talking about? Of course she is. She knows far more than most for their first year."

"I don't know." Jessie hesitated. "I'm thinking about keeping her home another year." At her remark, Sarah's face fell, and Jessie wanted to take it back—but couldn't. She'd do anything to keep her little girl safe.

"Jessie, I don't agree. I think—"

Jessie laughed and shook her head, hoping she sounded care-free. "Forgive me, Hannah, but it's time to go." She finished her tea and wiped her mouth, then set her napkin on the tabletop. "We still have a lot to accomplish before we start back to the ranch, don't we, Sarah?" She stood, feeling like the worst of friends. Hannah looked confused as she helped Sarah up.

"Jessie?"

"Don't forget the picnic. It's going to be a fun day," Jessie called, hurrying out the door.

CHAPTER NINETEEN

The feel of Hannah's body pressed up against his was still on his mind as Thom hustled into the stall and haltered Bertie, the large half-Percheron draft mare. Her hefty feet clomped as he led her down the center passageway, then turned her out into the small pasture out back. She ambled off toward Max and the tiny bison heifer.

Three more stalls. If he didn't hurry, he'd get a scolding from Mrs. Hollyhock for being late. Supper was on the table at five twenty-five and not a minute later.

With pitchfork in hand, Thom set about to strip Bertie's stall, reminding himself with each hefty, urine-soaked forkful that he was grateful to have this job. Hannah sitting on the bench popped into his head. *Nope, not going there.*

"He has a small crack on the outside of his right front hoof, due, I think, to improper shoeing." Win's powerful voice was hard to miss coming from the forge. "It's not bad enough to cause the lameness, though. Must be a stone bruise. Some time off it will do him a world of good."

"I know you can't work miracles, Preston. I tried to get him to you sooner but I've been busy. I hope I haven't made things worse."

The pitchfork froze midair. *Rome Littleton!* Thom hadn't seen him around since his first day in town and had assumed the rustler had ridden on.

No fighting. The doctor's words reminded Thom why he couldn't take Rome on here and now. The fact that Thom had to avoid giving Rome what he deserved produced a tangible fury. He'd been fortunate there had been no complications three days ago when he'd been yanked from his horse and then punched in the face. Thom didn't want to test Lady Luck too often.

Win came through the breezeway, leading a seal-brown gelding to the back of the barn. He quickly removed the animal's bridle and haltered him, then tied him to the hitching rail. It took less than a minute to strip off his saddle and put it in the tack room. On his way through, he paused at the stall door where Thom worked. "I didn't know you were back."

"Win." Thom stopped and stuck the pitchfork into the straw-covered floor of the stall, trying to mask his irritation. He liked Win. Owed him a lot.

Win's astute eyes remained on Thom's face. "Something wrong?"

Thom hated to mislead Win. For one, it was wrong. Two, his boss had been a friend when he needed one most. Nevertheless, what was in the past was going to have to stay there. If he fingered Rome for his part in the rustling all those years ago, it was the word of an ex-convict rustler against, most likely, one of a trusted ranch hand or owner. Thom didn't know what Rome's standing was in the community. Many years had passed. Anything was possible. Who did Thom have to vouch for him? *No one.* He'd do well to remember that when his Irish temper called for vengeance.

"Not a thing."

"How'd it go up on the hill? At the cemetery?" Win's Adam's apple bobbed nervously. *Probably sees my red eyes.* "You all right?"

"Had to face it. It's still difficult for me to believe."

The older man nodded in understanding. "Will be for some time to come, I'm sure. You let me know if there's anything I can do to help." With a quick pat on Thom's arm, he left the smithy and Thom to his thoughts.

"I don't know about you, Sarah," Jessie said, hefting Shane to the opposite side of her lap so Gabe could help her down from the buggy. They'd reined up in front of the Red Rooster Inn. "I'm getting tired. Good thing this is our last stop." Sarah slumped against her side, all but worn out.

With the bedraggled group on the ground, Gabe carefully lifted the chocolate cake from behind the seat. They started for the door, but a large long-haired dog jumped up and began barking, stopping them in their tracks.

"Hush, you hairy beast!" Mrs. Hollyhock scolded, stomping out of the inn to grab the dog by the collar. She shook her finger in his face. Turning, her eyes lit with pleasure and her lips tipped up.

"Jessie! Gabe! Sarah! Oh, and little Shane, too."

Jessie held them back.

"Come in, come in," she said, looking around expectantly. "Where's that husband of yours, Jessie? He run off yet?" Mrs. Hollyhock muscled the animal back, which, now up closer, Jessie saw was old and gray. Eyes a bit rheumy. They tromped up the stairs and went inside. Truth be told, the older woman loved Chase almost as much as Jessie did, but she'd never admit to such a thing. The table was set and dinner simmered on the old woodstove, filling the room with a hearty goodness. Gabe discreetly set the cake on the table.

"Whose dog is that?" Sarah asked, inching toward the animal standing in the doorway. His tail wagged back and forth as if waiting for an invitation to enter. "Look, Mommy!" she added, the smile in her voice infectious. "He's grinning at me."

"Ivan belongs ta my new houseguest, Thom Donovan. It was his ma and pa's out at the old ranch."

Gabe nodded. "That's right. I've seen that dog around a time or two, now that you mention it. Twice running through the meadow past town."

"Thom said that's 'cause Hannah took him home a couple o' times after Katherine—God rest her soul—passed on. Wanted to give 'im a home. Keep 'im fed. But the beast kept runnin' back to the ranch. Sort of makes my heart hurt if I think about it too long."

"Can I pet him?" Sarah loved animals. Any animal, it didn't matter.

"Go on—he won't bite you."

Everyone turned at the deep voice that came from just outside on the porch. The man came up to the doorway, and the dog sat by his feet. "Don't be shy. Ivan likes little girls."

Emboldened, Sarah went forward and rubbed the animal on the head, looking back at Jessie. "He's nice." Shane reached out his arms wanting to go to the dog, but Jessie held him close.

Maude hadn't exaggerated. Thom Donovan was incredibly handsome, with his thick, wavy brown hair and piercing toffee-colored eyes. Jessie felt her cheeks heat up, and she glanced away. She hoped her discomfort wouldn't be noticeable to anyone else. There was indecision written in his eyes.

"Thom," Mrs. Hollyhock said. "Come on in and meet some of Logan Meadow's finest citizens."

"I'd like to, Violet, but I'm not fit for company. Been working in the sun, then cleaning stalls."

He leaned in the door and looked at the old grandmother clock hanging above the fireplace. "I have exactly fifteen minutes to get a quick bath and get back here before suppertime." He gave Mrs. Hollyhock a wink. "I don't want to make my hostess angry."

Sarah ran her hand down the dog's back and came around Thom, already completely comfortable in Thom's presence. She looked over at the table set for supper. "Who's coming to dinner, Grammy?"

Sarah was putting her math skills to good use, but Jessie wished she hadn't asked Violet that question now.

The smile slid from Mrs. Hollyhock's face. "It's just Thom and me, honeybee."

"But you and him"—she pointed with her chin—"make two. I count three plates. See?" She ran over to the table and proudly counted aloud for everyone to hear.

Mrs. Hollyhock looked bemused for a moment, then went over and rested her gnarled hands on Sarah's shoulders. "Well," she began. "The third plate is for my boy. Remember I told ya one time that he went away but I think he's comin' back? Well, if I'm right and he does, I want him to feel welcome. I want him to know I've missed havin' 'im here with me." Her voice nearly cracked. "What's this?" she asked, looking at the cake. Jessie was sure it was her way of changing the subject.

"Your birthday present," Jessie said quickly. She blinked away the moisture that had gathered in her eyes. "From all of us. I'm sorry it's late."

"Oh, honey. You shouldn't have gone ta all that trouble for me. I mean that."

"Happy birthday," Gabe added, taking the cover off the keep so she could see it.

"Would you just look at that? It's the finest cake I ever did see. Would you all like a piece?"

"No," Jessie said. "It's for you. And Thom. We have to get home and get supper on the stove for Chase."

Thom was backing away. She had only a few moments to extend their invitation. Shane was squirming in her arms and he was going to erupt at any time. "Mr. Donovan," she began. "My husband and I would like to invite you out to the ranch for a picnic after church this Sunday. You, too, Violet. It's been much too long since we've spent the day under the cottonwoods."

Thom's foot rested on the second step, the large black-and-tan dog by his side. He glanced around at all the faces, coming back to hers.

"You're welcome to bring Ivan," Jessie added.

"I'd like that very much, thank you, Mrs. Logan."

"It's Jessie. You can call me that."

His concerned glance at Mrs. Hollyhock only endeared him to her even more. "You'll show me the way?"

"Of course," Mrs. Hollyhock said.

Thom nodded. "Fine. I'll get the buggy from Win."

After supper Thom lay on his bed, the letter addressed to his mother sitting beside him. Poor Mrs. Hollyhock. Her pain was so evident. All this time, waiting for her son to come home. Not knowing where he was. If he was dead or alive. *Is that what I put you through, Ma?* he thought with shame.

Ivan, next to his bed, heaved a long sigh and collapsed to his side. Thom picked up the post a third time and looked at it. The return address was from Shannon O'Hays, his mother's cousin. He opened it.

My dearest Katherine, it began. *I think of you often. If only we didn't have this wide ocean between us. Remember when we were wee girls and planned to marry a set of handsome brothers? Live side by side. Raise our children together. Share Sunday suppers and rock each other's grandbabies. It's been so long since I've heard from you. I know it must be hard now with Loughlan gone and worrying over Thom. I can't complain too much, though. I haven't written often enough either. The rheumatism in my hand makes holding a quill very difficult.*

My daughter Maggie has completed her studies in Dublin. If you remember, she and Thom were born on the same blessed day.

Times are changing so fast. You and I would never have considered leaving our homes as Maggie did, to further her education. She's a sassy one, to be sure. And much braver than I've ever been. And she's a bit too determined for her own good. I fear there isn't a man here, or in America, bold enough to take her on.

Thom threw his arm over his eyes, remembering how animated his mother would become whenever she'd remind him about his Irish-born female cousin and the fact they shared the same birthday.

Thom forced himself to read on, ignoring the pit of loss that burned in his belly.

Well, I must go now. There are chores to be done. Write me when you are able. Always know you and yours are in my daily prayers.

Your loving cousin, Shannon

Thom folded the correspondence and carefully tucked it back into the envelope. His mother had had dreams of her own. Young. In love. Ready to set the world on fire. He let the envelope fall to his side, suddenly aware of something he'd never considered. He did have family. Family besides his sister Anne Marie. Ireland. Of course, he had Hannah, too, and Markus, in his heart. What more could a man want?

CHAPTER TWENTY

*A*lbert reclined in his chair as Chase paced back and forth in front of the sheriff's desk, feeling like a caged mountain lion. Rustlers, again! His spread and the neighboring ranch. Despite the extra men he'd hired on.

"What is it exactly you want me to do, Chase? It's Saturday. Town's busier than I've seen it for a long time. I can't go door to door looking for a smoking branding iron. I promise you, I'm on it. We'll catch 'em. But these things take time."

Chase stopped at the window and stared at the livery across the street. Albert was right. Five unidentifiable horsemen sat their mounts outside Win's and he had no idea who any of them were. Some could be citizens of New Meringue, here for the announcement this evening. Choosing Logan Meadows for the important proclamation had to be an indicator the railroad was coming here. The Union Pacific was only fifty miles away.

"They got our best bull, Albert," Chase said as he turned. Anger built inside until he had to squelch the urge to shout. "Last year we went without to be able to afford him. Gave it plenty of thought before spending that kind of money on one animal. And it's not only me. Other ranchers around here can't afford to lose any more cattle either."

Dwight strode through the door and stopped. "Chase, you in town for the meeting?"

"Partly."

Albert leaned forward. "Rustlers hit his ranch for the second time last night. As well as the Cotton Ranch."

Dwight's brows dropped in concern. Going to the potbellied stove on the far wall, he poured himself a cup of coffee. "How bad?"

Chase glowered. "Bad enough. One steer is too many."

"I agree." Dwight sat in a chair and propped his boots on a gunnysack he'd filled with rocks to serve as a footstool. "Have any idea how many? Two, six, more?"

Damn the brazen deputy, sitting here questioning him. He should have the answers. "Looked like two riders from the tracks we found."

"What direction did they go?"

"You're just full of questions, aren't you? Why don't you ride out there and check for yourself. That's your job, isn't it?"

"Chase," Albert interrupted. "Don't take your frustrations out on us. I just spent three days combing the territory without finding a clue. It's never easy to catch rustlers. And these men are smart. The minute you get close, they clear out."

Chase checked his temper. "We followed their tracks to the high country but lost them in the sandy loam. Rain all but cleared them out. Have two men still out looking, but that's all I can spare. Can't leave the herd unprotected."

"I guess not, with all the land you own."

Chase turned on Dwight. "What the hell are you talking about? No one handed me that ranch—I *worked* for it!"

"Ain't what I heard. I thought the banker got it for you."

Albert stood. "Dwight. That mouth of yours is going to get you killed someday."

Chase put his hand on the doorknob, but turned and leveled a piercing look at the deputy. "I don't care what you think, Dwight." His voice was low, dangerous. "Your opinion is about as important as a beetle peeing in a rat hole. For the life of me, I can't figure out why Albert keeps you on."

Dwight jumped up, spilling his coffee down the front of his shirt. "Shoot!" His face scrunched in pain as he haphazardly wiped at the brown blotch marring his pressed white shirt. Coffee dripped to the floor. "Look what you made me do!"

Chase opened the door and walked out.

At the festival grounds, Hannah slipped into the second row of seats, taking the chair Jessie had saved for her. Paper lanterns hung from the trees and swayed in the breeze. She nodded to Chase, sitting on the other side of his wife. Excitement reverberated through everyone, as the all-important announcement would come any moment.

Jessie leaned over. "How was your lunch crowd today?"

Hannah hadn't had to say anything to her friend for Jessie to figure out what had been on her mind. "Pretty busy. We even ran out of one of our specials." It was impossible to keep back the smile of relief she felt coming on. "Now, if it could just keep going in that direction."

Jessie patted her leg. "It will. Now with the railroad coming through."

Hannah pulled her shawl more snugly around her shoulders. Mr. Peabody stood behind the stage talking with her uncle Frank and Sheriff Preston. She surreptitiously glanced about, looking for Thom. Nell Page was a few rows back, sitting with her brother, Seth. Maude was there, as was Win. Brenna Lane was all the way in the back, sitting alone. Penny must be home watching her siblings. And there were a host of faces Hannah had never seen before. The El Dorado Hotel must be as busy as she'd been today at the Silky Hen.

She nudged Jessie. "Where are the children?"

"With Mrs. Hollyhock. Markus?"

"Home with mom," Hannah replied, spotting Dwight at the forefront of the gathering. He caught her eye and smiled.

Jessie turned to her as if to say something and stopped.

"What?"

Jessie looked torn. "Oh, it's nothing."

"Come on, spit it out."

Her friend's brows drew down even as she tried to smile. "I'm sorry for snapping when you asked about Sarah going to school and then rushing out. I guess I was just tired. Had a lot on my mind."

She'd noticed Jessie's preoccupation the past few weeks and wondered if she was telling her everything. Keeping Sarah home another year would break the child's heart. "You don't have to apologize to me. You know that, Jessie. But if there is anything I can do for you, concerning anything at all, just let me know."

A real smile returned to Jessie's face. "Thank you. I'll remember that. By the way, how are things with your mother? I wanted to ask you about that on Tuesday, but I completely forgot."

"About the same, I guess. I am grateful for her help with Markus. I don't know what I'd do if she didn't look after him for me. I just wish she wouldn't try to run my life so much. You know, pushing Dwight at me all the time." *And criticizing Thom.* "I'm sure we'll work it out." What if her mother were more independent? Had a social life other than gossiping? Everyone needed a purpose in life. Right now, her mother's entire world revolved around her daughter and grandson. It had taken every bit of Hannah's willpower not to lose her temper about purchasing the fabric for the Christmas dress. Thank goodness Roberta had finally listened to reason, telling Maude to sell it to someone else if possible.

Jessie pointed. "Look. Mr. Peabody is taking the stage."

"Good evening, one and all!" Mr. Peabody's face lit up the stage. He did not look nervous as he had the last time he'd been there. "There is much excitement in the air tonight. And rightly so." He swept his arm wide. "As you know, the Union Pacific is only fifty short miles away. On my last visit, I stated the railroad would be making their decision in a few more months. Well, I'll bet you can guess by this meeting here tonight that that schedule has changed. The decision is final. Work on the rails begins tomorrow, and Logan Meadows is the winner. It won't be long before you have a train through your town once a week!"

Cheers went up and some boos and hisses. A few people tossed their hats into the air or clapped their hands. Hannah blushed when Chase threw his arm around Jessie and kissed her square on the mouth. *What a relief!* Hannah glanced over her shoulder, looking for Thom. She needed to share this wonderful news with him. Mr. Peabody held up his hands for quiet. "That does not mean the Union Pacific has waived the conditions it has asked of you. Those still hold. The railroad is ahead of schedule. Waiting a few months until you complete the enlargement of your school and add more services is not an option. The plan is to construct a depot just west of these festival grounds, approximately a quarter mile away. Union Pacific engineers will start on that this coming week. Congratulations, Logan Meadows!"

Frank, smiling from ear to ear, signaled the waiting quartet, and lively music soon filled the air.

Compelled to glance to her left, Hannah spotted Thom as he ambled in from the dark and leaned against a secluded tree, well away from curious eyes. He looked beat. Smudges of grime spotted his trousers and shirt. He took the kerchief from around his neck and discreetly swabbed his face.

He worked so hard. If he wasn't at the livery cleaning stalls, helping Win shoe horses, or out in the fields cutting hay, he was on top of some roof hammering on shingles in the broiling sun.

Jessie nudged her side. "There's Thom. You know he's coming to the picnic tomorrow, too, out at the ranch?"

"Yes." Was she only setting herself up for more heartache? Since talking with him at the cemetery, she'd not seen hide nor hair of him anywhere around town. Not even up on the roof of the mercantile. She'd been in the store a few times but hadn't had the nerve to ask Maude if he'd completed the job. Was he avoiding her on purpose? "I remember. I just wish I knew what he was thinking." Jessie put her arm around her shoulder. "He's just settling in, Hannah," she whispered into her ear. "Give him some time to—"

Hannah looked back around at Thom when Jessie's eyes went wide. Brenna Lane was at his side, offering him a glass of punch she had gotten at the refreshment tables. Hannah watched in grim fascination as Thom tipped his hat, took the drink, and drank it until it was gone.

"This means nothing," Jessie whispered quickly. "Brenna's just being kind."

Now that Mr. Peabody had made his announcement, everyone was getting up, talking, and milling around. Chase stood and waited for Jessie. It was amazing how Brenna's simple little gesture of offering Thom a glass of punch sliced to the quick. She chanced another peek as they talked, two outcasts finding solace with each other.

She hadn't known she'd made a noise until Jessie took her by her shoulders and gave her a good shake. "Stop this right now. Get a hold of yourself. Paste a pretty smile on your face and push out your chest." She glowered into Hannah's eyes. "Chin up."

"Jessie?" Chase was waiting, hat in hand. "I need to get back to the ranch."

"Give me one second, Chase. Hannah and I are just going over details for—the picnic."

His eyes took on a look of amused wonder. "You gals go right ahead with that important business. I'll be over at the food tables."

"Men!" Jessie watched Chase walk away. "They are so easily satisfied." She took Hannah by her hand and hauled her to her feet.

CHAPTER TWENTY-ONE

*W*ith Jessie and the children settled in at the house, Chase saddled up, checked in briefly at the bunkhouse, then made his way out to the north pasture. The temperature, downright chilly after slipping several degrees since the town meeting, forced him to shrug into his leather coat before riding out. He loped Cody for a good two miles before reining up, then they climbed to a lookout point on top of the bluff. From this vantage point, he could see much of the prairie that made up the Broken Horn. He bristled, remembering Dwight's comment.

The five hundred head below were calm. Chase could barely make out Jake as he rode slowly between the herd, but he caught a strain or two of some song he was singing softly to the peaceful cattle.

Chase relaxed in his saddle, taking in the sight. The night sky was clear. Because the crescent moon was no more than a sliver of a nail clipping, a blanket of twinkling stars stood out vividly in the inky black sky, reminding him of the first night he'd arrived at Jessie's small cabin. A sky like this one always made him remember.

A smile played around his lips as he recalled how young she'd looked when she'd first opened the door, invited him in. He'd been hungry as all get-out and distracted. Wondering how he'd fill his belly. He'd been trail weary and saddle sore. He aimed to deliver his message and be on his way.

He chuckled. *Hadn't quite worked out that way. At all.*

He'd been expecting a much more mature woman, someone closer to Nathan's age. Almost fell on his face when the beautiful slip of a girl admitted she was Nathan's wife.

His insides warmed; his body reacted. He was one lucky cowboy to have won Jessie's love. His life had changed. He would do anything for her. Ride to the moon and back if she asked. As if Sarah wasn't enough, she'd given him Shane, too. The boy was a combination of the two of them, with Jessie's inquisitive expressions and playful temperament and his looks and sometimes volatile nature. These were the best years of his life.

Cody cocked his hind hoof, getting comfortable, and Chase shook his head in disbelief of it all. Three years ago he'd been a loner, drifting wherever the wind blew. Thought it his destiny. How wrong he'd been. Glancing up at the heavens he heaved a hearty sigh, thanking God for showing him the error of his ways. Logan Meadows had welcomed them warmly. It was a good, wholesome town with honest, hardworking people. The perfect place to raise a family. That's why this rustling problem was so unsettling. Chase didn't want to see it go the way of so many bigger, rougher places. He didn't want Gabe or Jake, or anyone else, to get hurt or killed. So much was at stake.

Silence slipped by. Cool wind caressed his face. A coyote yipped far off in the hills, and instantly a chorus from several more erupted from the opposite direction. He'd promised Jessie he wouldn't stay out late. Something was up with her, but he couldn't figure it out. It had been tugging at the back of his mind, and he meant to ask her about it but things kept getting in the way. Thoughts of slipping into the comfortable bed beside her warm body chased away his concerns.

The unexpected scrape and clip of horseshoes slipping on shale shattered the quiet. Chase lowered his hand to Cody's shoulder, steadying the gelding so he wouldn't give them away. Whoever was coming up this way was not using the trail.

"There's the herd."

Chase recognized the voice of his hired hand, Blake Hansen. He and another man reined up twenty feet away.

"Seems quiet enough."

Dwight. The deputy actually did work now and then. Question was, what kind of work was he up to? Blake had been in the bunkhouse when Chase had stopped in. He was due to relieve Jake in about an hour. Could be he offered to ride out with Dwight and show him the way.

"How many head did they get from Cotton's last night?" Dwight asked.

The coyotes yipped again. Chase used the cover to quietly dismount, then creep a few steps behind his horse to a cover of large rocks. He wanted to see just what they were doing up on the ridge. And he didn't want to get blown to bits by mistake while doing it.

"More than enough to make it profitable."

A quality in Blake's voice gave Chase pause.

Cody stomped a hoof, and Chase swore under his breath as both men drew their guns.

"Hold it right there!" Blake shouted.

"Put your guns away," Chase said, coming out from behind the barrier. He kept his hand low, his leather coat pulled back. He didn't trust anyone in the dead of night. He mounted up and rode toward the men, Cody picking his way through the darkness. There was a moment of uncomfortable silence as both men holstered their firearms.

Blake was surprised. He looked from him to Dwight and back again.

"Thought you said you were heading south?" Blake said. "This is a damn good way to get yourself killed."

"Changed up."

Dwight's horse threw his head several times and nervously champed on his bit. Its strawberry roan coat practically glowed, even in the dimness. "Logan," Dwight drawled.

"Good to see you out doing some work, Hoskins. Where's Albert?"

Dwight holstered his gun. "He don't tell me his every move."

"You taking over for Jake?" Chase knew the answer to his question but wanted to keep them talking.

"Yeah. It's almost time for me to go now," Blake said.

Chase turned to leave. "Heading back, Dwight?"

"Not yet. Think I'll just stay up on this ridge and keep watch."

Dressed in a clean and pressed shirt and pants fresh off the line, Thom pulled the buggy to a halt in the sunny meadow next to the other vehicles. Nerves played havoc with his mood. As the buggy settled, he took in the wholesome sight under the cottonwood trees bordering a narrow creek. Ivan, obediently sitting at his feet, waited to be released. He let out a long complaint.

"Hurry up, Thom, and come around," Violet said impatiently. "Come help my ole bones out of this contraption." She'd been belting out directions and demands the entire forty-minute ride out.

Why had he accepted Mrs. Logan's invitation? *Jessie*, he reminded himself. She was among the men as they set up two tables and laid out several blankets under a grove of towering trees. *A picnic. Really?*

"Well, jist don't sit there—get the larder out!"

Thom hopped out and Ivan did, too—at the same time. Thom stumbled one stride but caught himself before he fell. Embarrassed, he rounded on Ivan. "You obey today!" he said, pointing in the dog's face. "No sneaking off with any of the goodies. Understand?" Ivan barked, wagged his tail, undaunted by his master's indignation.

Thom crossed behind the buggy, then reached for Mrs. Hollyhock's large basket. "What in the blazes you have in here? An anvil?"

"Quit your bellyaching and help me down."

A screech went up just as he took Mrs. Hollyhock's hand. Sarah had spotted the buggy, and now, with bouncing braids and a flutter of petticoats, raced toward them faster than any girl he'd ever seen. Then out from the trees popped Markus, and Thom almost pulled up short, which would have left Mrs. Hollyhock no better off than he'd been when Ivan had jumped out of the buggy between his feet. *If the boy's here, so is his mother.*

Sure enough, Hannah stepped out of the cottonwood grove a few feet behind her son and stopped by Jessie's side. The two women laughed as they watched Markus tear after his taller friend in vain, trying to catch up. Thom chuckled as the children passed by in a flurry of excitement and stopped beside Ivan.

"Here's the dog I told you about, Markus. He's big. Looks like a wolf."

"I know Ivan," Markus said, puffing out his chest. The boy grabbed the shepherd around the neck and squeezed. "He used to be Nana Katherine's before she died." Mrs. Hollyhock touched Thom's arm. Her soft smile said everything.

Markus turned and regarded Thom cautiously for a moment. Then a smile broke out. "He's your dog now, right?" He tipped his head in a very adult manner. His eyes, so much like Hannah's, searched his own.

All Thom could do was nod. He swallowed. "That's right, Markus," he finally got out. "Go," he said with a wave of his arm, releasing the animal. Ivan trotted off a few feet then stopped. He looked back at the kids as if waiting for them to follow.

"Seems I've been replaced by that beast!" Mrs. Hollyhock complained to Jessie as she and Hannah walked out to meet the buggy. The men were still setting up in the meadow.

"Morning, ladies," Thom said, tipping his hat. "You both look lovely today." Their smiles were his reward. "I'm going to take this basket and go help the men before they have everything done." He took a few steps toward the meadow.

"You don't need to do that, Thom," Jessie said. She glanced back. "It's all done. Come on and walk with us." She hooked her elbow into Mrs. Hollyhock's. "You know nothing could replace you." Hannah smiled her greeting, turning a pretty shade of pink.

After all the introductions were made, the group stood around talking while Shane toddled around in the grass looking for grasshoppers and the kids took off after Ivan.

"Donovan," Chase said. "We're glad to have you back in Logan Meadows. Frank Lloyd wanted to be here, too, have a chance to say hello. He sends his regards and says to drop by the bank when you have a spare moment to talk."

"Thank you. I'll do that," Thom responded, feeling much like a beetle at the bottom of a jar. Everyone, including Hannah, was looking at him. The two young men, Jake and Gabe, were letting Chase do the talking.

"You able to get out much?" It was Chase again, trying to be subtle. "I heard Win gave you the use of one of his horses. If you need a place to ride, or want to hire on now and then, just ask."

Thom smiled. "You'd hire me to tend your cattle?" *This is getting deep.*

"Why not?"

"I think you know."

Chase's eyebrow lifted.

CHAPTER TWENTY-TWO

*L*et's have a three-legged race," Jessie called as she hurried forward with a handful of gunnysacks.

"What?" All the men turned in surprise.

"It's perfect weather for one, a cool breeze, not a cloud in the sky." As if to prove her point, she held up a hand and her unbound hair rippled in a soft puff of air. "You men can just stop making those faces because there's nothing you can say to change my mind."

"I want to, Mommy. Can Markus and me be tied together?" Sarah giggled. Her face glistened from chasing after Ivan. The dog cantered into the group of adults, stopped, and flopped to his side, tongue lolling from the side of his mouth.

"Yes, honey," she said, handing Sarah a red bandanna. "Run down to that bush and tie this to a branch. That will mark the spot to turn around."

"But it's not very far."

Jessie nudged Sarah's little back to get the child going. "It's plenty far, sweetie. Go on now."

Jessie handed a gunnysack and a piece of twine to Thom. "This is for you and Hannah."

She almost laughed at Thom's pained expression as he looked at the length of twine. "Me and Hannah? You want me to tie this around her leg?"

Jessie nodded, her expression full of innocence.

His eyes narrowed.

"You don't want to be a stick-in-the-mud, do you?"

He started to protest, but the sight of Hannah tying Sarah's leg to Markus's smaller one touched his heart. She'd been there for him so often. Maybe this was one little thing he could do for her.

Jake and Gabe began backing away as Jessie turned in their direction. "Here you go, Gabe."

He shook his head. "I'm sitting this out."

Jessie's face fell. "Sarah will be so disappointed. Come on."

"No. I don't have a partner."

"Of course you do. Jake."

"*Jake!*" Both Gabe and Jake said in unison.

Jake took several long strides back, holding out a stiff arm to keep Jessie away. "I'm not getting' hitched to Gabe. No, sir!"

Jessie leaned in close. "If you don't, I'll bet Mrs. Hollyhock may want to join the fun. She'll need a partner." Gabe looked at Jake as Jake looked at Gabe. Jake took the brown sack and long length of twine with a shake of his head.

Thom almost chuckled as he watched Jessie. She was having fun. She picked Shane up and handed him to Mrs. Hollyhock, then hurried to her husband's side.

"Attention, everyone. Get tied up. Make it tight enough that you have to use your two legs together as one. No cheating!" She looked directly at Gabe and Jake. "When you're ready, come over here to the starting point. When Violet counts down, we'll race to the bush and touch the red bandanna tied there. Then race back. I have a little prize for the winning team."

Thom couldn't stall anymore and joined Hannah as she put the finishing touches to Sarah and Markus. The children stepped into the gunnysack, and Hannah pulled it up, handing them the edge.

"Now, hobble over there and wait for the rest of us," she said, sitting back.

The children promptly fell over in a gale of laughter. Hannah looked up at Thom, the smile on her face contagious. "Those two may not make it to the starting line."

Feeling suddenly shy, he held out the gunnysack but didn't say a word.

Hannah looked up at him with the most sincere eyes. "I'm sorry about this," she said in a choked voice. "Jessie came up with this ridiculous game and wouldn't take no for an answer. I tried to tell her it wasn't a good idea."

He shrugged. "Well, nothing to do about it now. Come on. We don't want to hold everyone up."

Jessie and Chase were almost ready, and Gabe and Jake stood sullenly at the starting line, their legs already bound together and set in the rough tan bag. Sarah and Markus had clutched together and were rolling over the tall grass toward the group.

Hannah hiked up one side of her dress to her knee while Thom stood alongside. He took the twine and, as quickly as he could, wrapped it around their legs, trying not to notice Hannah's shapely calf. *Hannah's right. Maybe this isn't such a good idea.*

Hannah wobbled. She gasped, then grasped on to his middle, clinging to him to keep her balance. Despite his efforts, they fell into the grass with a *thunk* amid her laughter and snorts.

"Oh, oh, *ouch*. That *hurt*," she wheezed.

He rolled, taking his weight off her. "You OK?"

She opened her eyes and looked straight into his, sending an invisible current zipping through his body. "Yes, I think so," she said, still laughing.

"Everyone's ready and waitin' on ya." Mrs. Hollyhock stood over them with Shane resting on her hip. Her crinkled eyes looked as sharp as an eagle's. She leveled them on his Hannah-filled hands. He jerked them up. "Stop playing patty-cake and get up."

Hannah, still on her back, stifled her giggles with a fist pressed to her mouth. Setting back on his heels, he rocked once and pulled them to their feet. She clung to him like a leech, her head laid tight on his chest and her arms circling his waist.

A round of applause went up. He looked down into her flushed face and shook his head. *Not a good idea at all.* Hobbling slowly, carefully, they made it to the starting line.

Mrs. Hollyhock stood off to the side, holding Shane. Ivan sat at her feet. "Get on your mark, get set...go!"

Sarah's shriek almost split Thom's eardrums. From the corner of his eye, he saw her and Markus fall into the grass first thing. Gabe and Jake, still standing motionless on the starting line, reached down and righted the tiny people-filled gunnysack, now three paces behind the two sets of grown-ups.

Chase and Jessie took a stride and then jumped together, finding a good rhythm. They led the race, and to Thom it almost looked as if Chase was carrying his wife. Challenged, and never one to give up easily, Thom slung his arm around Hannah's back and clenched her to his side. "Step," he ordered. "Hop. Step. Hop."

In the screaming, laughing excitement, Ivan bounded between the racers. He barked and ran back and forth as Mrs. Hollyhock screeched his name over the cacophony, demanding he return to her side.

Chase and Jessie would reach the red bandanna in moments. Chase was barking orders as the Logans kept a rhythmic pace over the grass. Thom glanced back to see who was closing in, and found the kids close behind and Jake and Gabe still standing at the starting line, laughing.

Distracted, Thom stepped a little too soon, throwing Hannah off balance. Before he knew what was up, they landed on the ground. Hannah gasped for breath, and his hip stung from hitting hard. The children whooshed past.

"You OK?" This time she lay on top of him, and he was acutely aware of her every curve. When he realized his right hand rested on her backside, he jerked it away as if it were a branding iron straight out of the fire.

She nodded and then laughed. "I'm sorry! I keep messing us up. We're going to lose for sure."

"Not if I have anything to do with it." Thom rolled them to the side and dragged her up with him. He was getting used to having Hannah in his arms, smack tight up next to him. It wasn't a surprise that he liked her feel more than he wanted to admit.

"Come on, Mommy!" Markus's little voice reached them. "Come on!"

"You're being summoned. Let's go."

Chase and Jessie had already reached the halfway mark and were on their way back. They were just about to pass Thom and Hannah, but Thom reached out his untethered leg and stuck it between Chase's. The couple went down.

Hannah gasped. "Thom!" She tried to turn her head to see her friend, but Thom wouldn't let her. "I can't believe you just did that."

"Pay attention, Hannah. Here come the kids."

Markus and Sarah passed them on their way back to the finish line. Even though she was taller, Sarah's arm wrapped Markus's back as the team struggled to keep their balance. Markus's face was one of total concentration, and Sarah's smile could outshine the sun.

At the marker, Hannah reached out and touched the cherry-red bandanna as Thom swirled her around. She was no heavier than a piece of pollen. She gripped his shirt in both her hands, leaving it up to him to keep a firm hold on the gunnysack. If it slipped too low, it would trip them up. He strained, not wanting to lose.

"Faster, Hannah. I don't like coming in last, unless it's to Markus and Sarah. If we hurry we can overtake Chase and Jessie. They're still down. They're—"

Thom broke off his sentence. Hannah craned her neck, trying to see why. Chase and Jessie were deep in the prairie grass, lost in a passionate kiss. They couldn't have cared less about Thom and Hannah galumphing by. Or about the dog barking. Or anything else. Desire surged through Thom's body.

Just as Sarah and Markus crossed the finish line and let out a whoop of victory, Thom stumbled, taking Hannah down with him. He'd thrown caution to the wind today, reaching out to Hannah like this, but what were the costs? He shifted. Took the impact. Hannah landed on his chest.

Thom came awake slowly to the sound of Hannah giggling and her lips close to his. For a moment, he just lay there. Pain shot through his head when he looked to the side. Poking out of the grass next to his head was a slab of shale.

CHAPTER TWENTY-THREE

*T*hom! Are you all right?" A collection of wrinkles lined his forehead as he gazed in silence at the puffy white clouds. "Thom?" Hannah gently shook his shoulder. "Say something, please."

A slow smile played around the corners of his mouth, and she let out a relieved sigh. "You scared me. You went dead white for a second there. I thought you'd hit your head."

She gave him a playful shove, and he surprised her by pulling her down. His lips found hers, and in the semi-cover of the tall grass he kissed her. A real kiss. A sizzling kiss. A kiss Hannah felt all the way to her toes. Warmth flushed her body, and she was keenly aware of his scent and taste. He didn't seem to be in a hurry about it, so she relaxed, placing her hands on his chest as he explored her mouth.

"Ma!"

It was Markus. He was free from Sarah and running their way.

Thom made a little sound from his throat—it might have been regret—and pulled away. Hannah sat up, pushed the sack off their legs, and began to untie the twine.

"We won! We won!"

In boy-like fashion, Markus skidded to a stop on his knees next to them, his face beaming with excitement. Ivan followed one stride behind and pushed his way in between, whining and demanding attention. "Look!" Markus held out a long piece of black licorice. "Our prize!"

"Oh, that looks delectable," Hannah said, pleased he was having so much fun. This was so good for him, so good to have a big family around. After the kiss from Thom, she didn't know how things could get better.

She nudged back the dog that straddled her lap so she could finish releasing Thom. Thom, who'd just kissed the stuffing out of her. She couldn't look at him. Caleb's kisses had never affected her like this. The longer she avoided his eyes, the hotter her face became. What had he been thinking?

Thom had pushed up on his elbows and was looking at the kids with amusement.

"You and Sarah are a worthy team," he said to Markus. His hair had tumbled over his forehead, and he looked very boy-like himself. Hannah resisted the urge to straighten it. "Once you two got moving, there was no catching you. You deserved to win."

At Thom's praise, Markus smiled from ear to ear and inched closer to him, curious and cautious at the same time. Both had dark hair and dancing eyes. They could easily pass for father and son. Thom would win him over just by being himself.

Chase and Jessie walked up arm in arm. "Guess you two came in second, if we're counting teams not crossing the finish line," Chase said. He glanced down into Jessie's face and smiled. "We don't mind losing. Do we, honey?"

Jessie shook her head, and her golden hair swayed from side to side.

Chase arched one brow at Thom. "But be warned. Next time you try tripping me, you better be ready for a push back."

Thom waved him off with a chuckle. "It was all in good fun, Logan. You certainly didn't seem to mind."

Hannah didn't quite know what to think about Thom. *This* Thom. And the kiss? What was that all about? Perhaps it was all the bumping and grabbing they'd had to do to stay on their feet. Her cheeks warmed, and she dared a glance in his direction as she climbed to her feet. She picked up the gunnysack and headed for Mrs. Hollyhock, wishing he would stay like this forever.

Why had he gone and kissed her? Was he crazy? His impulsive action would come back to roost, without a doubt. Confuse the already sticky situation they were in. He chanced a quick glance at Hannah just as the sun, low in the west, cast a soft amber light in all directions and a cool breeze ruffled the grasslands. She had donned her shawl, and the children looked plumb worn out. The tired group relaxed on several blankets, drained from all the activity. A few feet away, Ivan lay in the grass. His chin rested on his outstretched paws, and his eyes were horizontal slits. Thom took a deep sigh.

After the sack race, Sarah and Markus had insisted on flying the kite—or at least trying to. It took a good half hour for Chase to get it aloft before handing the reins over to Sarah and then to Markus for a turn. After that, the two children had played on the shore of Shady Creek, trying to catch frogs and tiny fish. All the while Shane had kept the women busy. The toddler had not been able to keep up with the older children, and an hour ago he had run out of steam. Now, as they ate an early supper under the trees, his eyes were at half-mast.

Hannah sat close by, fiddling with the food on her plate. He relived their moment in the grass. It was the sunshine, he thought. All the laughter and fun. It had clouded his judgment and got the better of him. *What judgment?* He grimaced inwardly. All the space he'd worked at putting between them was now for naught.

"This sure has been a perfect day," Mrs. Hollyhock said. "Thank you, Jessie, for inviting us."

Chase cleared his throat, then smiled.

"Oh, you, too, of course, Mr. Logan," she added. She set her plate aside and pulled some crochet from a bag.

"Anyone want to play horseshoes after we clean up?" Jessie asked. "I brought them along, just in case."

Gabe and Jake let out an exaggerated groan.

"It's getting late, sweetheart," Chase said. "We'll need to pack up and start home pretty soon. We still have a few chores that need tending to at the ranch."

No one moved.

"We still have dessert, Chase. I'll serve that up just as soon as everyone is finished."

Chase rocked back on his elbows. "I guess you've heard about the trouble we're having with rustlers." His gaze moved to Thom. "It started off light at first, but it's becoming a big problem."

Thom's hand stilled halfway to his mouth. He lowered the almost-eaten chicken leg back to his plate and wiped his fingers. "No. I've been keeping busy at the livery."

Jake and Gabe were watching him closely. *He's feeling me out. Everyone in town knows my past. Did he wait all day just to ask me this?* Thom's initial indignation got pushed back by hot irritation. "You have anything else you want to ask me?" he bit out. "Go on, Logan, don't be shy." The rancher should have just come straight-out, asked him about the rustling, and saved everyone the hassle of putting on such a welcoming show. Chase didn't want to hire him; he wanted to gauge his reaction.

The dazed, happy mood of the group fizzled. Hannah dropped her eyes to her plate. Anger sprouted inside Thom.

"I can see I've put you off," Chase said. "That wasn't my intent."

"I don't have anything to hide."

Jessie climbed to her feet and went to check on Shane, who was sleeping on a blanket a few feet past Ivan. She covered him with a light cover. "I made a fresh apple pie," she said softly. "Who'd like a slice?"

"And I baked a chokecherry pie." Mrs. Hollyhock climbed to her feet. "Raise your hand if you'd like a slice of that."

He was sure Chase had more things besides pie he wanted to talk about, so Thom took the bull by the horns. He'd have it all out tonight. "How many head did you lose?"

"I'm dishing everyone a slice of each," Jessie nervously interrupted. An uncharacteristic set of lines marred her forehead.

"I'd say almost fifty," Chase said. He raised a knowing brow at his wife.

Thom whistled. "That's a lot of beef. Worth a lot of money at market price. I can see why you're concerned."

Chase nodded. "More than that, they got our prize bull Friday night. If he's still in the territory somewhere, I'd like to get him back. Paid a pretty penny for him last year."

"You have any suspects in mind?"

Chase looked between Jake and Gabe. Shook his head. "Our little town has grown so much in the last three months, it makes it hard to keep track of everyone. It may not be anyone from Logan Meadows. It's hard to know."

Thom looked away over the grasslands. A bad feeling rolled around inside. It had been eight years since Rome Littleton's group was rustling up in Colorado. The man could have changed his ways, he supposed. Gone straight. Fingering him now without any proof of wrongdoing could easily backfire. Dwight could trump up charges that could send Thom back to Deer Creek, or worse. Who knew how powerful or connected Rome was. No. He'd not go to prison again.

A long silence ensued. "You got something to say, Donovan?" Chase asked.

Thom stood, his appetite all but gone. He took the slice of pie Jessie offered anyway, just to be polite.

"I'm not your man." He boldly met Chase's gaze. Explaining himself to Logan rankled just as much as it had with Dwight. "I wasn't guilty then, and I'm not guilty now. I'm working and minding my own business. Ask Win if you don't believe me."

He quickly ate his pie and handed the plate back to Jessie. "Thank you, Jessie. That was real good. You, too, Violet."

Everyone, including Hannah, kept their eyes trained on their plates. The clink of forks on dishes mingled with the solo chirp of an early cricket. Thom looked toward the buggy and the sleeping horses. "I'm going to get packed up," he said. Hannah had stood and now came to his side. "You need me to load anything for you?"

Just as the others were getting up and stretching out the kinks, a vicious barking ripped through the strained silence.

Thom swung around. Ivan was two feet away from Shane's blanket. The child was still asleep as his dog carried on like a wild animal, growling and barking at the toddler.

Chase ran to the wagon and grabbed his gun. "What the hell's wrong with your dog? Get him away from my son!" he yelled as he ran toward the blanket. Shane, stirring from all the commotion, lifted a small fist to rub sleepy eyes.

Thom grasped Chase's arm to stop him. "Wait. He's not barking at the baby. There's something else."

Ivan lowered his head and growled, then pounced up and down on his front paws. He stopped for only an instant and looked around before again taking up the alarm.

"Chase!" Jessie cried. "What is it? What—" She stopped as Sarah, who'd dashed over, buried her face in Jessie's skirt. Shane's frightened eyes blinked several times as the adults looked on helplessly. "Get my baby away from him!"

"Tell Shane to keep still," Thom demanded. Ivan looked at him for only an instant before launching into another barking tirade.

"*Ivan. Quiet!*" Thom inched forward, squatted, and took him around the scruff of the neck. Carefully he pulled the anxious animal away with a struggle. It was clear Ivan didn't want to go.

"Come on, boy," Thom said. "Come, Ivan." When he had him a few feet back, Mrs. Hollyhock took hold of him.

Jessie stepped forward.

"Wait!" Thom and Chase cried at the same time.

She looked at them, confused. Shane's face clouded, his eyes watery with unshed tears, surely frightened by all the commotion.

Thom held his hand up. "Just wait a second. Ivan wouldn't send up an alarm like that unless he sensed danger. There must be something wrong." Hannah stood by, holding tightly to Markus's hand.

Chase nodded. "You just stay still, Shane," he called out. "Pa's gonna pick you up. Just stay real still."

The toddler nodded and smiled as if this were some fun new game and looked over to Gabe and Jake standing close by.

Chase handed his gun to Thom and inched forward, begging God not to let anything happen to his son. *His son.* The incarnation of his and Jessie's love. Everything around him slowed as he carefully lifted the tiny blanket off the boy.

Jessie gasped. A three-inch-long scorpion scuttled closer to Shane's bare thigh. Its two main claws opened and closed threateningly, and the stinger rolled up over its thick black body, dangerously close to the child's skin.

CHAPTER TWENTY-FOUR

"Don't move, Shane," Chase ordered. "Stay very, very still."

Mrs. Hollyhock struggled to hold Ivan. The dog growled menacingly, as if begging to be let free, sensing a great need to get the deadly creature.

Chase glanced over his shoulder at the others. He wasn't quite sure how to get Shane free without his boy being stung.

Without saying anything, Thom handed the gun to Gabe and circled around to the other side of the blanket. Shane rolled his head to watch his progress. The scorpion crept closer to the underside of his leg, trying to hide. Shane started to reach down with his hand.

"Halt!" Chase barked. "You *must* stay still, Shane." Chase's tone said everything. "Thom is going to pick you up—fast. But you have to hold your body as—" Chase's voice cracked. He looked away, getting his emotions under control. Shane was so small. The scorpion's venom could easily kill him in minutes.

He inched a little closer as Thom did the same on the other side.

He looked up at Donovan. "On three."

Even the evening sounds seemed to hush, as if they knew something very dangerous, very life changing was about to happen. Ivan quieted. Chase didn't have to look to know the dog was sitting at attention, somehow understanding the seriousness of the situation. The only thing Chase heard was the rasp of his own breath.

Chase tensed. "One. Two. *Three!*"

Thom leaped forward, clamping Shane in a viselike grip under his arms and swinging him up. At the exact time, Chase swung his leg, connecting with his target just as the scorpion's stinger snapped. Shane screamed. Thom jumped back, the child gripped in his arms, and ran over to a frantic Jessie. Mrs. Hollyhock struggled to keep ahold of Ivan, who fought to get free. His snarls of anger were frightening.

Jessie sank to the blanket and set the screaming toddler down. She ran her hands repeatedly over his legs and arms, even his neck, looking for any spot where he might have been stung. Chase dropped to her side to help. Moments passed as the group crowded around.

Jessie looked up with tear-filled eyes. "He's OK." That's all she got out before she broke down in sobs. Shane stood up on shaky legs and wrapped his arms around Jessie's head, looking at his pa. Sarah squeezed in. Chase enfolded them in an embrace, a reminder that there were things more dangerous than rustlers—and more valuable than a few lost head of cattle. He vowed never to let anything in this wild, unpredictable world hurt his family.

As the rented buggy swayed along smoothly in the soft moonlight, Hannah ran her hands over Markus for the fiftieth time, thankful that her little boy slept safely in her lap. She'd not take a single day for granted. Life was precious. Look at Caleb, how his health had deteriorated in a matter of days. Now, this narrow escape for Chase and Jessie's toddler was one more reminder to cherish every moment.

She glanced up at the fluffy, cotton-like clouds that surrounded the moon. Random stars twinkled, and a silvery glow made the countryside look magical. The twitter from a night bird perched in the tall trees made Hannah smile. She resisted the urge to snuggle closer to Thom, who drove the buggy in silence. He'd insisted on taking her and Markus into Logan Meadows to save Gabe or Jake the trip. She'd gladly accepted and squished in beside him with Mrs. Hollyhock on her right and Ivan at their feet.

She tried to ignore the intoxicating feel of Thom next to her. The pleasing knowledge of his protective presence so close by. Would he kiss her again when they got to her house? After all those times pushing her away, she still couldn't believe that it had happened.

Mrs. Hollyhock's head softly plunked onto Hannah's shoulder, and then a tiny snore sounded next to her ear. Hannah nudged Thom's knee.

He looked down into her eyes, the moonlight caressing his face.

She tilted her head toward the old woman, and he smiled. "Guess *everyone* is wore out." He put the reins into one hand and with the other rubbed Markus's head. "This little cowpoke sure had a busy day. He'll most likely sleep for a week."

His breath, so near and warm on her face, sent tingles twirling inside. She hadn't been married all that long, but those kinds of feelings were hard to forget. Difficult to ignore the yearning inside.

She wished this buggy ride could go on forever. "We're almost to town," she said quietly. "I hate to wake her."

"I'll carry her in and then take you two home." There was a question in his eyes. "Is that OK?"

"Fine." The urge to lean up and kiss his lips, stroke his cheek, was strong. Hannah looked away.

They pulled up in front of the Red Rooster in silence. Thom handed her the reins and climbed down, circling around to the other side. "Shhh," he said as he gathered the old woman into his arms. Violet started to protest, but he shushed her again. He took the stairs easily with her cradled in his arms and disappeared inside the inn. A moment later in the doorway, he called to Ivan. The dog jumped out and trotted inside.

Thom closed the pine door and returned to the buggy. He looked at Markus. "You want to stretch him out?"

"No. He'll be fine."

"I was thinking of you. He must be getting heavy."

She shook her head, pretending at least for this short time that they were a real family. That Thom was her husband and Markus's father, that they were returning from a night out with friends, only to nestle into her large goose-down mattress until morning. The homey scene was an intoxicating thought. "I enjoy the feel of him. Besides, he's keeping me warm."

Thom nodded as he turned the buggy back toward Main Street.

Surprisingly, Logan Meadows was still awake. A lantern shone in the window of the El Dorado, illuminating the parlor, where a woman sat reading a book and several unidentifiable men talked. *Breakfast customers*, Hannah thought happily. Farther down the street, Maude, still up, swept the boardwalk in front of the mercantile, her white apron tied around her ample waist. As they approached, she stopped and squinted through the shadowy street. Her mouth formed an O when she recognized them, and she lifted her hand to wave.

Hannah's cheeks warmed. Thom waved back. Five horses tethered in front of the Bright Nugget dozed. Two men standing outside watched the buggy pass. The sounds of a lively piano tune floated through the swinging doors, punctuated with the sound of men's laughter.

"Town's busy," Thom whispered. He snapped the reins over the bay mare's back, and they trotted across the bridge and continued to Hannah's house. With disappointment, Hannah realized they were nearly home.

"Whoa," Thom called as they pulled up in front of Hannah's two-story. Several lanterns were burning inside. *Roberta. Up and waiting.* He hopped out and went to Hannah's side, taking Markus from her lap and extending a hand to assist her to the ground. The sleepy boy rolled his head onto Thom's shoulder and wrapped his arm around Thom's neck like a baby raccoon. His scent called to mind him wrestling with his brother and chasing his sister around the yard, laughing and screaming in fun. Memories, a mixture of joy and pain.

They took the porch steps side by side, Hannah moving ahead to open the door. Thom stepped over the threshold, and a warm, comforting aroma enveloped them. He took a moment to look around. The room was neat and clean, everything in its place. Some things he remembered from his childhood visits. The large hutch along the far wall, a tall grandfather clock with a crack at the top, the old rocking chair still in the same spot by the window. He felt Caleb in the room, in the emotions this house evoked.

Hannah touched his arm. "Do you mind carrying him up to his room for me? I hate to wake him."

"Of course." *Home.* He pushed the sentiment away.

At the top of the stairs, they passed the open door to Roberta's bedroom, where she sat in her night coat, reading. She closed the book, then stood. Her forehead creased and her mouth twisted as she recognized Thom carrying her grandson.

CHAPTER TWENTY-FIVE

*I*n here," Hannah whispered. She pulled back Markus's quilt and plumped his pillow. As Thom held the child, Hannah pulled off his boots. Thom laid him on the bed and stepped back, fully aware of Roberta hovering in the doorway. He could feel her eyes boring a hate-filled hole in his back.

Deftly, Hannah stripped the tyke of his pants, socks, and shirt, and then tucked the blanket around him. Leaning down, she kissed his cheek and traced a little cross on his forehead.

She turned and murmured, "They're only little for such a short time. Sometimes I don't want him to get any older." Roberta harrumphed from the doorway, causing a tiny smile to pull Hannah's lips up. "May as well face the music," she whispered, her eyes searching his.

"May as well."

They turned in unison, walked out of the room, and he closed the door with a soft click.

Roberta stepped back and then followed them down the stairs.

"Mother, you needn't stay up to visit with us. Tomorrow is the day you help in the restaurant. You don't want to be tired."

"Yes, Hannah, I know," she said, hurrying past and going into the kitchen. "I just want to make myself a cup of tea." She disappeared into the other room.

"Can you stay a moment?"

"Hannah."

"Just a moment, I promise."

Feeling more than a bit uncomfortable, he sat on the sofa. She sat, too, with a good, respectable space between them. Sounds of clinking and clanking from the kitchen made him chuckle.

"I know, I know," she whispered. "She's still the exact same."

"I don't know how you stand it."

Hannah's eyes gleamed with merriment. "She's my mother. I have to stand it."

He shrugged. "I guess that's so."

"Would either of you like a cup?" Roberta called. "Water will be hot soon."

"No, thank you," they replied in unison.

"She must have had the water hot from before," Hannah said. "Now, she's having another cup just to act as chaperone." She settled back against the cushions, getting comfortable. "Now that the roof on the mercantile and Maude's rental are finished, what will you do? Spend more time at the livery?"

Thom leaned back and crossed his feet at the ankles, resting one arm along the backside of the sofa. "That was my plan. Then yesterday, Albert came by and asked if I'd like to help on the construction of the depot when they get started. Right now, they're cutting lumber and digging the foundation. There'll be several men from the Union Pacific directing and helping, so it shouldn't take all that long."

She sat forward excitedly. "That's wonderful. You're meeting all kinds of new people, making contacts. Won't be long before you're not a stranger in town anymore."

He gave her a skeptical look, knowing what she was trying to do. "Maude really helped me get a leg up, and now this. I have to say I'm very grateful."

"Just what are you grateful for, Mr. Donovan? After all that's happened to you, I can't imagine you being thankful for anything." Roberta came shuffling out of the kitchen, unmindful of the woolen socks on her feet and blue housecoat. She held a teacup between her hands. Easing into the chair opposite them, she set the cup carefully on the table.

Hannah gave her a pointed look. "Mother."

"I've been hired on to help build the new railroad depot west of the festival grounds," Thom said.

Roberta tipped her head up and raised an eyebrow. "We can see the depot from here. There's a lot of activity going on." She cleared her throat.

He nodded. "Did I tell you, Hannah, even Win is primping up the livery?" he added, struggling for something to say. "Yesterday we built a small enclosure up close to Main Street on the west side of the livery barn. It's for the two pet buffalo, sort of an attraction for travelers. Everyone coming from the train depot will have to pass by. Win hopes they'll become the town mascots, so to speak."

Hannah's approving nod encouraged Thom to go on.

"He said there's fascination with bison, especially since they're disappearing from the prairies."

Roberta sniffed loudly. "The day those smelly creatures become our town symbol is the day I move out of Logan Meadows." She sipped her tea. "It's bad enough that on warm days I have to close my windows. Now, you say I'm going to have to see the object of my irritation every day as well? I'll have to talk with Frank about that tomorrow."

"You could take the long way around, Mother. So you wouldn't have to pass them. The doctor *did* tell you to get more exercise each day."

Great, Thom thought. Now, he'd gone and made trouble for Win. "They'll get moved out back each evening, Mrs. Brown. I can't see that being a hundred feet closer would make that much difference."

"You wouldn't, Mr. Donovan, but I do."

"Thom."

Roberta leaned back in surprise as if trying to figure him out. "Excuse me?"

"Thom. You should call me that."

Hannah's mother set her cup on the table with a rattling thud and stood. Thom blinked. Her image wavered before his eyes, making his stomach queasy. He looked away. Jammed his finger and thumb into his eyes.

"Thom?" Hannah's voice held concern. "Are you all right?"

Not wanting to make a scene, Thom opened his eyes. The outer edges of his sight were dim, fuzzy. He blinked and then smiled into Hannah's face.

"I guess falling down today knocked some sense out of me. I'm fine. Just a nagging headache coming on."

Roberta stepped over to the sofa and sat on his other side. She placed a warm palm on his forehead. "You fell today, Mr. Donovan? Did you hit your head?"

CHAPTER TWENTY-SIX

$\mathcal{O}$n the back porch, Chase pulled a chair over to another so he and Jessie could sit side by side. She was wound as tight as a spring after the close call they'd had with Shane. His son and daughter were now peacefully asleep in their beds, but he was sure it would be hours before he and Jessie were that lucky.

"Go on and sit," he said. "I'll be right back."

He went to the parlor and took two small crystal glasses from the sideboard and filled each with a good portion of sherry. The aroma drifted up, making his taste buds tingle. The bottle had been a gift from Frank three years ago, when they'd moved back to Logan Meadows and onto the ranch. They used it sparingly and only on special occasions. *Tonight is one indeed*, he thought, glancing at Shane's room. He carried the dainty, slim-stemmed glasses with care onto the back porch.

"For you," he said, handing a glass to Jessie.

"Thank you."

He sat. They sipped, lost in their own thoughts.

He took another, smiling to himself when Jessie did the same. It was a rare occasion when she took any spirits at all.

"That tastes good," she said. "Warm."

He grunted. The field out back rolled down the gently sloping hill to a flat spot where a small fork of the South Laramie flowed shallow a few months out of the year. Spring runoff from the mountains had it gushing, but come summer it dried to a bed of rocks. The main barn and several corrals were in the front of the ranch, a pretty picture for arriving or departing guests.

"You all right, Jess?" She was still, except for the rise and fall of her chest and the occasional lifting of the glass to her lips.

"Yes. Just thinking."

"I know."

"I couldn't have stood it, Chase. If something were to happen to Shane, I'd die myself. I couldn't go on."

"Don't talk like that. Nothing is going to happen to him. Or anyone." He set his glass on the railing and took her hand in his own, feeling it quiver. "But if something *did* happen—you *would* go on. That's a fact. I don't ever want to hear you say different again."

An owl hooted down in the draw, followed by the yip of a coyote.

The breeze lifted her hair, and it shimmered in the moonlight.
"You cold?" he asked.

"Not bad. This sherry is doing the trick and warming me from the inside out." She gave a small laugh, and he smiled.

"It does have a way of doing that." He stood.

"Where're you going?"

"Never you mind."

Chase entered the kitchen and crossed the main room to their bedroom. Opening the dresser, he rummaged around, looking for Jessie's shawl. As he took it from the drawer, a letter fluttered to the floor, coming to rest haphazardly on his boot.

It was a letter from the orphanage, from Mrs. Hobbs. He'd never met the woman, and from Jessie's stories, he didn't want to either.

He bent and picked it up. *It's not opened.*

Curious, he went back to her drawer. Pushing some hankies, a bonnet, and one unmentionable aside, he looked around. He was a bit shocked to find a letter she'd received several months back, opened, and another one still intact. *Why wouldn't she open the others? Letters? Unopened letters?* He turned them over, looking for some clue.

A chill crept up his spine. What was this about? He looked at the postmark. It had arrived this week, the other two, months before. He shoved the letters in his back pocket and picked up the shawl.

Jessie collected the two empty glasses, intending to take them inside. She was uneasy. Not in a mood to sit out here alone, pondering today and all the things that could have gone wrong.

Chase stepped out as she reached for the door. "Whoa, where you off to? I just got your shawl."

"I'm not in the mood to sit and talk, Chase. I need to do something. Keep moving."

"Oh, it's not all that bad." He took the glasses from her hands and set them down. She let him drape her favorite black-and-pink shawl, a gift from him, over her shoulders. "There. Now, come sit on my lap. That's not negotiable, Mrs. Logan. I'm telling, not asking."

It was a game they played. He'd never bully her into doing something she didn't want to do, so at times, this was their way of avoiding a fight. If one or the other said it was not negotiable, the other complied, no questions asked. And who knew, perhaps he felt as restless as she did and needed a little comforting himself but was too proud to ask.

He sat down and pulled her onto his lap, settling her in. His warmth cocooned her in safety, and she rested her head against his large, firm chest.

Chase.

My husband.

She ran her hand down the front of his shirt and back up, enjoying the feel beneath her fingertips.

"Comfortable?"

"Yes. This was a good idea." There was nothing an embrace wouldn't fix. The owl hooted again, familiar and soothing. "I feel better already."

"Good. We aim to please." He chuckled, and the rumble against her ear sent a ripple of warmth to her belly. She was safe. The children were safe. Chase wouldn't let *anything* happen.

"Tomorrow's going to come early. You tired?" he asked.

"I'm getting a little sleepy. I think it's the sherry."

He kissed the top of her head. "Me, too."

His hands massaged her back, his fingers doing magical things to her tensed muscles. "Tell me about the letters you're getting from the orphanage." He'd dropped his voice down a notch as if trying to purposefully sound mysterious.

Jessie slowly sat up, looked into Chase's face. Her dark eyes were pools of uncertainty. "What do you mean?"

He reached behind him and pulled her letters from his pocket. "I found these looking for your shawl. Can't begin to fathom what might keep you from opening up a letter from anyone, let alone bossy Mrs. Hobbs, so I didn't even try. I want to hear it from you."

It took her a moment to get her wits about her.

The letters.

Chase had stumbled on the letters she'd so foolishly stuffed in the bottom of her dresser drawer. She should have realized he was going in for her shawl when he'd asked if she was cold.

"Jessie?" He tipped her chin up. "Why didn't you open the other two? Months ago, when I brought you the first letter, you told me she was just sending a hello. Checking up on you. Is it more than that, darlin'?"

She tried to stand, needing secure footing under her before launching into this, but Chase held her back. "Chase, let me up." Worry made her voice thick.

"I don't want to. Now, you're keeping me warm," he teased. He nuzzled her neck. "Jess?"

Knowing he wasn't going to give up so easily, she gently plucked the letters from his fingers. "I didn't open them because all that busybody does is gossip. I don't want to be a part of that. If I don't reply, she'll get the idea without me having to explain."

She felt his body relax. "Fine then. You'd tell me if it were something more?"

"Yes."

Unable to look at him a moment longer, Jessie glanced down toward the creek, the letters practically burning her fingertips. Her heart shivered for telling Chase a lie. Well, it wasn't all a lie. But she couldn't share her fears with him now, not with all the trouble he was having with the disappearing cattle. He was already preoccupied enough with catching the rustlers. Distracting him might put his life in danger. Her conscience pricked, and she knew protecting Chase was not the real reason for her keeping quiet, but she pushed the feelings away. In all honesty, she expected the interest in Sarah to just die away. It had been so many years since they'd adopted her. It wasn't *her* little girl the woman who'd contacted Mrs. Hobbs was looking for. There were lots of young girls in orphanages. Surely they weren't looking for Sarah. Sarah was hers.

CHAPTER TWENTY-SEVEN

*E*arly Monday morning Thom headed straight for the sheriff's office. His vision had cleared—he'd not dwell on something he had no power to fix. But there was something he could fix. Rustling was bad business. It usually escalated into all kinds of other crimes, including murder. He wouldn't be able to live with himself if anything happened to Chase or Jessie or anyone else. All he could do was report what he knew and then stay out of trouble.

On entering the sheriff's office, he found Chase Logan there already in conversation with Albert. Albert was sitting behind his desk, and Chase was resting a hip on the top.

Thom removed his hat and held it. Chase's face went void of expression, and Thom wondered, after the strained day yesterday, which way Hannah's friend was leaning.

"Thom." By the red stains on the sheriff's cheeks, he figured they'd just been discussing him.

Thom tipped his head at each man.

Albert motioned to the chairs against the wall. "Pull up a seat and then get yourself a cup of coffee."

Thom nodded. *Why not?* He was tired of walking on eggshells. He hadn't done anything wrong. After pulling over a chair, he poured some black brew into a none-too-clean cup and sat down. Looking uncomfortable, Chase stood and retrieved a chair. He turned it around and straddled it.

"Chase was just telling me about the close call you had yesterday at the picnic with little Shane. Thank God you two were able to right the situation before the child was hurt."

"I want to thank you, Donovan," Chase said. "Your clear thinking helped save my son. I was remiss in not saying so yesterday. I owe you."

"You don't owe me anything." He took a sip of his coffee, remembering the size of the scorpion. "It was Ivan who sensed the danger."

"Well, the dog belongs to you. Jessie and I are indebted."

Thom accepted his thanks with a nod. "I have something I need to talk to you about." He looked at the sheriff. Chase stood to leave. "I'd like you to stay, Chase. It may or may not concern you. I don't know." That got both men's undivided attention. Logan sat.

"Go on," Albert said, sitting forward.

"Eleven days ago when I arrived in Logan Meadows, a man from my past was playing cards in the saloon. The head of the rustling outfit that I mistakenly hooked up with when I was a boy." He turned and looked directly at Chase. "Rome Littleton."

Chase jumped to his feet. "Rome Littleton!" His voice was hard, accusing. If he and Chase *had* come to a truce, it was now gone.

"That's right. The night the law closed in, he'd ridden out late and was nowhere to be seen. Everyone was hanged there on the spot, and I was taken in to stand trial." He gave Albert a look he hoped the sheriff would interpret correctly—he didn't want his medical history divulged, even to Chase. "Until yesterday, I didn't know there was any rustling going on. Now that I do know, I feel compelled to say something."

"Why didn't you come forward before?" Chase, a handful of years older, was wiser by a mile.

"I should have." Even though he knew Chase had a right to be angry, Thom didn't like the blame he sensed being tossed his way. He'd not broken any laws.

"Maybe my prize bull would still be in my pasture if you had." Thom's guarded mood veered sharply toward anger. His face went hot.

As if wanting to break the tension, Albert stood and went to fill his cup. "What's done is done. You can't place that at Thom's door, Chase."

"I'm a falsely convicted ex-convict. For rustling, no less." Unable to sit a moment longer, Thom stood. "How would the good townsfolk take it if I was to march into the sheriff's office and, first thing, accuse one of their own of cattle stealing?" Thom felt the tic in his jaw as he clenched and released. *Hang on to your temper*, he cautioned himself. "Littleton was never convicted of anything. Hell, no one alive but me even knows he was part of the gang. It's my word against his. And I don't feel like going back to prison."

Chase's eyes took on a glint of understanding.

"What's he do here in Logan Meadows?" Thom asked. "Own a ranch? What?"

"He's been around these parts going on two years. We don't know much about him 'cept he owns a spread over in New Meringue. Comes into town from time to time to play poker," Albert said, now back in his chair.

"He knows my man, Blake Hansen." Chase was shaking his head as he gazed at a spot on the wall behind Albert. Looked as if he was going over in his mind every detail he knew about the man. "Jake found him and another fellow riding around on Broken Horn land for the heck of it last Tuesday. Said they were looking for rustlers, since his ranch had been hit, too." He paused and looked at Albert. "I think we should keep this just between us until we know more."

Thom shifted his weight. "There *is* more. He brought his gelding into the livery. Horse threw a shoe and came up lame. Win pulled the rest and said the animal needed some time off. Littleton rented a mount from Win for the time being. Horse's still there." They exchanged glances, digesting that information.

The cling of spurred boots neared the door. Dwight stopped as soon as he entered, taking in the scene. His eyes narrowed imperceptibly at Thom.

Albert stood. "Morning, Dwight," he said, going back to the coffeepot. "We were just talking about the new depot. Word has it the men are breaking ground within the week."

"That so?"

"Indeed. A Union Pacific wagon arrived yesterday, and the workers are camping in the festival grounds. I want you to keep an eye out for any shenanigans. I won't stand for anyone starting trouble in my town," Albert said.

Dwight smirked. "How many?"

"About twenty. More will arrive in a day or two."

Thom pushed his hat on. "Well, I need to get over to the livery." He set his empty cup on a tray next to the stove. "Thanks for the coffee."

"Anytime, Thom," Albert said. Chase just watched him go.

CHAPTER TWENTY-EIGHT

*H*annah pushed through the line of people waiting to get into her restaurant and stopped in the doorway of the Silky Hen, her mouth agape. She had never seen anything like it in her life. Especially on a Monday. The note from Susanna asking her to get to the restaurant as soon as possible was crumpled in her hand.

Markus laughed in delight. "Can I help, Mommy?"

The room was loud, packed with customers, and hot. She knew some faces, but others were a complete mystery. People ate from heaping plates, and others looked at her with expectant eyes. Her mother clomped by, red-faced, her hair drooping in her eyes. Two bowls of stew tottered in her hands. "Don't just stand there, Hannah. Susanna needs your help in the kitchen!"

"Hey, lady. When are we gonna get some food?" a portly man yelled from the far wall. He pounded a weighty fist on the table-top. "Been here a good half hour and don't even have a glass of water to show for it."

His partner nodded. "Yeah. I'm hungry!"

"You're next," Roberta replied in a weary voice. "I'll be right with you."

That jarred Hannah out of her surprised stupor. Pushing past four scraggly looking men and a teenage boy, she practically ran through the swinging kitchen door, Markus in tow. A countertop filled with pots and pans and a sink overflowing with dirty dishes greeted her.

Susanna gasped, "Thank God you're here. We've been running since I first unlocked the door!"

Susanna's usual put-together charm was blown to bits. Her milky-white skin was drenched in sweat. Gravy and an array of other foodstuffs marred her white apron. Her always perfectly tied apron bow was totally cockeyed. That alone said just how hard-pressed she really was.

"We're practically out of *everything*," she said, gasping. "And we still have a passel of mouths, mostly male mouths, that we need to feed. Here." She shoved a large ceramic bowl into Hannah's arms as she blew a drooping hank of hair from out of her eyes. "You can finish the biscuits and get them in the oven. I need to slice the roast and make more gravy for six orders of beef and gravy."

Hannah took the bowl but set it to the side. They needed help. And fast. For as long as she could remember Thom had always been there for her. From the time he'd picked her up off the ground, to the afternoon he'd stood up to Roberta after Hannah had hidden in his wagon, telling her mother Hannah had fallen asleep in the back and hadn't known she was on her way to New Meringue. Yes, Thom would help her if he could. She snatched a pencil from her mother's pocket as the older woman rushed into the kitchen. As fast as she could write, she scribbled out a note on the back of the one Susanna had sent her and put it in Markus's hand. "Run over to the livery. Be quick. Maybe Win will let him come to our rescue." She gave Markus a little push. "Hurry, son!"

Markus raced through the back door, and Hannah grabbed her apron. She finished the dough, rolled it out on the floured countertop, and cut out two dozen biscuits with the rim of a coffee cup. Tossing them haphazardly onto two baking sheets, she shoved them into the hot oven. That done, she snatched the knife from Susanna's hands and turned her friend toward her. With a napkin, she wiped the sweat from her face. "I'll take over in here. You go out and help Mother. Those men are running her ragged."

"Gladly. Anything to get away from that hot beast." She gave the oven a scornful stare. "Now, don't forget about the biscuits in the oven—they're all spoken for—and start a new batch as soon as the six beef and gravy plates are ready. The railroad men are going through them like a lamb on fresh clover."

Roberta scurried into the kitchen. "Hannah, I need a chicken plate, two beef and gravy plates, and, and—" Her mother looked like she was going to faint.

"Mother, sit here." Hannah pulled out a chair and gently eased her down.

"I'm sorry, I've forgotten what the lady in blue asked for." Roberta struggled to get up as she rummaged through the pockets of her apron. "Where is the order? I'll go ask her again. She's been patiently waiting for a long time."

"No. You just stay put for a few minutes. It's not worth ruining your health over."

"But—"

"No buts. Susanna can ask her again."

Hannah worked the pump handle and caught some water in a glass. She set it on the table. "Now, take a sip, and then breathe. Try to relax. Everything is going to be OK."

Quickly, Hannah sliced up a loaf of bread and flopped the slices onto a dinner plate. "As soon as you feel up to it, you can go around and offer a slice to people who have been waiting the longest. It should hold them over. But not yet. Take a few more moments off your feet."

That done, she mixed up a new batch of biscuits and set them aside for when the others came out of the oven in three more minutes. She turned up the heat on the gravy and added a smidge more flour-water mixture to extend and thicken it faster, stirred it a few times, and then left it to simmer. Grabbing one of the last three clean plates, she sliced several good portions of the pot roast and put it on the plate, then added an extra scoop of green beans, since all that was left of the mashed potatoes was a dirty pot.

An angry voice rang out in the dining room. "Where's my supper?"

Thom pushed his way through the front door, Markus riding on his back. He was just in time to see a beefy man catch Susanna by the back of her apron sashes and pull her back. With her hands full of dirty plates, she almost toppled over.

"Why, you hooligan," she sputtered, her face clouding up. "I've never seen anyone with worse manners."

Thom set Markus down and strode over to the table. "Take your hands *off* the help."

The pudgy man's face scrunched up and his hands fisted. "Me and my men have been in this poor excuse of a restaurant for too long. She keeps ignoring us."

Susanna shook her head. "That's not true. I was getting to your table next."

Thom stood over the man with Susanna safely behind him. "I'm only telling you this once, so listen up. The next time you touch her, or anyone else working or eating here, I'll throw you out on your backside. Do I make myself clear?" Thom looked around at all the men and the few women in the restaurant, gauging the strength of his words. "Today's business was a surprise to the proprietor. Tomorrow, I can assure you, the place will be ready for you all."

Everyone clapped except the fat man. Smiles replaced scowls.

He found Hannah in the kitchen, red-faced and covered in flour. He almost laughed. "Thomas Donovan at your service."

She looked up. "Thom! Thank you for answering my cry for help."

Roberta watched them from a chair at the small table. She looked away and pursed her lips.

Rapidly scanning the room, Thom snatched a milk stool from the broom closet and set it in front of the sink. "Markus, how would you like to make two bits?"

The boy's eyes grew round, and a smile almost as circular as the horseshoe he'd been pounding ten minutes ago lit his face. "Two bits? *Sure!*"

"Climb on up. I want you to wash these plates and set them here." Thom cleared away a spot within easy reach for the boy. "I'll rinse and then dry them in a few minutes. Be extra careful because I have a feeling your ma is going to need each and every one in the months to come."

Hannah, still working to fill six plates, glanced at him as she worked. A sweet smile pulled the corners of her mouth.

"All right." The boy took the rag and plunged it in the sink of soapy water, then attacked the top plate of a ten-tall stack. Taking his job seriously, he scrubbed with force. Thom turned to find Chase Logan watching him from the back door. Hannah spotted him a moment later.

"What's going on in here?" Chase said, laughing. "All heck's breaking loose."

Hannah smiled. "You can say that again. It's the men from the railroad and other newcomers, too. Mr. Peabody was right—business is booming."

He stepped in a few feet and removed his hat. "Is there anything I can do to help?"

"Yes. I need more meat by tonight. Cut up and wrapped. Can you do that?"

"You bet. Anything now?"

She went over and handed Chase a cookie. Her expression said that was all she could spare. "Actually, yes. Can you stop by the mercantile and tell Maude to triple the things I usually pick up on Monday evening? I'll need plenty of canned goods as well as apples, raisins, and any other dried fruit that she has. I think I'll be baking for most of the night. Other than that, we're OK now.

Thank goodness Thom came to our rescue. If you can supply me the beef for tomorrow, that will be a huge help."

Thom looked at Hannah. "What's that smell?"

"Biscuits!" She dashed to the oven and yanked the door open.

"They're OK," he said from behind her. "Just getting brown on top." He grasped a pot holder and pulled them out, then took the knife from Hannah's hands. He motioned to the last roast in the work area. "I'll slice it up."

She nodded. "I'll make more gravy."

"And I'll get back to work." Her mother picked up the plate filled with bread and stomped out of the room.

An hour later, Hannah wiped a splotch of gravy from the plate rim she was filling with the last clean spot of her apron. *What a wonderful, exciting, money-making day.* It was hard to believe. Things were looking up. Now, she could pay Susanna her wages without worry, and she'd worked the whole afternoon with Thom. He'd cooked, cleaned, and even made several batches of biscuits. She'd been amazed by his culinary talents. He'd gotten her mother to laugh several times, too, although Roberta had tried her best not to. Sighing, Hannah scrunched her cramped toes, and pain radiated up her legs.

She set the plate on the shelf above the stove. "Order up," she called toward the dining room. She placed a note card Maude had made for her under the biscuit. After Chase delivered the message to the mercantile, Maude had put up her "I'll Be Back in Ten Minutes" sign and hurried over. They'd come up with an idea, and Maude had printed cards that apologized for the skimpy portions and promised a nice oatmeal raisin cookie upon redemption on their next visit to the restaurant.

Susanna shuffled in, picked up the plate, and was gone.

The crowd had dwindled. It was five minutes before seven—almost closing time. Thom helped Susanna straighten up out front, and Roberta had gone home. Markus was still at his job, albeit moving very, very sluggishly.

"Tired, Markus?" Hannah asked, rubbing his sweaty little back.

The boy nodded.

"You've done enough, sweetheart. I can finish that now."

He dried his rubbery red hands and climbed off the stool. He sat down with a plop and rested his elbows on his knees.

"You did a fine job. If you hadn't taken over when you did, we would have run out of dishware. You earned your pay today without a doubt." There was no response. She looked down to see he had fallen asleep.

The door swung open. Thom spotted Markus and stopped in his tracks. He caught the door, then closed it quietly. His gaze moved up to hers, and she almost melted. Tenderness filled his eyes. They held hers for several long moments, and she knew without a shadow of a doubt he loved her. He could protest all he wanted; she'd never believe him. What an extraordinary father he'd make for Markus. The two had bonded.

Thom gifted her with a lazy I-love-you smile. "What a good-hearted little cowpoke," he said, nodding to Markus. "And a hard worker t'boot." He reached out and took her hand, dragging his thumb slowly across the back.

He's finally come to his senses.

He led her over to more privacy by the back door. All was quiet in the dining room. She closed her eyes and pursed her lips. Her heart did an excited somersault in anticipation.

A second passed.

"Hannah?"

Opening her eyes, she read the confusion on his face. She straightened and cleared her throat, embarrassed.

"You should take Markus home. He's all but worn out. I'll pick him up so he won't awaken."

Hurt, she looked at the sink and all the hours of work that remained. "I can't leave. There's still too much left to do before tomorrow." Susanna came in, saw them standing hand in hand, twirled around, and left. Thom's amused expression added to her disappointment.

"Susanna's been here for hours," Hannah protested. "She can take him home for me, and Mother will put him to bed." A pang of guilt pricked her insides. "That way I can clean up and get prepared for tomorrow. I have roasts to cook and pies to bake." Her excitement over such a profitable day paled as she contemplated Thom. Couldn't he feel her love? What was holding him back?

Thom shook his head. He strode over and gently picked Markus up without waking him, then placed him in her arms. "Can you manage?"

"Of course. But—"

He cocked an eyebrow. "He needs you, Hannah. You're his ma. Later, after he's asleep and you've had a few hours to rest, then you can come back. Susanna told me she has been helping you for a long time and knows everything you do. We'll wrangle this place into shape and then start cooking and baking. Tomorrow, after my chores at the livery are done, I'll stop back to help."

Markus mumbled something in his sleep and snuggled into her breast. *What can I do? He's right. Markus does need me.* "Fine," she said and headed for the back door.

CHAPTER TWENTY-NINE

$\mathcal{B}$y ten o'clock, Jake had delivered the packaged beef Hannah had asked for to the Silky Hen, where Thom Donovan and Susanna still toiled. He'd also brought along some baked goods from Jessie, made after she'd heard the story of Hannah's full house.

Now free of responsibilities, Jake headed toward the saloon, curious about all the new faces. The usual sleepy street had people coming and going, rare for this late in the evening. He stopped short of entering. He knew too well the things that happened beyond the swinging doors. He'd cooled off a lot since last week, accepting that he was what he was. Nothing more. Chase had offered him a lot, letting him tag along three years ago. He'd do well by being grateful for the second chance he'd been offered and not screwing it up.

The jaunty song on the piano ended and the player started in on "The Streets of Laredo." Philomena's voice joined in, bringing a lump to his throat.

"Thought I saw you out here, Jake," Daisy said, stepping through the doors. Her soft voice wrapped around him like a warm blanket.

He smiled, taking in her pretty dress and happy expression. She was doing better. He was glad. "You're busy tonight." He nodded toward the saloon. "Lots of new people in town."

She sidled up close and took his arm. "But none like you, Jake. I haven't seen you around for a while."

"Been busy, I guess."

A man burst through the doors, stumbling down onto a knee. Jake swung Daisy behind him, out of harm's way.

"Heck of a way to treat your neighbor," the drunken man shouted into the bar, as he shook his fist in the air. He swiped his hand over his face and looked around. "I'll be looking for you!" When he saw them, he pulled up. "What're you staring at?" Not waiting for an answer, he mumbled something unintelligible and wobbled off into the night.

"You be careful," Jake said, watching the drunk fall into the dirt.

She lifted a shoulder. "I can take care of myself."

He really liked Daisy. She was sweet, with a good heart. She'd been dealt a bad hand, but she never felt sorry for herself, as he'd done the other day. Philomena started the second verse where the cowboy tells the passerby that he's dying.

Jake cocked his head. "That sure sounds pretty. This song always gets me right here." He thumped his heart, then chuckled when Daisy curtly folded her arms over her bosom. "You're not jealous, are you, Daisy? You know you're the prettiest gal in this territory."

"Daisy!" It was Kendall. He sounded aggravated.

Jake turned. "I better get back to the ranch."

"Don't go yet, Jake. Come inside, just for a little while." He felt the warmth of her smile. A burst of laughter resounded from inside.

Why not? He was off until tomorrow. He'd just go in and take a quick look around. Wouldn't stay more than five minutes.

He nodded and followed Daisy through the swinging doors. The place was jammed with bodies. "'Twas once in the saddle I used to go ridin'. Once in the saddle I used to go gay. First led to drinkin', and then to card playing. I'm shot in the breast and I'm dying today."

Something about that song always sent a niggle of unease scratching up Jake's spine. Perched on top of the piano like a songbird, Philomena swung her shapely, ankle-crossed, black-stocking-covered legs with the music. She smiled when he came in. "Jake!" Blake bellowed. He stood at the bar, drinking with some fellows. Kendall would be happy tomorrow after the walloping business tonight. "Come over here so I can buy you a drink."

Jake ambled over, and Daisy made her way through the tables, checking on the men.

"Evenin'," Jake said. Blake was the only man there who he knew.

"Jake, boy, what brings you into town? Kendall, pour my young friend a drink on me."

Blake had already had a snootful even though he had watch later tonight. Kendall poured the liquor into a shot glass and slid it over to Jake.

"Go on. What's stopping you?" Blake turned to his friends and said something under his breath. They all laughed.

Jake picked up the glass and tossed the whole thing back at once, squelching the desire to cough up the fireball plunging to his belly. His eyes watered, but he blinked back the moisture.

Blake did the same and wiped his mouth with the back of his hand. "That's darn good. Been too long since I had any time off."

Two men left the farthest card table, aiming for the door. "Blake," Rome called. "A spot just opened up for you. If you're playing, now's the time. Bring along Jake."

Before he knew what had happened, Jake found himself at a card table with Blake, Rome, and two strangers. The whiskey that had pooled in his belly now slithered through his veins as it brought a nice, weighty feeling to his limbs. He nodded when Rome held up his bottle in invitation, then filled the players' glasses.

"Let's see your money, boys." Rome shuffled a well-worn deck as he looked from face to face.

Jake was amazed at the wad Blake drew out. He slipped off a money clip and peeled off several ten-dollar bills. Saddle tramping didn't pay *that* well. Yesterday was payday, and Jake still had his twenty dollars in his pocket. He pulled it out.

Philomena ended the song, and everyone clapped. The piano player helped her down, and she made her way over to the bar.

The men anted up. "Five card draw," Rome said, dealing the cards.

Daisy came over and ran her hand up Jake's back, letting it linger then stop on his left shoulder. It felt good. He looked up. The corners of her soft-looking mouth turned upward in a charming smile. Jake sipped his drink slowly. He wasn't going to get drunk. And after a hand or two, he'd leave. He folded the first hand, along with Blake and two others. Rome won the pot, albeit a small one.

An hour passed with Jake holding his own. He was up thirty dollars, having gotten the hang of reading faces. He'd played plenty in the bunkhouse, but this was his first time with strangers. Lady Luck seemed to be smiling his way. The other men appeared to be watching him, as if he'd passed muster. He liked the approval, as well as the whiskey he'd consumed. He blinked, clearing his vision.

Rome shuffled. Before he could deal, one of the players got up and left, leaving just the four men. Jake picked up his cards. Two kings, two queens, an eight. *Holy smokes! Best hand I've had all night.*

Rome tossed in five dollars, followed by everyone else.

Blake drew three cards, Rome one, the third man—a railroad employee—two.

"Jake?"

"One."

He rolled the corner of the card Rome placed in front of him. *Queen.* A full house.

Hefty betting went around several times.

Jake calculated the pot. Over one hundred dollars. He swallowed. He could sure use that money. He studied Rome over the rim of his cards. *I'm not the only one with a good hand.*

It was past midnight, but the saloon was still going strong. Philomena had disappeared upstairs, and Daisy glided around the room picking up empty glasses, delivering whiskey bottles, and smiling at the men. Blake tossed back another whiskey and studied his cards. Looked undecided. Wiped sweat from his forehead.

"Blake?" Rome prompted.

"Fold." He stood, swaying dangerously to the side as he picked up his money. "I needs to get back to the ranch. Got four o'clock watch." He waved his arm over the table. "Thanks, boys."

The railroad employee clenched the toothpick in his mouth and pushed his money forward. "All in."

CHAPTER THIRTY

The clock on the dining room wall chimed quarter past one as Thom slopped the mop into the water bucket for the last time and stretched his tired back. Earlier, he'd gone over to fetch Hannah back. They had sat down for a quick ten-minute meeting and had decided which three meals would be the easiest to make up in big batches. They'd settled on stew, cottage pie, and roasts for the beef and gravy plates that had been so popular yesterday. Hannah sent Susanna home, telling her to get rested for the busy day ahead. Since then Hannah had chopped and diced, putting together a large kettle of stew that was bubbling away on the stove and filling the room with a savory aroma. Fixings, ready to start another stew in the morning, sat covered and stored in the ice room.

Thom hefted the bucket, balancing the mop handle across his shoulder, and trudged through the propped-open kitchen door.

Hannah glanced up. "All done?"

"That's it. How about you?"

"I think I'm finished. Ten batches of flour mixture premeasured for biscuits. Three dried apple pies, cooked and cooled." She ticked off the items on her fingers. "Stew, enough to feed an army. Six roasts, roasted." She laughed, but her eyes drooped as she slouched to the right. "Six pans of cottage pie. I don't know. This may be heavy-handedness, but I'd rather be prepared than live through another day like yesterday."

Thom leaned against the counter and crossed his arms. *She gets more beautiful every day. Even looking like a bedraggled little field mouse.* She went about storing the food for the next day.

"Thom?"

"Oh. I agree. And if it is too much, all of it can keep a day or two, making your job a trifle easier for the rest of the week."

"It was kind of Jessie to send out that batch of oatmeal cookies and huckleberry pie. I'm going to see if Brenna wants to do some baking on a regular basis. I know she can use the work."

"Brenna?"

"The woman who offered you punch at the town meeting on Saturday."

Thom held his smile. "Oh, you mean *that* Brenna? Yes. That was very kind of her."

Hannah gave him a disbelieving look, then plopped down in the chair at the table. A small giggle slipped between her lips.

"What?"

"You should have seen me before Susanna arrived a year ago. I'm ashamed to say that I was a horrible, *horrible* cook. Customers left the Silky Hen in droves. One time I actually spilled a full box of wallpaper paste into my biscuit mix by mistake and almost killed a man!"

Thom barked out a laugh and slapped his leg. "Really? No!"

Hannah nodded, an embarrassed furrow lining her forehead. "Don't laugh, Thom. He actually broke off one of his teeth. It was awful!" Her mouth pulled down as she remembered. "Ferdinand. That was his name," she added. "I still feel real bad about him breaking his tooth. He left town and never came back."

She stifled a yawn. "If Markus had been older, he could have used the biscuits for projectiles in his slingshot. It was years before Albert let that one die. Still, every once in a while he brings it up, and I have to live through my humiliation all over again."

They were so comfortable together, he and Hannah. It would be so darn easy to slip back into his old life here. Take her for his wife. Have home and family again—*even Roberta*—to take care of and love. But he couldn't. He'd not set her up for another dead husband and more heartbreak. He loved her more than that. If all they could have was friendship, then so be it.

He took her hand, looking forward to a good night's sleep. "Come on, I'll walk you home." He trudged toward the coat tree with her in tow and took down her shawl. "Here you go," he said, draping it over her shoulders. The silver key hung on the wall nearby, and he grabbed it.

She hesitated. "You don't have to do that, Thom. I can manage. I've been making the walk for years."

"You better get used to the idea that Logan Meadows is not the quiet little town you grew up in. Early evening is one thing, but not when it's dark."

After seeing Hannah to her door, Thom descended the steps of the house and stopped in the yard, taking in the festival grounds across the way and the growing throng of workers camped in the large open area. A bit disconcerted, he shifted his weight. A fire flickered, muffled voices. Well, they wouldn't be there for long. Just until the depot was finished.

He headed to the livery to retrieve his horse. Inside, he led his mount from the stall, placed his saddle pad on the horse's back, and threw up his saddle. Hannah and the biscuit story made him smile as he drew the cinch tight and fetched his jacket. A rustling sounded from the loft, and then the barn cat looked down, her yellow-slit eyes glowing in the dark. She jumped to a stall divider and then down onto the hard-packed earth, coming to rub against his leg.

Thom chuckled. She tried to brush against his gelding's fetlock, but the horse stomped his hoof on the hard-packed dirt, leaving a slight outline of his shoe in the soil. Thom stared at it for several seconds. The cat walked back and forth over the mark. Then, straightening, Thom went to the stall where Rome's seal-brown gelding slept peacefully and opened the wooden half-door.

Startled, Jake stared at his cards. He'd thought Rome was his competition in this hand, but he'd been wrong. He mentally calculated his winnings. He didn't have enough to stay in the game. Ned would win this hand by default.

Rome whistled. "That's a lot of money." It was his bet, and it was obvious he was weighing the situation heavily. He swore under his breath and slapped his cards facedown on the table. "I'm out."

Jake felt like cussing. The whiskey soured in his belly. *That pot should be mine.*

Rome leaned over and glanced at his cards. Didn't say a word but pushed his money over to Jake in invitation. "A loan. Worth ten percent."

When had the room gotten so hot? Jake resisted the urge to pull at his collar for air. Sweat gathered on his forehead. One bead trickled down his temple, and he wiped it with the back of his fingers before it dropped onto his shirt.

Rome's money was tempting. Full house, queens over kings. How could he lose? Ten percent was little to pay for such a pot. The men in the saloon quieted, sensing the tension in the air. Daisy watched with troubled eyes from across the hall.

Jake pushed Rome's money forward. "Call."

Time seemed to stop. Jake's heart ricocheted around his chest like a bullet in a canyon. Rome's beady eyes glowed in wicked excitement, even though he wasn't the one playing for the pot. The railroad man smiled, and Jake suddenly felt unsure.

"I hope you can beat a royal flush, young pup. Because if you can't, you've sure dug a deep hole for yourself throwing in with that devil." Ned nodded toward Rome as a gut-wrenching laugh blasted through his lips.

Jake wasn't sure he'd heard anything past *royal flush*. He sat dead still, staring at the cards he'd tossed faceup on the pile of money.

"Well, what've you got? The suspense is killing me."

The tone stung. He was toying with him. The man sat back proudly, puffing out his chest while Jake felt like the biggest fool in the world.

Jake stood. "It's yours."

"The drinks are on me," the burly man shouted. The room exploded in celebration. With his arm, Ned corralled the money and scraped it into his hat. Daisy took a step in his direction, but Jake stopped her with a scowl. *I don't need anyone's pity.* Angry, he headed for the door.

"Hold up there, my friend," Rome drawled. "Aren't you forgetting something?"

CHAPTER THIRTY-ONE

$\mathscr{T}$uesday morning Thom dressed quickly and hurried out of his room. The sun had yet to top the mountains. He had a few chores he'd let go that he'd complete now before going to work. In the kitchen, he found Mrs. Hollyhock busy making breakfast and four place settings on the table.

"Mornin'," he said.

"Came in pretty late last night." She looked over her shoulder at him as she stirred her pot. "Seems that dog's good for something."

Thom patted Ivan on the head and shrugged. The dog had raised the alarm before Thom could hush him, and he'd wondered if he'd awoken his hostess. "We have guests?"

"Yes. Two. Men from the Union Pacific."

"I thought the railroad men were camping in the festival grounds?"

"That's true enough. I suspect these two are bosses. Looked like important people. They should be up anytime." She pointed her oatmeal-covered spoon at Ivan. "Be sure that beast don't hurt 'em."

Ivan whined, then trotted to her side and sat down. Seemed she'd won his dog over, even if she pretended otherwise. Mrs. Hollyhock went over to the table, picked up his plate, and filled it with biscuits, bacon, and gravy.

Thom sat down and practically inhaled the food. It was good. Warm. Deadened the dull ache that usually woke him up around three o'clock in the morning. Seemed the more he ate and gained weight, the more food he needed. He wiped his mouth and said, "I'll get to your chores this morning, Violet. Fill the wash kettle, chop wood, fill your inside wood bin, clean out the chicken coop and stalls. Anything else you want to add to the list?"

She shook her head.

"Oh, I almost forgot." Thom pulled out two dollars and placed it next to his plate.

"What's that?" Her tone was suspicion mixed with hurt. He would have to walk softly not to wound her feelings. She poured him a cup of coffee and looked at the money.

"Just a little something toward my keep. I know you're buying a lot more food since I've arrived."

Turning, she proceeded back to the counter and clunked the coffeepot atop the woodstove none too softly, then turned to face him. "Deal was your muscle and help for room and board."

"I know. And it still is. You charge five dollars a week. Maude paid me a good amount to reroof her two buildings and that helped get me back on my feet. I'd like to pay something, now that I can afford it." He stuffed the last strip of bacon into his mouth and chewed. He swallowed and took a sip of coffee. "Besides, you never have that much for me to do around here, and I'm feeling plenty guilty about that. Like I'm taking advantage of your goodwill." Maybe he was laying it on a little too thick.

Mrs. Hollyhock picked up his dirty plate and slipped it into the water bucket on the counter.

He suppressed his smile. He'd won—for now. "When will those chickens start to lay?"

She smiled, and a warm look came into her eyes. "Well, I'm not exactly sure. Usually takes 'em five or six months before they start. Not knowin' how old Rose, Iris, and Buttercup really are makes it a tad bit difficult ta know. Their combs are startin' to turn, though. I'd guess 'bout a month, give or take a few weeks."

In other words, she had no idea. "Buttercup?" He chuckled, drawing an irritated look from her. "What'd you name the rooster?"

She pulled out a chair and sat beside him, shaking her head. "That poor, confused creature, I ain't never seen another like him. Thinks he's a hen. Goes around with the girls scratching and pecking, and cuddlin' close. Cockerels usually stay apart—thinkin' they're superior, jist bidin' their time till the pullets come into their own, iffin' you know what I mean." She wiggled her eyebrows up and down suggestively. "I hope he has it in 'im when the time comes. I'd like to grow my flock and sell eggs to the mercantile again, like I used to."

"The name."

She fidgeted in her chair. "Pansy."

He couldn't hold back and laughed from his gut.

"*Shush.* You're gonna wake the others."

He stood. "I better get to your chores so I won't be late to Win's." He shook his head. The old woman had turned into a good friend, one he'd needed badly. "I hope Pansy doesn't live up to his name." He patted his leg. "Come on, Ivan, let's get you out on your line."

Finished at the Red Rooster and cleaned up, Thom rode down Main Street on his way to work. Two fellows, faces he remembered from the brawl he'd had the first Saturday in town, stood in front of the bakery and watched his approach. He reined up next door at the mercantile, ignoring their angry stares.

"Thomas," Maude called from the window, feather duster in hand. She rushed over and wrapped him in an embrace even before he had a chance to remove his hat. Warmth crept into his face as she held him much longer than he felt comfortable. He finally broke away, thanking her. "Good to see you, too," he said, swiping the Stetson from his head.

"Thank you for helping Hannah in the restaurant yesterday. The three of you—no, the five of you—really had your work cut out. Markus is growing up so fast. It's just wonderful that Mr. Peabody's words are coming true. I've had three exceptional days here at the store, too."

"Yes. It's happening faster than anyone expected, I think." Thom scanned the shelves as she went on. The bell above the door tinkled, and two unfamiliar ladies stepped in.

"Excuse me for a moment." She hurried over to the newcomers.

Thom breathed a sigh of relief. He went to the wall and picked up the boots Hannah had rejected a few days ago. She hadn't had a chance to come and get them yet, and he wanted to surprise her. He took them to the counter and waited for Maude.

The shopkeeper came around the counter and stopped. Smiled when she saw the boots. Pulling the pencil from behind her ear, she wrote up his tag. "Would you like this on your account?"

He nodded.

"Anything else?"

"A sack of flour."

Maude's gaze jerked up to his. "Violet feeling poorly? She usually picks up her staples on Thursday."

"No. She's fine."

Maude harrumphed at having guessed wrong. "Must think you're her personal slave."

"No, ma'am."

"Maude," the shopkeeper corrected.

He nodded. "And some wallpaper paste. I didn't see any on your shelves."

Her eyebrow crooked up. "Wallpaper paste?"

Thom shifted his weight. He didn't like fibbing, but there was no help for it now. "Uh, yes."

When he didn't offer a clarification, she asked, "Is Violet *finally* doing something with the interior of that rustic barn?"

The Red Rooster was hardly a barn, but he knew better than to get between two women. "Yes. She's always doing this or that."

She turned to fetch what he'd asked for. "Thank heavens for small favors," she muttered, as she walked behind the long counter toward the back room. "That old place could use some loving care, I should think. Especially now, with all the new citizens that'll be moving here. Ever since Dora Lee sold it to that country bumpkin…"

Thom couldn't hear the end of Maude's sentence as she disappeared through the alcove. He felt the presence of someone behind him, so he turned. The two ladies, one young and one older, smiled up at him, twittering. The young one looked away immediately, but the other—her mother?—nodded.

"Ladies," he said, turning back to the counter. What was taking Maude so long?

"Here we are," Maude exclaimed, hurrying back. She handed him a good-size cardboard paper box and a five-pound sack of flour. "Tell Violet that if she needs help picking out a pretty paper, I have many years of experience decorating. I'd be glad to help."

Thom put his hat on and made for the door. "I'll do that, ma'am. And thank you."

"*Maude*," he heard her call to his back. "Anytime, Thomas."

CHAPTER THIRTY-TWO

*O*nce Win had gone out to lunch, Thom pulled the big barn doors closed and hurried into the tack room, where he'd stashed the wallpaper paste and flour behind the stack of grain sacks.

The barn was warm. Sweat, generated from nerves, gathered on his forehead. *Am I crazy?* This just might be the lamest thing he'd ever thought of, but all the same, he had to try something. Opportunities like this didn't come along every day.

He dumped the whole five-pound sack of flour into a bucket with a whoosh, his face and arms getting covered with a light white film. Dusting off, he added a small amount of water. When it was sticky, he added a good amount of the paste. Remembering Hannah and her recitation of her biscuit story last night made him chuckle. This was all guesswork and might end up as nothing more than a big mess to clean up.

Finished, he set the chalk-white mixture aside, haltered Rome's gelding, and brought him out of his stall, tying him at the hitching post. He carefully picked pebbles and hay out of each hoof, now divested of any iron shoe.

He needed to act swiftly. If Win caught him in the act, he'd think he'd gone completely off his rocker. Using a trowel, he spread out a thin layer of the mixture on a board he'd found leaning against the wall of the toolshed. A glob fell off the edge of the trowel and plopped onto his pants.

It was fortunate Rome's gelding was gentle. The horse didn't resist as he lifted each hoof and placed it on the board, making a nice, distinct print of each. Thom made sure to take extra time with his front right, to get the outside crack in the print.

Whamp, whamp, whamp.

Someone was outside. Grasping the long board, Thom climbed quickly to the loft and laid it atop the hay to dry. He stashed the bucket in the gelding's stall and swung the gate closed. Hustling for the front doors, he prayed it wasn't Rome, here to collect his gooey-hoofed horse.

One door slid open. "Anyone here?" Street sounds filtered in, people talking, horses trotting past.

Frank Lloyd stepped inside, blinking and looking around just as Thom arrived up front.

"Mr. Lloyd." Thom wiped his hands down the front of his pant legs, then offered one to the banker. They shook. The poor man was trying to ignore his untidy appearance.

"I've been meaning to stop by sooner, Thom, but everybody and his mother has been keeping me busy. Welcome back to Logan Meadows."

"Thank you. I'm glad to be home."

A moment of awkward silence passed. "I'm sure you are. I'm sorry about your parents and brother. It must be very difficult for you. Let me know if there is anything I can do to help you settle in."

"I appreciate that," Thom responded. "I remember coming over to your place with Pa and Roland to clear your pasture when I was just a kid."

Frank's eyes crinkled. "Yes. That was before I moved into town." The banker looked around expectantly.

"Win isn't here right now," Thom said. "Lunchtime. Is there something I can do for you?"

"It's sort of personal, but I guess you can pass on the message to Win. Then if he has any questions, he can come over to the bank and talk with me."

Thom waited. Hoped it wasn't what he was thinking.

"There's been a complaint about Win moving the two buffalo out toward the street."

Roberta. She didn't waste any time.

Maximus took that moment to let out a loud, bellowing complaint from the rear of the property.

"I see," Thom said. "We started on the enclosure a few days ago but haven't had a chance to finish it yet. Does this mean Win can't go ahead with his plan?"

"Not exactly. It's only one person. One person can't dictate to the other business owners and such. Nevertheless, if *said person* got angry enough and decided to force their hand, they could get a petition going and the city council would have to address the situation."

Roberta would definitely do that.

"My advice would be to hold off building for a while and let it blow over. Perhaps *said person* would be more receptive to the idea later. Personally, I really like the idea. A tourist attraction of sorts."

Thom nodded. Darn that stubborn-headed woman. It amazed him how cantankerous she was.

Frank turned. "That's all. I'll let you get back to what you were doing." His eyebrow crooked up. "Whatever *that* is. Oh, did Chase Logan relay the message I asked him to? I'm serious about your coming to me for anything, young man. You understand? This town needs good, strong men like yourself."

"Yes, he did," Thom replied, touched by the kindness of Hannah's uncle. "Thank you. I may take you up on that at some point." *About Roberta, your sister.*

The chill of May's early mornings gave way to warmer temperatures and anticipation of Sarah's approaching birthday. When

June fourteenth finally arrived, Jessie could hardly contain her excitement. She gathered the children together, and Chase helped them all into the wagon as they prepared for the celebration of the noontime arrival of Logan Meadow's first train *and* Sarah's birthday. It would be a day of festivity, food, and fun. Maude had sent a message via Gabe that Sarah's present had arrived in one piece and was everything they'd hoped it would be. The shopkeeper had wrapped it for Jessie and said it was ready whenever she'd like to pick it up.

"Excited?" Chase slapped the long reins over the team's back, and the wagon lurched ahead.

"Yes," Jessie replied. She held Shane in her lap, and Sarah sat between them. "It's going to be a delightful day. I can feel it in my bones."

"What's delightful feel like, Mommy?" Sarah's brows scrunched as she tried to figure out what that meant.

Chase laughed. "Yes, Jessie. I've wondered that myself."

Shane was on the move and crawling, with help, over Sarah and onto Chase's lap, where his father squashed him between his thighs and let him grasp the end of the reins. "Gooo horses," he cried, a big smile splitting his freshly washed face.

"It means," Jessie began, "that since I have such a beautiful family, and a nice day planned, that a warm, sort of fuzzy feeling is cuddled inside my heart."

Sarah tipped her head. "But you said bones."

"And bones," Jessie added quickly. "Absolutely."

Sarah nodded approvingly as if that made total sense to her. Chase just smiled as he drove the wagon, concentrating on the road ahead. "I couldn't have said it better myself."

With her arms now free, Jessie encircled her daughter and gave a hug, knowing that Sarah was going to love the pretty tea set that waited for her at the mercantile. She was all girl. A lovely, sweet girl, too. Jessie's eyes prickled, but she blinked her emotion away. Sarah was seven today, or as close to that as they could figure. Three years had disappeared like melting snowflakes.

Changing the emotion-filled subject, Jessie said, "I thought Gabe and Jake were coming with us. Did they ride in earlier?"

"Yeah, they're meeting us in town later, in time for supper and other things." Chase tipped his head toward Sarah. "Since they both helped on the depot's construction, they're in celebrating with the other men. I have to say, it really turned out nice."

Jessie's excitement grew. "I can't wait to see it."

"Am I going on the eggnog ride, Pa?"

Chase chuckled. "Not today, sugar." He patted Sarah's leg. "But soon. I promise. That just didn't work out."

Sarah shrugged happily. "That's OK. I forgot to bring Dolly McFolly anyway. I wouldn't want to go without her."

Hannah stood at the window of the Silky Hen and saw the Logans' wagon navigating slowly through the crowded street. She stuffed her order pad and pencil into the pocket of her apron. "I'm sorry," she said to the man and woman who had been waiting patiently for service. "I'll be right back. I'll only be a second."

Running out the door, she looked both ways before venturing out to meet the tall, wooden-planked vehicle. "Good morning," she called, taking in Sarah's excitement and Shane's little-boy energy. Chase pulled the horses to a stop.

"Good morning," Jessie replied, her face beaming with happiness. "Just look at your restaurant. I can't believe how it's taken off these last two weeks."

Hannah laughed. "Yes. I've had a deluge of customers for days. I feel like Noah after the flood. I'm tired, but it's well worth the effort." She lifted her skirt a few inches so Jessie could see the boots she was wearing. "But these help enormously."

"New?"

Hannah nodded. She could feel her face turning red. "Yes. A mysterious someone left them for me in the broom closet." She gave Jessie a knowing smile.

"Ahhh, how romantic," she whispered. Jessie lifted her eyebrows in question, and Hannah nodded again.

"That's wonderful, but do you have enough help?"

Dwight, atop his leggy roan horse, rode through the townspeople from the opposite direction, having already seen her in the street. The animal tossed his head and pulled on his reins, reacting to the excitement in the air. Dwight didn't stop, but tipped his hat and smiled.

Hannah smiled back stiffly. "For now. Brenna is baking every night, and I have Lorna Brinkley, my mother's friend, coming in four days a week to prepare a few extra dishes for the next day, and she helps clean up. We're getting by and learning, too." She laughed, still overjoyed at the sudden explosion of business. She was not only paying the bills, but had opened up a savings account that was building nicely, all thanks to the railroad and construction people. What would it be like when the train actually deposited travelers? "It's all about thoughtful preparation the day before. If we have plenty of side dishes already prepared and ready to go, it's doable for Susanna and me."

"Well, you seem to have it all figured out. I'm glad. Are you going to be able to join us in the park for supper? We have plenty, and you've most certainly earned a break."

"I don't think so, Jessie. That's the busiest part of the day." Both Jessie's and Sarah's faces fell in disappointment. "But I'll try," she added quickly. Sarah's birthday party was all Markus had talked about the entire week. "If there's any way at all, I'll be there."

A gunshot rang out from three buildings down, startling Chase's horses and sending Hannah's heart careening in her chest. Shouting came from inside the saloon. Chase pulled back, settling the team in their traces, a scowl on his face. "Albert needs to hire another deputy. You had better get out of the street, Hannah. Today is busier than most."

She waved. "Be sure to have some of Maude's walnut fudge. She made up a triple batch and has a table set up in the park. If I can sneak away at lunchtime, I will. Mother will meet you in the festival grounds at noon with Markus."

Hannah hurried back inside. Every table was filled, and people still waited for a seat. "I'm so sorry to keep you waiting," she said to the older man and woman at the table. They looked prosperous.

"That's no problem," the man said. "We're in no hurry." He wore a suit, and a cane rested against his knee. His hair was white, and round silver spectacles rested on the bridge of his nose.

"You're new to town?"

"Yes, came in on the stage yesterday and have a room here in the hotel. We had no idea today was a day of celebration. If we'd known there was going to be a train line coming to Logan Meadows, Bridget and I would have opted for that. Six weeks on the stage is a bit too long for our aging bones."

"And a bit too dusty," the woman added softly. She had an elegant beauty about her that had nothing to do with her tailored green-and-white chiffon dress and stylish little hat. Her eyes all but glowed with gentle kindness.

"Six weeks." Hannah sucked in a deep breath. "That's a long trip. Where were you traveling from?"

The woman smiled over to her husband, and his head tipped slightly as if they had a wonderful secret. "Santa Fe, New Mexico."

CHAPTER THIRTY-THREE

$\mathcal{J}$ake followed along behind Gabe, feeling tense. Noon had arrived, and the crowd gathered in the festival grounds now spilled down the narrow road toward the depot, waiting anxiously for the arrival of the Union Pacific. The train, overdue by ten minutes, had a four-hour stop planned, giving everyone a chance to tour the train and enjoy the celebration in Logan Meadows.

"Look at that," Gabe said, laughing. He stopped and waited for Jake to catch up.

Jake glanced around. Suddenly, a large man dressed up like the giant from "Jack and the Beanstalk" came through the throng of people on stilts, head and shoulders above everyone else. A furry vest exposed powerful arms; his long, unkempt hair swirled around his face. A toy goose hung from one stilt and a golden egg rested atop the other. Children swarmed and ran ahead. "Fee-fi-fo-fum," he cried out in a loud voice, eliciting screams and cringes of fear. "I smell the blood of an Englishman. Be he alive, or be him dead, I'll grind his bones to make my bread." He chortled from his gut as he wobbled on the tall sticks, and when he smiled, a row of golden teeth glittered in his mouth.

When Jake didn't respond, Gabe looked at him. "What's wrong? You've been quiet for days now."

"Nothing. Just taking it all in."

What could he say? Friday was his deadline, and it would be here before he could scrounge together the seventy-five dollars he owed Rome. He'd saved every cent he could over the past two weeks, but where was he supposed to get that kind of money? He wouldn't be able to. That was just it. And Jake wasn't sure what Rome would do when he showed without the full amount.

Gabe nudged him and then motioned with his head. Sarah and Markus stood rooted to the spot, hand in hand, as they stared up at the scary fairy-tale giant. Their heads craned up on their little necks, trying to guess his next move. When he looked their way, Sarah dashed behind Gabe, came around, and grabbed Jake's legs. "Save me, Jake," she cried. Markus had disappeared into the crowd. "He's gonna get me." Her voice was a mixture of laughter and fear and put a hurt so big inside of Jake's heart he almost gasped. He'd messed up bad. He stood to lose everything he held dear. He'd not go to Chase—to see the disappointment and disgust in his eyes would be the last straw. He was thankful Blake had taken off for the ranch and hadn't heard about the outcome of the poker game. Somehow Jake had to find a way out of this mess. He reached down and picked Sarah up. She threw her arms around him and buried her face in his neck to hide.

Hoot, hoot, hooooooooooooot.

All heads turned. A quarter mile away, the black-and-silver engine of the Union Pacific rounded the bend; the tall stack puffed gray smoke into the air and left a trail of soot billowing in its wake. Sarah looked around excitedly at the sound and scrambled out of his arms. She ran off toward Jessie.

The train got closer. Flags attached to the sides whipped in the wind. Ladies waved handkerchiefs out the windows. The band started up, and a jaunty tune filled the air. Everyone moved toward the depot with the giant, on his stilts, bringing up the rear.

The engine slowed. Thirty yards out, brake pads met metal wheels and great clouds of steam whooshed out from below, followed by an earsplitting screech. It pulled up gradually at the spanking-new depot platform and rolled to a stop.

"Logan Meadows," the conductor called loudly from inside. It was only a moment before the door opened and short Mr. Peabody stepped off, followed by several smiling men and women. The conductor set a wooden box in the middle of the platform, and the railroad man climbed up.

"Hello, one and all. It is with great pleasure that the Union Pacific's inaugural trip to your fair town, arrived"—he flipped open his pocket watch and looked at it for a moment, then snapped it closed—"exactly twelve minutes past noon. Everyone is welcome to board this beautiful machine and take a look around. The train will remain for four hours and will depart precisely at four o'clock. Not a minute after."

The townspeople swept forward, anxious to get, for some, their first look inside a train car. The conductor stood at attention by the door Mr. Peabody had appeared from, helping the ladies by taking their hand and steadying them as they climbed the three steps. Another conductor stood ready at the rear door for exiting.

Gabe looked at him. "You want to take a look inside?"

"Sure. Thought that's why we're here."

Gabe stopped. "Hold up—here comes Blake."

Blake swaggered over, on his face the typical smirk he wore whenever Chase wasn't around. "Boys," he said and slapped Gabe on the shoulder. He looked at Jake and nodded. "You fixin' on taking a look?"

The train was short, three passenger cars long, plus engine and caboose. It wouldn't take but five minutes to tour the whole thing.

"Yeah," Jake responded. His troubles weren't Blake's fault, he reminded himself. He could have refused the whiskey. Could have declined the poker game. The responsibility for his actions belonged to him, no one else.

Sarah stuck her head out the window and waved.

"Hey, Sarah," Gabe called to her and waved back. "How is it?"

"Nice. I like it."

Markus, always her shadow, did the same. "I like it, too," he chorused.

Thom took notice when Rome rode into town. The man had picked up his gelding four days ago and turned in Win's rented mount. He and Rome had yet to meet face-to-face, but even if they did, Thom doubted Rome would remember him. The outlaw believed everyone in his band had perished and along with them anyone who could point a guilty finger at him. Still, Thom was careful to avoid being near the man. He intended to clear his name. His plan wasn't perfect—it could backfire—but one thing he'd learned from all those years locked away: nothing was certain.

Laughter came from the train. Markus, in the middle of a passel of children, walked down the aisle, his hand landing on one seat back and then the next.

As they exited, Jessie called everyone over. "We're having Sarah's party in the park now. I've brought along a nice big cake if you're interested, Thom."

Markus ran up to him. "Are ya comin', Thom?"

Thom smiled. The boy seemed to have lost all his distrust of him. Hannah was still in the restaurant, serving away. He'd gone over to the Silky Hen to check on them before coming to the gathering, but she had everything under control and had shooed away his help. He crouched down to Markus's height. "I wouldn't miss it."

CHAPTER THIRTY-FOUR

*J*essie's conscience pricked. *I need to talk with Chase. He has a right to know.* Lost in thought, she brushed her unbound hair opposite the bedroom mirror. She'd never kept a secret from Chase. It was eating her alive.

Chase came into the room and toed off his boots. With deft fingers, he ran down the buttons on his shirt and shrugged out of it, then tossed it on a chair in the corner. "Why so quiet?"

Through the reflection, she tried to smile, but it was impossible. Not when Chase looked at her with love and respect written all over his face. Today was meant to be a very special day. Sarah had loved the tea set and the doll from Markus. She'd been showered with love from Gabe and Jake, and Thom Donovan, too. But Jessie had been nervous and jumpy. So many newcomers at the festival grounds. She'd been suspicious of each and every one. Hot, painful prickles made her blink and look away.

"Hey, what's wrong?" Chase closed the distance between them and went down on one knee. He lifted her chin with a calloused finger. "I can see it in your eyes, Jessie. What's troubling you?"

Should she tell him? Maybe there wouldn't be any more letters. With all the trouble happening with the rustlers, Chase didn't need to be distracted. The outlaws had hit the Cotton Ranch again just last week down at the widest part of Shady Creek. One of Seth Cotton's men had been gunned down in cold blood. "Just tired, I guess."

His expression said he didn't believe her for a moment. "Sarah really loved the tea set, didn't she? I'm so glad we spent that money. What good is it if it just sits in a bank and—" Her voice broke.

"Out with it." His tone was sharp. He stood, looking down at her. "Something is upsetting you. You've been anxious all day. The secret I kept from you three years ago almost broke us apart, and I won't stand for any more." He shot her a stern look. "What's troubling you?"

Jessie set her brush aside and stood. Took a deep breath. "It's about those letters that you found in my drawer."

His eyes narrowed. "Go on."

She swallowed. Wished she hadn't started this tonight. They were both worn out from the busy day. What could a day or two more matter? He wasn't going to make this confession easy.

He released a slow breath as disappointment crossed his face. "Fine. If you don't trust me enough to share this gossip, this meddling—whatever it is—I'll read it for myself." In two steps he was at the dresser. He yanked it open. Riffling through her things, he pulled out the three correspondences and took the pages from the opened envelope.

Minutes ticked by. He was a good reader, but slow. Jessie wanted to run to him and take them and hurry and read them aloud. She didn't, though. Over the years, she'd learned he hated to be read to. He'd take as long as he needed to figure out the words, the sentences, work for an hour on a difficult page—but he always persevered. She respected him for it all the more.

His arm dropped to his side, his fingers pinching the two rumpled pages in his hand, the unopened letters in the opposite fist. She stepped away when his anger all but jumped at her. "When were you going to tell me, Jessie? When they drove up to our door and took Sarah from her bed?"

"You don't know that it's Sarah they're looking for. There were lots of babies at the orphanage."

"Not many with a birthmark that resembles a butterfly on their shoulder blade, or am I wrong?" His expression clouded.

"How could you keep this from me? Something so important? She's my daughter, too."

Jessie knew it was pain, or fear, that made him speak so harshly. He turned away and went to the window, staring out into the darkness of the night. She longed to go to him, but something held her feet grounded to the floor.

"Did you think you could just bury your head in the sand and they'd go away? You're smarter than that, Jessie." He'd never shouted at her before. Sure, they had had disagreements, but someone always gave in before it got this far. She worried that the children might hear and be frightened.

"Chase, please. Sarah and Shane will be scared if they hear you."

He nodded. Looked at the wall for several moments. "It's time we find out what the other letters say."

Jessie nodded.

He went to the bed, sat down, checked the postmark, and opened the second envelope.

Jessie's hands shook, so she clutched her fingers together and sat by his side.

"Dear Jessie," Chase began. His voice no longer sounded angry, just old and sad. "Since I did not get a response to my first letter I have pre-presumed"—Chase struggled with the word—"it was lost en route to you." Chase started and stopped. Emotions clogged his throat. "I'm writing today to ask you again if the child you and Mr. Strong adopted three years ago has a *bi-birth*mark on her back, just above her shoulder blade. It is no larger than a nickel. It sort of resembles a butterfly. We are interested in know-ing. Yours truly, Mrs. Hobbs."

He tossed the letter on the bed and ripped open the last letter, the one that had arrived two weeks ago, turning her world upside down. "Dear Jessie, I still have not heard from you. The reason for my last letters was ob-obvious, and now the child's kin have already started for Logan Meadows to see for themselves if your girl is the one they are searching for. Please help them. They have money. It would be in the best interest of the child if she went back with Mr. and Mrs. Stockbridge. Yours truly, Mrs. Hobbs."

Chase stood. "It's Sarah."

"What if they're here already, Chase? What can we do?"

"I don't know. I need to talk with Frank."

Jessie wished he would hold her, silence her fears, but she knew he didn't have any more answers than she did. This one Chase couldn't fix. She said the only thing that would come out. "I'm scared."

"So am I. I don't know about all this, Jessie. I know cattle, when to breed and when to brand. I know horses, how they think and how to grow 'em strong." He looked her in the face. "I don't know a thing about the law pertaining to adoption and such. Do you remember the day Sarah was left at the orphanage? Did somebody drop her off?"

Jessie nodded. She remembered the day as if it were yesterday. It was the day after she'd turned thirteen, and for months all she'd prayed for was that God would send her mother back. As a birthday present. Jessie had been waiting so long, so many heartbreaking years. Before leaving her, her mother had promised she would be gone only a few days. But days turned into months and months into years. Still, Jessie begged God to let this birthday be different. But the day came and went, no different from other years. No fanfare, no cake, no mother.

"It was about four o'clock in the afternoon," she whispered, not trusting her voice. "I finished my household chores and sat on the front porch steps watching people go by. The July heat was stifling. Flies were thick. Mrs. Hobbs, as she did every summer day, disappeared into her room until the cool of the evening. Mr. Hobbs was gone. I went around to the back of the house to get a drink from the well. When I returned there was a wicker basket on the porch by the front door. A newborn swaddled in a pretty pink blanket slept peacefully inside, unaware she'd just been given away."

"So no papers were ever signed?" he asked.

"No."

Chase slung his arm over her shoulder and pulled her close. "I'm so sorry, Jessie. I know how much you love Sarah. We'll get through this." He practically choked on the words. "I promise." He swiped at his eyes with the back of his hand and buried his face in her hair.

"I'm sorry I didn't share this with you, Chase. I told myself it was because you had the rustlers to worry about. I didn't want to add to your burdens. But honestly, it was more. Once I told you, I'd have to face the fact that we might lose her. I couldn't do that. I still don't think I can."

Chase leaned back. Still close, she could see the tiny brown-and-gold flecks in his eyes. The fine lines that time had etched on his face. *My beloved. My Chase.* He'd made it possible three years ago for her to keep Sarah; somehow, he'd do it again. "Can you ever forgive me?"

"You were only worried about Sarah." He brushed a strand of hair across her forehead. "Just wish I knew if, or when, the people Mrs. Hobbs is talking about are going to show up here in Logan Meadows." He paused and picked up the last letter. "Mr. and Mrs. Stockbridge. I feel like I need to get a plan together, but there is no plan to get. Facts are facts. We'll just have to wait and see."

CHAPTER THIRTY-FIVE

Three days passed with no further attacks from the rustlers. Jake hefted the last sack of grain into the back of the wagon parked in front of Winston's Feed, then wiped his hands down the sides of his pants. Glancing across the bridge and down the street, he contemplated the Bright Nugget, wondering how he was going to get out of the mess he'd created. He climbed into the box, took up the reins, and hauled the horses around. He started back up Main Street for the ranch.

Tonight was the night.

Tonight he'd ride out to the south fork of Shady Creek and meet Rome, explain that all he had now was twenty dollars. Somehow he'd get the remaining fifty-five dollars, plus the seven fifty interest. His guitar was worth five to a tenderfoot; there were more and more of 'em in town these days. Other than that, all he had of value was his horse and rig, but without those he wasn't able to work.

Rome seemed a decent man, a bit of a braggart perhaps, but other than that, Jake felt sure he would work with him until he could repay what he owed. At least he hoped he would. However they worked it out, it still didn't change the fact that he'd lost a heck of a lot of money. Hard lesson learned.

Discouraged, Jake swiped his hand across his moist brow and pulled the horses to the side of the road to give ample room to a man driving several milk cows and a goat down the middle of the street.

"Jake," a female voice called.

Daisy waved to him from the balcony of the Bright Nugget. Seeing her brought back a fresh rush of embarrassment. He forced a smile and waved back. Philomena stepped out beside her. The older girl saw him and then whispered something into Daisy's ear.

"Jake," she called again. "Can I talk with you?"

"Sure, Daisy. I'll come in."

Just as he set the wagon brake, Nell Page and Seth Cotton, brother and sister, trotted up the street on horseback. Nell pulled the reins and squeezed with her legs, fighting her good-looking paint every step of the way. The horse tossed his head and jumped sideways at people walking by. He shied at stationary objects, too, like hitching rails and chairs. He even jumped back at his own shadow. White foam dripped from his sides and from between his legs. Nell didn't look all that much better.

"He *still* not broke, Nell?" Jake laughed. Seth pulled up. From his perch in the wagon, he was eye to eye with the two on horseback.

"Hush up, Jake," Nell replied hotly. "I don't need you pointing out his shortcomings. He's high-strung." The horse stood still for a full three seconds, his sides quivering and eyes wide, taking in one scary thing after the other. She reached down and patted his sweaty neck.

"What's wrong with him? He should be plenty gentle by now. Is this his first trip to town?"

Seth rolled a toothpick between his teeth as he contemplated the horse next to him. "Nope, his fifth. His dam was exactly the same. Took me a good six months before she was safe for anyone to ride. Even then, you had to be on guard or she'd leave you in a pile of dust. She turned out to be a great stock horse, though, and we're hoping the same for this one."

Jake glanced up, recalling his promise to go in and see Daisy. She was gone, but Philomena stood there, hands on hips, glaring down at him.

"Uh, 'scuse me." Boot to wheel, he climbed down to the boardwalk. "I have some business in the Bright Nugget."

Jake strode into the saloon. He didn't see Daisy right away, but Dwight stood at the bar with two other fellows. His foot rested on the brass footrest, and his hat was tipped back.

"I'd bet money that Donovan is our man. He has a history of rustling. A dog can't change his spots even if he tries."

Jake hadn't made it past third grade, but he knew slander was wrong. Dwight didn't have any evidence on Thom. If he did, Albert would have arrested him already. It rankled to hear a good man talked about like that. *Don't get involved. You're in enough trouble already,* he reminded himself. *I don't need Hoskins on my back, too.*

Dwight's friend shrugged. "Could be. Why would he come back here where everyone knows his past?"

"Maybe he thinks this town is easy pickings. So far, he'd be right about that. The Sunday the Triple T was hit—twice—the mick was nowhere to be found. I know because I was looking. I don't trust him around women either. I caught him looking at—"

A flash of anger hit Jake like a freight train. *Ah, horsepucky. Why'd Dwight have to go and say that?*

Dwight finished off his whiskey as he caught Jake coming toward him in the mirror's reflection. "You got something to say—*Jake?*"

There it was. The insinuation that he didn't have any name but his first. Same ole, same ole. Jake balled his fist. "Yeah, I got something to say, Deputy. You ought not go ruinin' a man's name just because you don't like him." They stood toe-to-toe. Dwight didn't scare him. "Thom Donovan was out at the ranch that particular Sunday you just mentioned—in a gunnysack race with Hannah Hoskins." He paused, letting his words sink in. Everyone knew Dwight had been sweet on Hannah for a very long time. "They didn't win, in case you're wondering."

The stench of Dwight's heavy perspiration, mixed with whiskey, coiled thick in the air. His eyes narrowed dangerously when his two companions laughed.

Jake felt the corners of his mouth tip up. He couldn't stop himself from driving the nail a bit deeper. "Offered to save me a trip into town by taking her home. Yep, I'd say a romance is blooming."

Dwight lunged. The other men scattered. Disadvantaged by Dwight's extra thirty pounds, Jake fell backward on the wooden floor with Hoskins on top. The deputy drove several painful punches into Jake's face. Jake wrestled a hand free and socked Dwight's side, knocking the wind from him. That gave Jake a moment to heft the lawman off and jump up. Dwight stood and grabbed the whiskey bottle he'd been drinking and smashed it against the bar, leaving long, wicked spikes on the bottom half. The lawman leaped forward. Jake reacted quickly, but a shard flew off the bottle and hit him on the lower edge of his eyebrow. He flinched.

The metal click of a shotgun brought them up short.

"That's enough!" Kendall held his shotgun steady from behind the bar.

Jake dabbed the corner of his mouth with the back of his hand, ignoring the sting above his eye.

Daisy ran up and grabbed his arm. "Come on, Jake, let me get that out." A drop of blood dripped into his eye.

He set her away, unsure if Dwight was finished.

"Go on," Dwight sneered. "Have your *saloon girl* fix you up. She don't care if you're a by-product of a wild night out on the town."

A blast filled the room, hurting Jake's ears. Little bits of the ceiling rained down on them. "I told you to shut up, Dwight. That star don't give you the right to do anything you darn well please."

Jake stepped forward, but Kendall leveled the gun on him. "When I said that's enough, I meant it. Now, git, Jake."

Jake didn't want to let it go. The tinny taste of blood in his mouth fueled his anger. Dwight slurring Daisy's name made him the maddest of all.

Philomena slid between him and Dwight, one finely plucked eyebrow arched in censure. She put her hand on Jake's arm, and he had no choice but to follow. They went into the back room where Kendall kept the whiskey and Daisy waited. Without a word, Philomena backed out and closed the door with a click.

"Come over here." Daisy's voice was soft, reminding Jake of something pretty. Like butterfly wings in the spring. She guided him to a barrel on end, and he sat without saying a word. By now, his eye stung like a son of a gun, and he clenched it closed.

A tiny smile pulled at her lips.

"What's so funny?"

"You look like a pirate," she said, carefully plucking the shard of glass from beneath his eyebrow. She placed a piece of cloth over the wound. The light pressure felt good.

Sounds of men's voices filtered through the thin wall. With a wet cloth she blotted away the drying blood, all the while ignoring his steady gaze.

"You're a sweet girl, Daisy," he said, unable to take his eyes from her face. She moved slowly, letting her fingers linger on his skin. "Anyone ever tell you that before?"

She shook her head. A dusty pink colored her cheeks.

"Well, that's a shame because it's true."

"Hush, Jake. I need to clean you up. It's been awhile since you've been in. I was getting worried."

He tried not to let her statement please him, but it did. Much more than he'd like to admit. Compared to Dwight, Daisy smelled nice, a sort of spice mixed with a maple-syrupy kind of smell. Took him back to the days he'd stay some nights at the old store in Valley Springs with Mrs. Hollyhock and she'd feed him pancakes in the morning and make him bathe. The memory made him smile.

"What?" She was smiling, too, as if she knew what he was thinking.

He shook his head. Suddenly he realized what he'd been needing those months ago when he'd first thought he was in love with Hannah. It wasn't really Hannah he'd been longing for, but the approval her affection would mean to him. She was a person of high standing in the community. Her love would have been the proof he desperately sought that *he* was indeed someone. He stared down at the grimy, litter-strewn floor of the storeroom, struggling to grasp the understanding that thundered around inside him. Everything he'd ever needed was here, in this room, in Daisy's eyes. He didn't need anyone's approval except his own.

Daisy's unexpected stillness drew his attention. A worried frown replaced her smile, and her hands hung at her sides; the fire in her expressive green eyes almost misted over. She must have misunderstood his contemplation for rejection, because she turned and headed for the door.

"Wait." The word came out with a needy rasp. Jake reached for her wrist and pulled her toward him and onto his lap.

"I'm a saloon girl, Jake. Probably always will be." She placed a hand on his chest as she looked up into his face. Her gaze flicked to the wound under his eyebrow and then back to his eyes. The sorrow he saw there hurt deep in his heart.

"Maybe. Maybe not." He didn't know himself what it was he wanted, except to feel her sweetness next to him. To hold her close. When her chin tipped up, he softly pressed his lips to hers.

The door banged open, and Jake pulled back. Kendall came in and stopped. Daisy jumped to her feet, and Jake followed.

"I wondered where you'd gone off to, Daisy." His tone wasn't angry. He gave Jake a look that said he'd just been caught raiding the cookie jar. The bartender took two bottles of whiskey off the top shelf.

"I was just doctoring him a little," Daisy offered. "I'll be out in a minute."

"Good. A group of railroad men just came in and need some entertainment." He cocked a brow, then turned and hurried out.

She took a step to follow him, but Jake beat her to the door. "I need to get to work, Jake." She reached up and checked the spot under his eyebrow one last time.

"I know. I just wanted to tell you that I've been preoccupied for the last two weeks. That's why I haven't had a chance to stop in. All the rustling and such."

"And Rome? I wondered. After the poker game…"

"I know. I stormed out. I've never lost that much money before." A grim laugh slipped out between his teeth. "I've never lost *any* money before. It was foolish. After tonight, though, everything—" He closed his mouth.

Her gaze snapped to his, her eyes huge in her heart-shaped face. "Are you meeting Rome tonight? Where, Jake? Do you have the money?"

"Not the full amount yet. But he seems like a pretty decent man. I'll work it out to pay some each month with interest."

"Daisy!" Kendall bellowed. The word was drawn out so long, the men in the saloon laughed.

"I'm coming, Kendall." She grasped Jake by the front of his shirt. "He's *not* a decent man. There's something about him that scares me. Don't go alone, Jake. I'm begging you."

"He's fine, Daisy. He's no outlaw."

Her nostrils flared. "I've been saving my earnings. It's not all that much, but it can help you make up the difference. You can have—"

"No. But thank you. I'm not taking your hard-earned money because of my stupidity."

The sound of Kendall's flat-bottomed boots clomped toward the storeroom. Daisy went up on tiptoe, coming close to his face. She gave him a strong shake. "Tell me where, Jake. Where're the two of you meeting?"

The door rattled as Kendall got closer.

"Jake!"

Her distress made Jake speak. "South fork of Shady Creek. Ten o'clock tonight."

CHAPTER THIRTY-SIX

$\mathcal{U}$pstairs in her bedroom, Hannah reached around to unbutton the waist of her skirt and slipped the yards of material toward the floor. *Oh, how I'd love to be free of long skirts and dresses. A nice pair of pants would suit me just fine.* A sharp pounding resounded loudly at the front door. Surprised, she snagged her foot in her pantaloons and spilled onto her quilt-covered bed, floundering in all the fabric. "Oh, for heaven's sake. Who in the name of anything good knocks like that?"

A little over an hour ago, she'd returned from the restaurant and now she was changing before fixing something for Markus's dinner. Righting herself, she tussled her foot free and tossed the gravy-splattered dress into the corner for washing. She glanced at her bedside clock.

"Mother, can you get that, please?" she called loudly through her closed door. Whoever it was pounded again, setting her teeth on edge and lighting her temper.

"One moment," she called out the window.

Bang, bang, bang.

Where is Mother? She quickly pulled on a new skirt, buttoned up her blouse, and ran down the stairs. She flung the door open just as the offender struck it again, rattling the door in her hand.

"Dwight!"

"I want to talk to you, Hannah," he said, stepping past her even though she hadn't invited him in.

A noxious odor floated in with him, and she took a step back. "Can't it wait until tomorrow? I'm busy."

He scowled. He looked wildly around the room as if he expected to find someone hiding behind the furniture. When he seemed satisfied that they were alone, he turned on her. Stringy blond hair stuck out in a mess, and he had a shiner forming on his right eye. A long tear opened his shirt under the pocket, and his deputy's star dangled. Someone had gotten the better of him.

"No. It can't wait. I've been waiting for years. I don't intend to wait anymore."

She squared her shoulders. "What in the blazes has you so aggravated?"

Hatred shone from his eyes. "Well, let me see. Maybe it's the fact you've been stringing me along. I'm sick of it. Today it ends!"

How dare he? "I've *never* led you on. Either apologize or get out." She pointed to the door with all the grit she could muster. "Actually, I prefer the latter."

Instead of leaving, he stalked around the room like a man gone mad. Fear inched up Hannah's spine, but she pushed it away. Dwight was not going to cow her. Not now. Not ever!

"You've been consorting with that Irish mick. Even after I told you—have been waiting patiently for you. You're going to be my wife whether you like it or not."

Hannah laughed. She couldn't stop herself. "That is the most ridiculous thing I've ever heard. I never—I repeat *never*, encouraged you. The romance you've cooked up was only in your head. I repeatedly told you there would never be anything between us. I'm never going to marry you, Dwight. I don't care if you are Caleb's cousin. I don't care if we already share the same last name. I don't care if you're the deputy sheriff of Logan Meadows. I'll not marry you now or ever. I'm going to marry Thom Donovan. I *love* Thom Donovan. It'll be Thom Donovan or no one. Do you understand?"

Dwight's face turned three shades of purple. He clenched and unclenched his hands, and Hannah thought out in her mind the different escape routes she could take if he stepped her way.

"So you're going to marry Thom." It was a statement said in a flat, nasally tone.

"I would if he wanted me." *Good.* It seemed her tirade had burst his bubble. "Which he doesn't. He knows my feelings, and still he stays firm in pushing me away. Now, are you happy?"

The back door slammed, and the sound of running feet echoed into the living room. Roberta burst into the room. Her eyes were wide as she looked back and forth between them. Markus was next. He ran to Hannah's side as if to protect her.

"What in the heavens is going on in this house?" Roberta gasped. "We could hear you all the way from the creek." Markus held a slimy frog cupped in his hands. The bottom of his pants were wet up to his knees.

"She's in love with him, Roberta," Dwight yelled. "I can't believe my own words. Thom Donovan!" He looked back and forth between her and her mother as if they were in the third grade and he was telling on her. Maybe he thought she'd get ten swats and then be sent to bed without any supper. "I wouldn't be surprised if they've already—" He looked at Markus and shut his mouth.

Hannah's heart twisted as her mother stepped toward the tall, crazy-looking deputy and poked a straight finger into his chest. "I'm going to have your job for this outrageous stunt, Deputy Hoskins. I suggest you get your whiny mouth and dirty mind out of Hannah's house and never step foot into it again. Do I make myself perfectly clear?"

Dwight stumbled back, clearly shaken. "What? But—" He held out a hand to Roberta, a lost-little-boy look in his eyes.

Hannah reached down and picked up Markus. He wrapped one arm around her neck and clung to the frog with the other. His presence bolstered her resolve. "I'm sorry, Dwight, about whatever

happened to you today. I can see that you've clearly been upset."
*Was it Thom? Had the two finally come to blows? Was Thom hurt,
bleeding somewhere, needing help?*

Dwight brushed at his pants as if he could fix his appearance
with the small gesture. "You and Thom," he muttered and took
a step toward the door. "I never thought I'd see the day. Never
thought…" He yanked the door open and stomped out.

CHAPTER THIRTY-SEVEN

$\mathcal{T}$he usual peaceful feeling Chase got from the barn did little to calm his ragged nerves. He moved from one stall to the next, checking on the young horses bedded inside. Five of the finest of this year's two-year-old crop were spending their first night ever in a barn. They'd run free until now, growing strong and clever. A colt, three stalls back, snorted and kicked the wooden slats keeping him from his prairie home.

Chase stifled a grin as he carefully opened the last gate on the aisle. The golden-colored filly swung around in fear, crowding into the corner, her silvery mane and tail rippling with movement. Her large, intelligent eyes, brilliant even in the dusky light, distrustfully looked him over. The aroma of damp horseflesh hung thick in the air. She snorted, then stomped her right foreleg in warning. Chase put out his hand in supplication, but didn't go in. "Easy, girl." She was a beauty. Was sure to bring a high price this fall if they decided to sell her.

He rubbed his gritty eyes and closed the stall door. A sigh slipped out. Nothing mattered except fixing this horribly cruel mess with Sarah. When would the Stockbridge people arrive? What would it do to Jessie if they took Sarah away? *And to me? Gabe and Jake? Shane?* So many questions. So few answers. He felt castrated. Unable to protect his family when they needed him most.

"Chase?"

He turned and saw Gabe silhouetted in the door. The young man entered, his footfalls silenced in the soft-packed dirt. "Hoped I'd find you out here."

"Yeah, just finishing up." It was just a small lie. He'd been avoiding Jessie at every turn. The pain in her face was killing him inside. He needed to do something, but he didn't know what. Long hours in the barn, riding the pastures, and checking with Albert in town helped him stay away. As of yet, he and Jessie hadn't shared the information about Sarah with anyone.

"The stock look good," Chase added, motioning to the stalls. "How many more are still running up in the high country?"

Gabe offered a lopsided grin. "A good ten. We should have 'em corralled at Devil's Gorge by the end of next week. By then this batch will be started and able to be moved to paddocks. I have my eye on her." His nod indicated the filly in the last stall. "I think we should keep her."

"My thoughts, too." He opened her gate again. This time she pinned her ears and shook her head. "She's a beauty, all right. Her dam's as spirited as they come. Seems this girl will be the same. The wilder the colt, the better the horse."

Gabe nodded.

Chase glanced around. "Where's Jake? Thought he'd be with you."

"Actually, I thought he was with you in the barn," Gabe said. "He's not at the house. I checked before I came out here."

"Well, he's probably gone into town to let off some steam. It is Friday night."

Gabe shrugged, then looked away.

Gabe's boyhood diversion tactic was not lost on Chase. "What? Is there something about him going to town that I should know about?"

"Nope. A man has the right to rein his life in any direction he wants, I guess."

They were walking toward the large barn door and Chase stopped. "What's that supposed to mean?"

"Exactly what I said. Jake's been chewing on a bitter pill of late. Just think he has some hard knocks ahead of him before he gets it out of his system."

"All this from you, two years younger and still wet behind the ears," Chase teased. Gabe knew how valuable he was to this ranch. They couldn't have come so far so fast without him.

"I don't have to be old to have good sense."

Chase shrugged. "Guess not. Go on and say what you have to say about Jake and don't feel guilty. We all love him like family."

The two moseyed out to the hitching rails, and Chase leaned back against one. Gabe needed a little time before spilling the beans, he thought, as he looked around the tidied yard. Everything in its place, ready for the next day of work.

"It's just that I hate to see him in any kind of trouble," Gabe finally said.

Chase rolled on his elbow and faced Gabe. "Now, you're getting me worried. Tell me what's on your mind. Does it have anything to do with Hannah Hoskins?"

"No. I think Jake gave that up a few weeks ago. It's something else. Something I heard through the grapevine."

Thank goodness for that. After the display Thom and Hannah had made at the picnic, Jake didn't stand a field mouse's chance in a snake pit. "I'm listening."

Gabe scuffed his boot in the dirt. "A coupla weeks ago Jake got fleeced in a game of poker at the saloon. Seems he lost a bunch of money."

"You know what they say—a winning poker hand is like a cowboy's legs, few and far between." He chuckled at his own joke. When Gabe didn't respond, he said, "I didn't know Jake was interested in gambling."

"As far as I know, he's not. The way it's told, he came into the Bright Nugget and Blake, who already had a snootful, goaded him into drinking. One thing led to another and they both joined a game in progress."

"Well, that's too bad," Chase added, looking up at the overcast sky. It was quiet. Dark. "That's a hard lesson, but I hope he learned it well. He has his eye on a nice patch of property I've said I'd sell to him at a good price when the time is right."

"That's not the worst of it."

What could be worse than that? Chase thought. Both boys worked hard for their pay. Didn't want anything handed to them. "Give me the rest."

"Seems he was gambling with Rome Littleton."

Rome.

"Seems there was a huge pot, and when it came down to Jake and some other fellow Rome lent him money to stay in the game. He not only lost his pay, but now owes Littleton a large chunk, too."

Chase lunged toward the corral.

"Where you going?" Gabe called, jogging to catch up.

"See if Jake's horse is here. Maybe we're worrying for nothin'."

He didn't think so. A bad sentiment had punched him in the belly when Gabe mentioned Rome's name. He hoped he wasn't too late. He prayed Jake hadn't gotten mixed up with something that could kill him.

Hand over hand, Chase scaled the corral fence and moved through the large herd of ranch horses. Some snorted and trotted away. Others slept on in the cool evening air, gentle and dead broke. A shotgun could go off and they'd not care. "I don't see his gelding anywhere."

Gabe stared at him through the poles. "What's wrong?" His voice was tight.

"Not sure." Albert didn't want him showing their hand about Rome, but to heck with that—Gabe was a trusted part of this family. "Actually, yes, I do know," he said, climbing back over the fence. "We believe Rome is part of the rustlers we've been chasing and keep coming up short. I don't want him to sucker Jake into anything."

Gabe straightened and started for the barn, his face grim. "I'll get the horses saddled."

Hannah set Markus on the floor. "Run and put that frog back in the creek, son," she said softly, looking at her mother standing in the middle of the room. Roberta's mouth was a hard, straight line, and indignant outrage seeped from her every pore. Her hands gripped her hips, and she leaned toward the door as if she wanted to run after Dwight and give him a good whipping. "Do it and come directly back."

"Yes'm." Markus took off, none the worse for wear. Thom, and what might have transpired between the two men, popped into her head, and she hurried over to the hall tree.

Roberta's hands dropped to her sides. "Where you going?"

Hannah flipped the cape over her shoulders. "To see if Thom's all right. He's the only one I can think of that Dwight would want to fight."

"The Red Rooster is all the way on the other side of town, Hannah. It's not safe anymore for you to go out at night alone. I'm sure Thom Donovan is fine. It was boxing that got him into trouble all that time ago, remember? He can take care of himself—especially against someone like Dwight Hoskins."

She came over, took Hannah by the shoulders, and pushed her toward the sofa in the middle of the parlor. "Sit down. There's something I'd like to talk to you about." Her eyes were soft. It was something Hannah hadn't seen for a very long time.

The back door slammed, and Markus was back. "I'm hungry."

"I know you are, honey. I'll make you some roast beef with gravy right now."

BEFORE THE LARKSPUR BLOOMS

"She'll do it in one moment, Markus," Roberta said, holding Hannah by her side. "And while she does, I'll heat water so you can have a bath. You need one, young man. First, though, your mother and I are going to sit here for ten minutes—undisturbed—and talk. Can you wait for me in your room, please?"

His eyes went wide as if his ma was in big trouble, and he started up the stairs.

"Mother—"

"I'm only asking for ten minutes, Hannah. If Markus can give me that, so can you."

Hannah watched Markus scamper up the stairs. He glanced back once, catching her eye before disappearing around the corner. She prepared herself for the tongue-lashing she knew was coming. Thom Donovan this and Thom Donovan that. She didn't think she had the energy to hear everything her mother would throw her way.

Roberta delicately cleared her throat. "Hannah," her mother began in a voice so soft she didn't recognize it. "I know this will come as a shock to you, but I've been known to be wrong a time or two in my life. Now, I don't like to concede that, but it's true. I was very wrong about Dwight Hoskins."

"Mother—"

"I should never have thrown him at you all these years." She sat tall, dignified. She kept her gaze on Hannah's face. "Encouraged him. Helped him get closer to you. I'm sorry."

Her mother's words were like a balm, smoothing over her ragged nerves and warming her heart. Never in her life would she have expected her mother to concede to anything, let alone Dwight. "Mother, we all make mistakes. I make them every day. Just—"

Roberta patted her hands, shushing her. "Please, Hannah, let me finish. This is hard enough without you interrupting and contradicting my every other word. I overheard you tell Dwight that Thom Donovan has rebuffed your every advance. Is that true?"

Embarrassed, Hannah nodded. Her face warmed under her mother's observant gaze.

"Why do you think that is?"

Hannah tried to stand, but her mother kept her in her seat. "Mother, I really don't want to talk about Thom with you. I'm sorry, but considering everything that has happened since he's come home, it just doesn't feel right. Besides, I thought you couldn't stand the sight of him, let alone talk about him courting me." It was as if a hot iron had been placed on each cheek. How embarrassing. Her mother needn't keep running Thom off. He wasn't interested in her at all.

"Answer me, Hannah. Do you think it's because of all the things I've said?"

Hannah shook her head. A jumble of emotions clogged her throat.

"Hannah?"

"No. When Thom sets his mind to something, nothing stops him. There's more to it than you. As hard as it is for me to accept, he doesn't feel the same about me as I do about him. It's as simple as that. I love Thom. I always have. I always will." She gazed at her mother through a watery shield. "But why do you ask? Now, it's you I can't figure out."

It looked like her mother had just bitten into a sour lemon. "As much as I hate to say it, or admit it, I was wrong about Thom. Getting to know him as an adult, I've actually come to like him. He's good with Markus. Seems Markus has taken to him, too." She inhaled, holding the deep breath a moment before continuing. "But most of all, I don't want you to end up all by yourself."

Hannah almost chuckled. Her mother—the one she knew—was back. If Hannah weren't so flabbergasted by the words coming out of her mother's mouth, she would have. "I don't care about what others think about me. Or Thom. I just want to make a good life for Markus, and I hope someday I'll be able to have more children. A whole passel. But that's never going to happen because Thom's made it perfectly clear how he feels about me."

Roberta harrumphed, but there was a twinkle in her eye. "*No man* in his correct mind would pass up a catch like you, dear. You're not only lovely, but incredibly smart, with a twenty-four-carat-gold heart. That thickheaded Irishman rebuff you? We'll just see about that!"

CHAPTER THIRTY-EIGHT

*C*hase reined up in front of the Bright Nugget Saloon, found a spot at the crowded hitching rail, and hurried inside. The place was packed. Kendall must be making a fortune with a Friday night turnout like this. Piano music filled the room amid laughter and shouts. Philomena and Daisy worked the room.

"Evenin', sugar," Philomena purred, stepping over. She ran her hand up his arm as her perfume tickled his nose.

Chase scanned the faces looking for Jake, a bad feeling in his gut. His horse wasn't outside.

"I'm looking for Jake."

Her eyebrow peaked sharply. "He in trouble?"

"Not with me."

She tipped her head. "He was in, but that was earlier in the day."

"Did he say anything about where he was going tonight?" Chase wouldn't sleep a wink if he added Jake to his worries. The kid had a good heart and a good head on his shoulders, if he'd get past feeling inferior to everyone. And it didn't hurt that he'd taken to ranching as if he'd been born to it. Chase would be sore put to find someone to fill his shoes. He gave himself a mental shake. Jake wasn't going anywhere. Not if he had anything to say about it. Just because he'd lost some money in poker and was indebted to Rome didn't mean anything.

Chase wondered why Gabe and Albert had not shown up yet. Before coming in, he'd sent Gabe over to Albert's office, and he expected them any second.

"Not to me. He did spend a little time with Daisy getting patched up."

"What do you mean, patched up? Did something happen?"

"He got into a scuffle with the deputy."

"Dwight Hoskins? What in the blazes would they fight over?"

"I wasn't privy to that information, Chase." She briefly touched his arm again. "Wait here."

Philomena hurried over to Daisy, smiling and flirting as she went. She whispered something into the girl's ear, and Daisy looked over to where he waited in the doorway, the dark night at his back. She hurried over.

"May I help you?" she asked, over the pounding of the piano. "Philomena said you wanted to talk to me."

"I hope so. I'm looking for Jake. Philomena said he was in today and that you spent time with him. I hope you can tell me where he is."

"We spent time downstairs," she said quickly. Her face turned rosy even in the dim light. "We only talked for a few minutes. That's all."

Chase nodded. "He didn't mention his plans tonight?"

She looked at him distrustfully. Albert and Gabe rode up and dismounted. He turned. "I guess if you don't know anything…"

"Wait." Daisy's expression appeared torn. She knew something she wasn't saying. Was she protecting Jake?

"What is it, Daisy? What do you know? I'm afraid Jake may be involved in something over his head."

She nodded and leaned closer, so no one else could hear. "He's meeting up with Rome Littleton tonight. South fork of Shady Creek. I'm worried about him."

A terrible sinking feeling all but smothered Chase. *What in the blazes is going on?* "Thank you for telling me, Daisy. You did the right thing."

Just as Albert came in, followed by Gabe, Chase grabbed both by the elbow and turned them around. Thom Donovan was behind them.

Gabe's face was grim. "Thom was just leaving the livery and saw me at the sheriff's office. He wants to help."

Chase nodded. "Fine. Come on, boys. We have some riding to do."

Jake got off his gelding and tied him to a branch, feeling the weight of his gun strapped to his leg. Rome wasn't there yet. He needed to get this behind him, the sooner the better. Get on with his life.

He looked around, half expecting Gabe to step out from behind a tree. *Keeping an eye on me. Worried I'll get in deeper.* A halfhearted smile crinkled the corners of his mouth. Gabe was a true friend. Without him he'd never have had the courage to leave Valley Springs, a town that held nothing for him but heartache, thanks to his mother. Gabe had also badgered him into trying things he'd never do on his own—like reading. They'd made a pact to read two books a year. Every time Jake got frustrated and wanted to quit, Gabe would help him work through it and teach him silly little rules to make it easier.

Jake looked across the creek, deep and wide here at South Fork, thinking of a certain short story he'd just as soon like to forget. He wasn't ashamed to admit that "The Tell-Tale Heart" had scared the heck out of him that snowy night last December. It had a way of sneaking into his subconscious on dark nights. Or when he was alone tending the herd. It rolled around in his head like hot coals. Poe sure knew how to weave a tale. Jake hated to think of the vulture eye, and worse, the crazy boy sticking his head in his benefactor's room in the dead of night, murdering him and dismembering the poor old man. Stuffing him in—

"Jake."

He jumped, his heart thwacking painfully against his ribs. It was Rome. The cowboy reined up in the clearing but stayed on his horse.

Jake didn't like it. Maybe it was the story he'd just been thinking about, but the hair on the back of his neck rose, and not because of the cool breeze. Leaves whispered softly in the trees as if trying to tell him something. He took a step toward his horse but didn't get far.

"You have my money?" Rome's tone was harsh.

Jake stopped. Turned. "Not all of it. Twenty dollars for now."

"I ain't running no bank, Jake. I gave you more time than you deserved. Why, if you weren't good for the money you ought not have taken my loan."

Rome was right.

"So. What should I do with you?" Rome scratched a match and lit the end of a cigarette. "You tell me."

Jake followed the glowing line when Rome tossed the match into the river. His palms slickened. He'd been a stupid fool to come out here tonight all alone. Daisy was smarter than he was.

"I know," Rome finally said. "I'm moving some cattle tonight. Ten head over in the next valley. I want you to take them to Casper for me. A few days' work is little to ask for that much money. That'll take off the remainder of what you owe."

Cattle.

"I'm not rustling."

Rome laughed. "Who said anything about rustling?"

"It's damn obvious to me."

Rome drew his gun and leveled it at Jake. "You'll help, and shut up about it. It's my word against a no-named nothing."

Clattering hooves sent rocks rolling into the riverbank. Both men turned. Dwight plunged his horse down a sharp drop and reined up next to Rome. His horse dripped sweat. Dwight's clothes were rumpled and his face bruised from the earlier fight. "I found cattle over the draw. And the bull from the Broken Horn." He nodded toward Jake. "What's this?"

Rome smirked. "I caught one of your rustlers, Hoskins."

Dwight pulled up, as if startled at Rome's words.

"Who knows the land and ranches around here better than him?" Rome pointed to Jake with the end of his pistol. "It's the perfect cover. If we take him in, Preston will just release him, being he's such good friends with Logan. Best we take care of this here and now."

CHAPTER THIRTY-NINE

*J*ake itched to reach for his gun, but if he did he was a dead man. "I'm not a rustler, and you know it, Rome!" He knew his time was running out. "*You're* the rustler," he blurted. He chanced a glance at Dwight. The moon was just bright enough that Jake could see a satisfied smirk right under the purple shiner he'd given him in the saloon. His taunting words about Hannah and Thom Donovan slipped back. He wished now he hadn't pushed that point quite so hard. Dwight wasn't going to believe a thing he said, but Jake had to try or else this would be his last night on earth. "We were meeting out here so I could pay Rome the money I owed from the poker game. Look in my saddlebag, Dwight. You'll find twenty dollars."

Rome laughed. "I never would have suspected *you*, Jake."

"It's *not* true," Jake insisted.

Dwight looked between them. "Now, why would you ride all the way out here just to pay back a little money? Don't make any sense at all. I don't think that passes the honesty test, Jake, ole boy." He untied the lariat looped on his saddle. "You know range law, Jake. Easier and faster than waiting on the circuit judge. Scares off other rustlers, too."

Jake jerked back, and sweat broke out on his brow. Rome's gun—Dwight's lariat. *This might be it. My end. An ugly way to die. And what about Chase and Jessie? What will they believe?* Regrets a mile wide rendered his heart as he fought to stay in control of his emotions. *Daisy.*

Dwight glanced around in the trees, looking for a suitable branch. He tossed his rope over a limb several feet above him and caught the end, pulling it into his lap. He quickly tied a noose. "Yes, sir. Albert's going to be darned pleased to hear we rid the territory of vermin like him."

Thundering hooves echoed up the draw. Whoever it was wasn't trying to cover their arrival.

"Do it!" Rome commanded. "String the boy up."

Jake backed away, preparing to dive headfirst into the river. He'd take his chances there. He couldn't swim, but he was a fast learner.

Dwight spurred his horse. It jumped forward, cutting off Jake's path to the river. The deputy dropped a noose around his neck, then pulled his gun and struck him on the head. Pain exploded, and everything went black.

Hat pulled low, Thom stayed behind Albert, Chase, and Gabe as they rode into the clearing. Jake lay unconscious on the ground, a noose looped around his neck.

"What in the devil is going on?" Albert shouted. He reined up first, followed by the others. Their horses danced around on the rocky soil, creating a clamor.

Dwight puffed out his chest. "Rome caught himself a rustler red-handed. Ten head over yonder to prove it. Your bull, too, Logan. Range law says we have the right to string him up on the spot."

"They don't pay us to murder people, Deputy," Albert said forcefully. "If he's a rustler he'll get an impartial trial."

"Jake isn't a rustler," Chase gritted out. "Get that rope off his neck." He dismounted and handed his reins to Gabe. He started toward Jake, but Rome cut him off.

The crazy look in his old adversary's eyes gave Thom pause. Rome was a cold-blooded killer. He was sure none of the others, with the possible exception of Chase, could outshoot him. Still, Jake's crumpled body urged them to hurry.

"I didn't go to all the trouble of doing your job just to see him walk free, Preston. That's what will happen if we let you take him in," Rome shouted at Albert. He jerked his reins cruelly, and his horse tossed his head. "Chase Logan has you in his back pocket. Everyone knows it. He says jump and you ask how high. The ranchers are sick and tired of losing their beef. Hanging this one will set an example for the rest."

It'd be a bloodbath if anyone fired. Albert's quick glance told Thom the sheriff knew the fine line they walked.

"Everyone, just stay calm." Albert put out his hand in supplication.

Rome let go a string of curse words. Spittle flew from his mouth. "Dwight, you're a lily-livered coward. Give me that rope!" Rome's horse leaped forward when stuck with two-inch spurs. He ripped the lariat from the deputy's grasp and wrapped it around his saddle horn. Chase, still standing close, grabbed Rome's horse by the bridle, halting it in his tracks. He held firm as Rome kicked and struggled with his horse.

"How do we know Jake's the rustler?" Thom asked, riding forward.

Something in his voice must have touched a memory in Rome. The man twisted in his saddle and looked directly at Thom for the first time. "I caught him with stolen cattle. How much more proof do you need?"

A thrill shot through Thom. His heart beat faster with the unquenchable thirst of triumph. *Finally! I have you now!* After all these years, he'd have his revenge. Repay the man who'd stolen his future, his life. If it hadn't been for Littleton, he wouldn't carry the bullet that was robbing him of happiness with Hannah.

"Been talking to Stinky Slim lately?" Thom asked slowly. "His ghost tell you where to find the stolen cattle?"

Rome sat back in his saddle, startled. "Who? What?" A tremor rattled his voice.

"Stinky Slim. Surely you haven't forgotten. Him hobbling about, one leg longer than the other."

Thom could almost see Rome's mind turning. The man believed everyone from the old outfit was dead. He'd gone about his life with no one left to point any fingers. No one would know that name unless they'd ridden with him in Colorado. He squirmed in his saddle. Looked around suspiciously.

The night sounds went quiet. Dwight, for the first time, looked mixed up. He kept glancing at Albert as if waiting for direction. The only sound was the water as it splashed over its rocky course.

Thom snagged and kept Rome's gaze.

"You don't remember me, do you, Rome?" No one wanted a gunfight. With four guns to Rome's one, and possibly Dwight's, they could take him down but not before he got a few shots off himself. Someone would be killed. Everyone needed to remain calm. Collected. Not only did Thom want proof of Rome's nefarious deeds, but he wanted vindication for himself.

"It's me, Thomas Donovan. Surely you recall the Irish lad you hired on in Colorado."

It was as if Rome snapped out of a trance. He sneered and again tried in vain to free his horse from Chase. "Get back, Logan," he said, ignoring Thom's remark. "I'm hanging this rustler. Cleaning out the prairie."

Jake moaned. His leg moved.

"I'm eight years older now, Rome. Sat in a stinking jail all because of you."

"I don't know what you're talking about. I've never seen you and never heard of some bum named Stinky Slim. You're cracked."

"Am I?" Thom dismounted, but when he reached for his saddlebag the silver buckle wavered before his eyes. He stumbled, caught himself with the saddle.

"Thom?" It was Albert, watching him closely.

He pushed on, worked the buckle, squelching the pain that throbbed behind his eyes. A moment later, he withdrew the molded hoofprint he'd tossed into his saddlebag before riding out. It was still attached to the board. When the prints had dried rock-hard, he'd sawed the board into four squares. He held this one up for everyone to see.

He smiled, enjoying every minute of Rome's alarm. "I've been doing a little detective work myself. I took these prints when the rustlers hit the Cotton Ranch after the rain. Shows one of the rustlers had a horse with a sizable crack in the outside of his right front."

Again being careful not to set Rome off, Thom slowly reached back into his saddlebag and pulled out a pair of nippers. He tossed them to Chase. "Pull off that front right, Chase. You'll find all the evidence you'll need to watch Rome Littleton swing."

CHAPTER FORTY

$\mathscr{L}$ittleton spurred and pulled back at the same time, causing his horse to rear. Chase was jerked off the ground by his firm grip on the bridle. Chase yanked his body back, avoiding the animal's striking hooves. Rome moved his gun back and forth from Thom's chest to Gabe's. "Anyone draw their gun and I kill Gabe Garrison first!"

"Calm down," Albert said evenly. "No one is drawing their gun. We're all giving you as much space as you need."

Chase struggled with his footing, staying clear of the frightened horse. Thom had been right. Rome was the leader to react like this.

Rome jabbed his gun at Thom. "I should have *killed* you. Killed you when you were nothing but a hungry, stupid kid. Couldn't even tell we were hiding from the law!" He looked at Chase. "Let go, Logan, unless you want a bullet through your brain."

A flash lit up the night as a six-shooter boomed in the tight area. Acrid smoke burned Chase's throat. Rome fell from his saddle and landed on the ground with a thud, still clutching his gun. His horse jerked free and took off at a gallop.

Jake! Chase dove for the lariat. A zinging sound filled the air as the rope scorched leather as it pulled free from the saddle horn, painfully burning Chase's hands. The rope snapped off, flipped into the air, then fell limply to the earth.

Jake wobbled on his feet, his smoking revolver hung at his side. He wrested the rope from his neck and threw it to the ground. Chase ran to his side.

Albert turned on Dwight, his gaze suspicious. "What are you doing out here so far?"

"What! I'm not a rustler! I was just doing my job!"

"Of hanging innocent people?" Albert said angrily. "You're fired."

Hoskins snapped straight. "What are you talking about, Albert? I tracked—"

"Shut up! You're relieved of your badge until I find out what's going on. Toss your gun away."

Albert rode forward, dismounted, and picked up the gun. "Gabe, you go catch Rome's horse. We'll need him to get Littleton back to Logan Meadows."

Gabe nodded and took off.

Two hours later, the town's young physician worked to remove Jake's bullet from Rome's side. The men stood around in a wide circle, making sure the half-conscious outlaw didn't somehow get away.

Chase looked at the group through gritty eyes. Jake slumped in a chair. Thom and Gabe stood beside him. *Getting too old for shenanigans like this*, Chase thought. *Just glad we're all here and alive.* The doc had finished Jake's examination ten minutes ago. Except for a lump on his head, he'd be fine.

"I still owe him seventy-five dollars," Jake said quietly.

Albert shook his head. "Considering it was stolen money in the first place, I'd say anything you owed Rome was paid in full tonight."

"Thom, I'm still trying to figure out how you got those tracks," Gabe said. "That plaster is hard as a rock."

"I was just wondering that myself," Albert said, the square piece of wood with the print dangling from his hand.

Thom shrugged. Lines of exhaustion etched his face, and he rubbed his eyes. "Well, actually I didn't."

A smile crept over Albert's face.

Thom nodded. "You're correct in your thinking, Albert. I was bluffing my way through."

"But the plaster prints?" Albert insisted. "It's right here."

"Remember I told you Rome's horse was stabled at Win's? Had a stone bruise and needed time off. As long as I had access to his horse, I knew I should be doing *something*. But I didn't know what. Then Hannah shared a story about how she'd accidentally spilled wallpaper paste into her biscuit makings. So I took the gelding's prints and waited for my chance to use them. I felt certain that if Logan Meadows was having problems with rustlers and Rome was here, the two went hand in hand. I could've been wrong."

Gabe's smile split his face. "You were banking on his reaction to your made-up story."

"That's right, Gabe."

From the operation table, Rome gave a loud moan. Dr. Thorn tossed the bullet into a tin bowl at his side.

Albert whistled. "That's interesting thinking. I could sure use a deputy like you. Someone who uses the brains God's given him, not going off half-cocked all the time. What do you say, Thom?"

Jessie paced to the window and looked down the road. She'd lain awake last night for hours waiting for Chase. When he'd returned, he'd told her how Thom had tricked the leader of the rustlers and Jake had saved the day. It was an amazing story, and she was happy about the outcome. But she couldn't concentrate.

Frank had ridden out last night with a message. As she'd feared, Mr. and Mrs. Stockbridge had shown up in Logan Meadows a few days ago and were coming out today. They wanted to talk about Sarah. About her little girl. Jessie's heart thundered in her chest. *How, Lord? How has this happened? And why now?* Chase had gone out this morning to talk with the ranch hands, but he'd promised to be back as soon as he could.

Jessie fiddled at the table, making sure everything was perfect. It was set with her best dishes and linen. Her first larkspur of the season had just bloomed that morning, so she'd cut several velvety-blue stems and a handful of pink roses and had arranged a pretty bouquet. It now sat in the middle of the table.

Last night, she'd been too keyed up to even think about going to sleep once the children were put to bed. Instead, she'd baked a chocolate pound cake and a batch of huckleberry oatmeal cookies. Now, she turned at the sound of hoofbeats and ran to the door.

Chase came in and hung his hat on a hook. "Anything yet?" He strode over and wrapped her in his arms.

She shook her head. "I expect them anytime."

"And the children?"

"Gabe and Jake took them on an outing to the meadow for me. They're confused but didn't ask why." She stepped out of his arms. Chase looked worried and tired. Any other day he'd have skipped shaving and gone to work. Not today. He'd bathed at five even though he'd gotten home at three. Neither of them had slept a wink.

He tried to smile, but the corners of his lips pulled down. "It's going to work out, Jessie." He couldn't hold her gaze and looked away. He didn't believe that any more than she did.

"How did the men react to the news about the rustlers?" she asked, wanting to take his thoughts off Mr. and Mrs. Stockbridge.

"Funny thing. Blake cleared out sometime last night. I don't know how he found out about Rome, unless he was hiding somewhere in the dark. No one's seen hide nor hair of him."

"Blake?" Bile rose in her throat.

Chase nodded. "Hurts, doesn't it?"

"I would never have suspected him." She fiddled with the lace on the collar of her best Sunday dress. "I guess you don't really know someone at all."

"No. Don't be suspicious of everyone, though. One or two rotten apricots don't spoil the whole tree. Here's a bit of good news. Happy Jack is back in the pasture with the heifers. He was in the group of cattle retrieved last night."

"Chase, that's wonderful!" *Chase.* What would she do without him? Always looking on the bright side.

A soft knock sounded on the door.

She gasped. She'd been so wrapped up with Chase she hadn't heard the buggy arrive. "How do I look?" She smoothed her hair with a shaky hand.

"Prettier than you've ever been."

Maybe Mr. and Mrs. Stockbridge didn't care about pretty, or pound cake, or that Sarah was an important part of a loving home. Maybe they wanted her back no matter what. Jessie gathered her courage to face them with dignity.

They went together and opened the door.

"Please, come in," Chase said.

She was shocked to find that Mr. and Mrs. Stockbridge looked to be in their sixties. In awkward silence, they filed into the parlor, Mr. Stockbridge bringing up the rear with his cane. Remembering herself, Jessie quickly asked, "May I take your shawl, Mrs. Stockbridge?" The woman smiled kindly and handed the delicately crocheted garment to Jessie. She folded it nicely, placed it on the table in the entry, and hurried back to Chase.

"You seem shocked by our arrival, Mr. and Mrs. Logan," the old gentleman began after he'd settled onto the sofa. He was dressed in business-type attire that spoke volumes about their finances. White hair capped his head, and his face, crisscrossed with wrinkles and embellished with silver glasses, was thoughtful. Jessie tried not to be drawn to him, but that was next to impossible.

"Yes." Chase's tight voice was so uncharacteristic. Jessie chanced a quick peek in his direction. "We are. We've had Sarah over three years. We thought you were her parents."

Mrs. Stockbridge smiled and shook her head. "Her uncle and aunt." She was delicate. *Cultured*, Jessie thought. Her hair, not white like her husband's, was chestnut and streaked with silver. Her soft emerald dress looked expensive.

Jessie found her voice and asked, "How do we know, Mr. Stockbridge, that you are who you say you are? I'm sorry to be mistrustful, but…" It was the question that had been rolling around in her head ever since the first letter had arrived.

Mrs. Stockbridge reached over and patted her husband's hand. "First, you must call us by our given names. I'm Bridget, and my husband is William. Do I have permission to call you Chase and Jessie?"

Chase nodded. "Of course."

"Thank you." She pulled a small book from her satchel. Black ink splotches dotted the cover, and the pages were worn. "I told William you'd ask that very question, so I've brought along the way we found out about Sarah." She opened the book and skimmed through the pages. "This belonged to my twin sister, Bethany Camble. When she passed away last year, we traveled to Texas to settle her estate, her being a widow. I found this diary in the attic. It first belonged to her daughter, Emma Camble, Sarah's mother."

Unable to control her shaking hands, Jessie huddled close and pressed them into Chase's. His warm skin calmed her soul. This was all too familiar and yet very strange. Sarah's relatives sat right before her eyes. Her mother's name was Emma. Did Emma have Sarah's dancing blue eyes and soft chestnut hair?

"Although you might think it wrong, I read it. I learned Emma had been engaged to a man named Eugene. I'm sorry, but I don't know his surname. Before the nuptials had taken place, she found herself with child. When she told her betrothed, it seems his true colors surfaced, and he ran off, abandoning her. He never contacted Emma again. Emma was the only child my sister had, and her father, strict as the day is long, worshipped the ground his daughter walked on. Fearful of his reaction, Emma planned an extended trip to visit her cousin in New Mexico Territory. She stayed almost a year. After the birth, her cousin put the baby girl in a basket and left her at the orphanage."

Tears slipped from Jessie's eyes as she struggled to control her emotions. She remembered that day very well. How sad for Emma. And Sarah. And everyone concerned. Chase wrapped her in his arms, holding her tight. Shivers racked her body as the memories came thundering back.

"Please, go on," Jessie whispered. "I'm all right." She wiped her eyes with a white cotton hankie Bridget had pulled from her pocket.

"Are you sure, dear?" Bridget waved the hankie away when Jessie tried to give it back. "You might need it again when I read this page. It will erase any doubt that we are Sarah's kin." She cleared her throat, brought the book close, and began reading. "'My precious tiny girl is perfect in every way. Although we thought it best that I give her up the moment she came into the world, I just could not do it. I fed her and bathed her, and she never even cried. Her eyes, so full of wonder, took in her surroundings as if trying to figure out where she was. Her birth was easy, nothing like I'd heard from others. How I wish I could take her home to my mother, and share this miracle with my auntie Bridget. On her tiny back, just above her shoulder, is a birthmark that reminds me of a beautiful little butterfly. Oh, if only I could keep her. Love her. That is all my heart yearns to do. I long to feel her in my arms already, even though that is where she is now. Oh, my sweet girl. I pray God will keep you safe.'"

Jessie was drowning. A million sensations swirled inside, and tears ran unchecked down her cheeks. *Oh, Sarah. So tiny,* so precious. She remembered thinking those exact same things when she'd opened the wicker basket and looked inside. Jessie's heart cried for her own mother, too. Had she suffered like Emma?

"W-what about Emma? Is she still—" Jessie put her hand over her mouth to stop what she'd almost asked. But she needed to know.

"Still alive?" Bridget finished for her. "No, I'm afraid not. She passed on at an early age, only twenty-two. She'd never married. She contracted tuberculosis and spent some years in a sanitarium, but it didn't heal her. Bethany and Robert were devastated."

CHAPTER FORTY-ONE

$\mathscr{C}$hase cleared his painfully tight throat. "The journal, and Sarah's birthmark, leave little doubt that you're who you say you are. We believe you." Chase's voice faltered. It felt like a raspy-edged peach pit sat lodged inside somewhere between his Adam's apple and lungs. The diary, written by Sarah's mother, was tough for him to hear. What about Jessie? Under the protection of his arm, she quivered uncontrollably. He patted her back and gave a little squeeze. What if they demanded to take Sarah back home with them today? How long did they have? They needed to know. "Don't keep us in suspense any longer. What are your intentions for Sarah?"

Both Stockbridges sat up straight and then looked at each other for several long moments. Bridget stood and came over to them, putting her arm around Jessie. "Didn't Mrs. Hobbs tell you in her letters?" Bridget's face had drained of color and her hands were shaking. "Oh, dear child! We're not here to take Sarah away from you. We just wanted to see her. And, if you are agreeable, meet her, get to know her. She is all we have left in this world since William and I were never able to have children of our own and my sister has passed on."

That was all it took. Jessie turned in Chase's arms and let her tears flow. Months of fear and anticipation came coursing down her face like a great thaw after a long winter, wetting his neck and chest. Chase felt a smile stretching across his face. He looked up at the old woman and wanted to kiss her.

He rocked Jessie from side to side. "Uh, just give her a minute. She's been awfully upset these last few months."

Jessie sat back and used Bridget's hankie again, drying her eyes, and then gave her nose a good, hard blow. Even with watery eyes, tearstained cheeks, and a nose that would rival the darkest cherry on her tree, she looked beautiful. Soft. Lovely.

Mrs. Stockbridge turned back to her husband, her eyes sparking with anger. "Why would that woman mislead them in such a way? It's terrible—inexcusable. I have a good mind to take this matter up when we get home. It's the most unfeeling thing I can think of to do to a mother. Threaten to take her child away."

"Where is your home?" Chase asked. He wanted to give Jessie time to pull herself together.

William sat forward, now totally at ease. "We're Virginians, actually. Bridget and I were both born and raised in Westmoreland County, the birthplace of George Washington," he said with great pride. A warm glow in his eyes made Chase like this man very much. "Then after we married, we moved to Richmond, where I set up my medical practice."

"You're a doctor?" Jessie, now composed, tried a wobbly smile. Bridget had reclaimed her spot next to William.

"I am. A surgeon. I still practice, but with my advancing age I find myself lecturing more and cutting less. I enjoy the medical students very much."

Love beamed from the little woman's face. "Don't let my husband fool you. He's highly respected. He's done some amazing surgeries that were thought near impossible." She reached over and patted his hands, a gesture Chase was getting used to seeing. "He's the most amazing man I've ever known."

"And you, my dear, are an amazing woman. She's worked on the hospital committee for twenty-five years, been the annual bazaar chairwoman innumerable times for our church, taking on all that entails."

"That's nothing," Bridget said softly.

"And she's been an active member of the women's suffrage movement since I can remember. It's been, and still is, a long, hard struggle."

Revived, Jessie now sat straighter. "We have the vote here in Wyoming. Since December 10, 1869."

"That's so," Chase added. "But I heard it wasn't in an effort to give women a voice, just necessary to get some to come to this wild, wide-open territory."

Bridget giggled and pointed a finger at him. "Whatever the reasons, young man, it's made your territory a better place."

Chase nodded. "I agree wholeheartedly." He glanced at Jessie, thinking how alone she'd been in her little Wyoming cabin in Valley Springs. "I wouldn't have it any other way. I'm hoping for statehood soon. Governor Hoyt believes we're moving in that direction."

A commotion outside brought Chase to his feet. "I'll see what that is."

Before he made it to the door, Sarah burst through, her braids flying behind her, and she ran to Jessie and threw herself into her mother's arms. "Mommy! Mommy! Shane got stung by a bee!"

Both William and Bridget sat transfixed. The looks on their faces made Chase tear up himself, and he had to wipe his eyes with the back of his hand. Jessie was holding Sarah, probably longer than the current bee catastrophe called for, but he knew it was really the long-percolating threat of losing her daughter that made his wife so sentimental now.

The moment Gabe came through the door, Shane, who he held in his arms, reached for Chase. Jake was close behind. The toddler blinked tear-filled eyes several times before he launched into another round of sobs. "Arm, my arm," he said, pointing to a red swollen blotch above his elbow. "Hurts…"

"I'm sorry, Jessie," Gabe said. "We should have watched him better. It all happened so quickly."

Jake twisted his hat in his palms, and concern pulled the corners of his mouth sharply.

Everyone stood. "It's not your fault," Jessie said. "We've all been stung before. I'd like you to meet William and Bridget Stockbridge. *Family* from Virginia." She winked at the boys' confused looks.

She took Sarah by her small shoulders and turned her toward the waiting couple. "Sarah, this is your uncle, William Stockbridge, and your aunt, Bridget Stockbridge. They have traveled many, many miles to meet you."

Sarah, not really understanding what was going on, tilted her head back against Jessie's tummy and looked up at her with all the love in the world. Jessie smiled and then let her gaze touch each face until it came to Jake's, where it stopped and lingered. "We're a quilted-together family, some lineages known, some unknown. But whatever our roots, we couldn't have more love and respect for each other if we tried." She glanced over to the Stockbridges. "Welcome."

"Thank you," Bridget whispered between Shane's cries. She took a step toward Sarah. "She's the most beautiful little girl I've ever seen."

"And, of course, I agree with that, my dear. But right now, we have a little patient that needs tending." William slowly walked over to examine Shane's arm. "No stinger. That's good. Jessie, would you happen to have some witch hazel and a little bit of honey?"

When Jessie looked at Chase, he knew everything was going to be all right. Actually, much better than that. Of course they would welcome the Stockbridges into Sarah's life. Both being orphans, he and Jessie longed for any knowledge about their own heritage. To actually have relatives was a great blessing. Jessie must have read his expression because she gave him her special smile before hurrying off to the kitchen.

Bridget called Sarah over, taking something frilly from her handbag. "This is for you, sweetheart," she said. "I made it on our trip out. I hope it will fit." She gently placed a blue velvet bonnet on Sarah's head and carefully tied the bow underneath her chin. "Do you like it?"

Sarah nodded. When she smiled, her missing front tooth made Bridget laugh softly.

"May I give you a hug?"

Chase nodded when Sarah looked for his approval, but he couldn't watch.

He glanced down at Shane after Sarah's aunt wrapped her in her arms and rubbed her cheek across the top of Sarah's head. He felt his face heat up for the hundredth time today and wished Jessie would hurry up with that concoction. Things were getting plenty sentimental out here.

CHAPTER FORTY-TWO

$\mathcal{S}$ince it was Saturday, Thom stayed at the Red Rooster before heading to the livery, ignoring the dizziness that had seemed to plague him since Rome's arrest. He had too many tasks to fulfill to worry about that or the headache that had gripped him last night. His symptoms would pass. They always did. With the new plaster-flour mixture Hannah had invented, he went around patching cracks in the inn's chink, which had made the place drafty. Now, with the warm weather, it didn't seem so important, but once winter rolled around and snow started to fall, Mrs. Hollyhock would feel a difference.

Would he still be here by then? A hollow feeling pressed in his belly. He was restless. Needed a plan. Seemed with the catching of the rustlers last night, and then Albert offering him a job, a burning need to know what the future held was nipping at his heels.

He paused and gazed out the kitchen window. Mrs. Hollyhock made her way around the chicken coop, tossing cracked corn to her pets. Thom smiled. Ivan lay by the wire fence, chin on paws, gazing in.

She turned, then waved. Thom went to the front window and looked out. Hannah, with Markus in hand, rounded the corner. Hannah let go, and Markus ran into the coop. The two women talked for a moment, and then Hannah headed for the inn.

"Good morning," she said, smiling. "Violet said you were here." She came up and gave him a hug and peck on the cheek. "Actually, so did Win."

"You looking for me?"

"Of course." She looked around the room. "The place looks nice. I'm glad you're here with Violet. I worry about her being out here alone. Are the railroad men still here?"

Thom shook his head. Hannah looked different. As always, she was pretty as a picture and smelled incredibly good, but there was just something different in her eyes. Something he couldn't make out.

"Do you have a moment to visit? I have a little while before Susanna needs me at the restaurant."

"Sure." He set the pot of plaster on the counter by the stove.

She went to the sofa and sat down. He followed suit. The room seemed darker than usual this morning; he squinted, trying to see what she had in her hands.

"What's that?" he asked, trying to ignore her close proximity and her light, clean scent.

"A little something from my mother. It's good for headaches like the one that came over you when we were talking the other night. It's a powder she sends for back east." Her long eyelashes lowered over the softness of her cheek as she glanced down at the packet in her hands.

He couldn't help but cock his brow. "You sure it's safe? It might be her way of getting rid of me once and for all."

Hannah laughed, her eyes sparkling. "Now, don't be so hard on her. I thought it was thoughtful."

He took the small white packet and turned it over in his hands. Grains of powder slipped around inside, reminding him of sand.

"You just mix it in a tall glass of water."

"Fine. Next time I have a headache I'll give it a try."

Hannah cleared her throat and sat up a little straighter. "Thom, Albert told me about what happened yesterday. How you tricked Rome Littleton into confessing. How he cleared your name. How the Logans got their bull back thanks to you." She raised her eyebrows. "How you used *my* wallpaper biscuit paste to make hoofprint molds of his horse."

His cheeks warmed. He had hoped that silly fact would stay between the men who had been out at South Fork. "There's more of it in that bowl." He pointed to the counter. "I'm finding lots of things it's useful for."

"Albert also told me he offered you Dwight's job." A moment passed as she studied his face. "Are you going to take it?"

As appealing as it sounded, he knew he couldn't. What if he dropped dead at some critical moment and an innocent person was hurt, or even killed? Everything in his life revolved around that darn bullet. He cursed the day he'd taken it and lived.

"No. It's not for me." He'd told Albert in private last night. He couldn't risk it. Besides, he needed to put space between him and Hannah. He'd let slip to his friend that he'd marry Hannah in a second if he was whole. More than anything he wanted a normal life; he'd risk *anything* for it, but he couldn't risk damaging her.

She sat back into the sofa, causing little specks of dust to pop up and float around in a beam of sunshine streaming through the window. Her eyes were searching. "Why not? You're perfect for it. The townspeople, if you're worried about them, surely can't object now that Rome admitted your innocence."

Thom looked away. "I'm thinking about visiting Anne Marie. Now that I've cleared our family name as much as I can, I think that's what I should do."

Hannah's face blanched. "Why?" she finally said. "Everyone here loves you. You're making a home. I'll miss you. Markus will miss you. Please tell me you're not serious." She reached out a hand. "I *love* you," she whispered. "Doesn't that make any difference to you at all?"

The affection shining in Hannah's eyes made it impossible not to see how much his constant rejection was hurting her. She was bound to whittle him down sooner or later and he'd admit his feelings. It would be so easy to fall into her waiting arms and spend the rest of his life there. He needed to put a stop to it.

Reaching out, he cradled her cheek in the palm of his hand. "Hannah."

She pulled away from him. Her chin lifted. "I can understand your wanting to see Anne Marie. Are you planning a visit or staying for good?"

"Just don't know."

"I see." She stood and he followed. Her face was an unreadable mask. "When?"

"Next week."

"Well, that's just *fine* with me, Thom Donovan. I should have known. You're as stubborn now as you've—"

"Hey, hey, hey," he said softly. With his finger, he tipped her chin toward him. "Let's not say anything that we'll later regret. If truth be told, you're the finest thing that has ever happened to me. If it weren't for you, I'd have moved on long ago."

Her eyes gazed up at him—eyes that could challenge him and comfort him and dissolve his heart with just a glance. He knew he shouldn't, but he couldn't stay the words from crossing his lips. "I'm going to miss you, Hannah. Markus, too. More than you could ever know." Sick and tired of hiding his feelings, he pulled her into his arms. His lips found hers. Warm and pliant, they tasted of sassafras, smiles, and growing old together. He thought he'd die from the pleasure.

"Oh, Hannah," he murmured against her hair, "I love *you*. It feels so good to finally say it. It's been inside me for so long. I've loved you for as long as I can remember." Her response was instantaneous, pulling him close, running her hands up his chest and through his hair. Her need seemed as great as his.

When she pulled away, he tucked her head into the curve of his neck. This was their moment. There wouldn't be another. He wanted to savor it for as long as possible.

"Why? Why didn't you tell me?" Her whispered plea almost broke his heart.

"Back then, well, I never felt good enough for you. We were very poor. Your mother never let me forget our differences. Loathed the ground I walked on, actually. And then Levi happened. I had to go away."

Hannah tangled her fingers through his and brought them up to her lips. She kissed softly, sweetly. "Mother doesn't run my life. I'm a grown woman, free to choose whomever I want. You and I, we have our chance now."

He kissed the top of her hair, searching for words that didn't sound foolish. "I'm sorry, Hannah. There are reasons I can't explain, that I won't share because they don't change anything. It just can't be between us. That's all."

Hannah pulled back, looking up into his face, her confusion and frustration evident. "Even after this? Even though you love me?"

He shook his head slowly.

She stared. He couldn't tell if she was raging mad or if her heart was shattering into a million pieces, like his. She pulled away, crossed the room, and picked up her bag.

"I won't listen to you another second, Thom! You say one thing but mean another. You don't make sense." Her face flushed as she searched his eyes. "You're afraid. You won't admit it to yourself, and I can't fight what I don't know. Please, just tell me what's really going on!" Tears threatened to spill down her cheeks. "I think we're worth that, at least!"

The door opened and Markus tumbled in, followed by Ivan. The boy's face was candy-apple red. "Time to go, Ma," he said, totally missing the intimate way they stood together, the tears glistening in Hannah's eyes. "Church tower is donging eleven."

Hannah forced a smile and reached down to push a strand of hair out of her son's face. "Thank you, sweetheart. You're right. It *is* time to go." She looked Thom straight in the eyes. "It's time to get on with our day and our lives." She went to the door and waited while Markus slung his arms around Ivan's neck and buried his face in the dog's fur.

Mrs. Hollyhock came in and stopped just beyond the threshold, looking back and forth between them. Her hawklike gaze didn't miss a thing. Her eyebrow rose slowly. "Did ya have a nice visit?" she asked. "Or are you bickering again like the brainless birds I have out in that pen?"

Hannah gave her a pained look. "Just business as usual, Violet. Come on, son, say your good-byes." She went over and gave him a peck on the cheek. "Be sure to send a post now and again."

"Well, I just don't know what's wrong with that Irishman," Roberta said to Hannah as they walked across the bridge and past the livery. They turned onto the footpath between the bakery and Dr. Thorn's office and proceeded up the hill toward the little white church. "Except that it's exactly what I've been saying since the moment he came back into this town. He's thick-skulled. Mind like a mule. Gets an idea and there's no changing it." She looked over at Hannah and winked. "We just have to be more clever."

Markus was between them, playing with a cricket he'd found outside their door. The Sunday midmorning air chilled as the sun disappeared behind a billowy white cloud hanging in the sky. It was only a moment before it popped out on the other side with happy golden rays.

"I don't want to change his mind anymore, Mother," she replied softly, feeling mulish herself. No matter what she'd tried that morning, she couldn't fix her puffy red eyes. Anyone who saw her would know she'd been crying. She'd skip church if she hadn't promised to talk with Maude afterward about the coming fall social.

As they approached, several ladies smiled and waved. Buggies and wagons were parked about, and trees were surrounded by horses already sleeping in the sunshine. A mill of voices greeted them as they entered. Roberta led the way to their usual pew halfway up the left side of the nave.

"Hannah," a hushed voice called.

She looked over Markus's head to see Chase and Jessie directly across the aisle. Shane was perched on Jessie's lap. Surprised, she recognized the Stockbridges, the couple she'd met in her restaurant on the day of the railroad celebration, and wondered at the connection. Sarah sat between the old man and woman, looking happy as a chipmunk. Hannah wiggled her fingers. Smiled as best she could.

The small building warmed as the townsfolk all gathered inside. Hannah wished the service would get started so she could get her day over with and get home. Ashamed of herself, she glanced down at Markus sitting next to her, knowing she had much to be thankful for. She needed to pull her emotions together. Stop feeling sorry for herself. The restaurant had record-breaking sales every day now, and she needed to talk with Uncle Frank about the possibility of expanding out back.

Brenna walked past with her scraggly brood. Indeed, Hannah was well-off, and she had just better remember that.

"Can ya scooch over a tad?" someone whispered into her ear.

Violet stood close with a solemn-faced Thom directly behind, hatless and clean-shaven. Their eyes met and held. A burst of butterflies filled her chest. Her lips tingled at the memory of his kiss. She jerked her gaze away.

"Of course," she replied. She gently pushed Markus over toward his grandmother, and Roberta looked over. Her eyes opened, then widened, but she didn't smile. *Oh, she's a cool cucumber when she wants to be*, Hannah thought.

At ten sharp, Reverend Wilbrand greeted his congregation. It was difficult to concentrate on the preacher's words with Thom sitting so close. Without turning her head, Hannah was able to see him struggling to find space in the cramped area for his long legs. Fiddling with his song sheet. Gazing at the ceiling. *We would have been perfect together.* Filled with hurt, and a good measure of anger, she forced her attention away.

Before she knew it, people stood and began the closing hymn. Roberta exited into the main aisle, and Hannah came face-to-face with Jessie.

"Just wait until I tell you our news," Jessie whispered into her ear. Her friend glanced over her shoulder and smiled at the woman who held Sarah's hand. Hannah smiled, too, painfully aware of Thom's tall presence close behind.

Out in the bright sunshine, people gathered in groups. For many, this was the only social time they had each week. Maude hurried over and pushed in between Roberta and Thom, giving Hannah a big smile. Markus had long since run out back with the other children, where laughter sounded from a game of tag.

When the shopkeeper spotted Violet, she pulled up short. "Good morning, Violet," Maude said, nodding to everyone in the group.

"Mornin', Maude," Violet responded. Her taciturn tone could freeze a forest fire.

The innkeeper's attitude was not lost on Maude. "How are those poor little pullets? Still alive?"

Oh, no! If those two got going, Sunday would be ruined. Hannah elbowed her mother into action.

"Mr. Donovan," Roberta said, without missing a beat. "I want to tell you I've had a change of heart."

Hannah almost gasped. What was she up to?

Roberta smiled charmingly. "What you said the other day. I've been thinking."

"About?" Thom asked slowly, carefully. He looked around the small circle of women, clearly uncomfortable.

"The buffalo. I actually believe the idea has merit. Would be beneficial for the town. And, although I sincerely hate to admit it, especially to you, I've grown fond of the aromatic creatures. Particularly the little one."

Thom looked back and forth between the women, skepticism written in his eyes. "That's good to hear. Win's attached to his pets and I'd hate to see—"

Thom's sentence cut off. A look of confusion crossed his face, then his eyes closed and he collapsed to the grassy earth.

CHAPTER FORTY-THREE

$\mathscr{H}$annah dropped to her knees. "Thom," she cried urgently. "Thom!" She stroked his face in an effort to wake him. Something very bad took hold of her heart and squeezed. What was wrong? "Get the doctor!"

Dr. Thorn pushed through the group of women. "What happened?" he asked as he knelt down and picked up Thom's wrist.

"We were talking and he just passed out," Hannah heard her mother say. Hannah hadn't taken her gaze off Thom's face. Crushing fear sliced her heart asunder as a voice whispered in her mind, *Oh, God, don't let Thom die.*

Hannah glanced up when Jessie called her name. Her mother huddled together with Violet and Maude, the three women whiter than a snowy Christmas morning. She scrambled to her feet. "Don't let Thom die!" She looked around wildly. "Please, somebody do something!"

"Get a wagon," Dr. Thorn yelled. "Chase, Jake, Albert! I need some help over here."

Instantly, all the men in the yard hurried over. They carefully lifted Thom's unconscious form into the back of a wagon.

"Has this ever happened before?" Dr. Thorn asked.

Win stepped forward, his brows crinkled together. "I noticed he's been stumbling a lot in the livery the past two days. I wouldn't have thought a thing about it 'cept he dropped a sack of grain on our cat and we laughed about it after we made sure she was unhurt and only mad."

Roberta stepped forward. "What about that draining headache he got at our place last Sunday?"

Hannah nodded. "And I noticed he had a hard time seeing what I had in my hands at the inn," Hannah whispered. It was impossible to keep tears from trickling down her face. "At the time I thought he was just tired from the night before with Rome."

Albert cleared his throat as his face drained of all color. When he looked away, Hannah grabbed his arm. "What? What do you know?"

"In light of all this, I feel I must speak up," he said. "Thom confided in me that he has a bullet lodged in the base of his skull. Got it years ago. He didn't want anyone to know. Didn't want their pity."

Jessie's arms came around Hannah to steady her.

Mr. Stockbridge stepped forward as Gabe climbed into the driver's box. "Drive slowly and take your time," he cautioned. "We don't want to jostle him. Chase, you climb in and hold his head completely still."

Dr. Thorn stood with questions in his eyes.

"We don't have time for proper introductions, Doctor," Mr. Stockbridge said, climbing into a buggy Jake pulled to a stop by his side. "I'm a surgeon visiting from Virginia. We best get that young man down to your office before it's too late."

Thirty minutes later, Hannah, along with what seemed like half the town, filled the waiting room of Dr. Thorn's office. Silence was thick. More people gathered outside in quiet contemplation, waiting for news. Children looked through the window with cupped hands. Reverend Wilbrand sat in the corner, reading the Bible.

The two doctors had promised they'd pass on information as soon as they had any. After a short time in with the doctors, Albert left and returned twenty minutes later, disappearing again into the examination room without an explanation. Every nerve in Hannah's body felt as if they had just gone a round with a meat cleaver. She'd run to the privy several times with an urge to throw up.

The door opened. Albert stuck his head out, looking around the crowded waiting room, down the row of faces. "Hannah," he said softly. "Can we speak with you in here for a moment?"

Feeling as if she were in a cocoon, Hannah stood and walked slowly into the examination room, knowing the worst had come to pass.

Thom had died.

He was gone.

She couldn't breathe. It was as if her heart literally stopped beating. *Thom! Oh, why—why couldn't you tell me? We should have lived each day we had instead of letting happiness slip through our fingers. I'd have loved you no matter what. I'll love you forever...*

Once inside, Albert quietly closed the door behind her. Without asking, she went to Thom's lifeless body stretched out on Dr. Thorn's tall table. She placed her hand on the side of his face, loving everything about him. The men followed her over and circled around.

"I want to tell you what I told the doctors," Albert began. "Yesterday, when I offered Thom the deputy's job, he turned it down flat. Wouldn't even think of taking it. Was afraid something like this would happen at a bad time and didn't want some innocent person to suffer because of it. He also said that it's because of this situation he wasn't able to follow his heart and marry you, Hannah. He was afraid not only of dying, but of becoming an invalid. He didn't want to be a burden."

No! She couldn't hear this! She shook her head softly, never taking her gaze from Thom's face. Dark hair fell over his forehead, drawing her eyes to his dear face, as if he was only asleep. She wanted to lay down next to him, refuse to let him go. She couldn't accept that their chance for love was gone.

Albert touched her hand, regaining her attention. "When he was shot, the doctor who treated him was little more than a self-taught sawbones. At least he had the good sense not to try. Thom healed with the bullet inside and was sent to prison." Albert held up a piece of paper from the telegram office. "This is a response from the doctor in Cripple Creek. Not much to go on, but it's something. More than anything, Thom wanted the bullet out of his head. Wanted his life back. He told me he would risk *anything*, even death, to accomplish it."

Her head jerked up. "He's *not* dead." Her heart welled, and new tears rushed to the surface.

"Oh, sweetheart, no. Unconscious." Albert took her hand. "I'm sorry for scaring you."

"Hannah," Dr. Thorn said. "Thom needs surgery. Dr. Stockbridge is a skilled surgeon with many years of experience. Taking into consideration what the sheriff told us, we feel compelled to try."

Her dry throat felt as if it'd crack. "What are the risks?"

Dr. Thorn shrugged. "Huge, of course. I don't even like to think about them."

Dr. Stockbridge ran his hand over Thom's forehead, then lifted each eyelid and looked closely at each eye. "Mrs. Hoskins, the operation is very chancy. If we move the bullet and are not able to extract it, he could be blind, or never walk or talk again—if it doesn't kill him instantly. However, and let me be clear—if the bullet is *not* taken out, I'm certain he will die soon anyway. Because of the signs and symptoms he's been experiencing, I feel quite certain his time is near. Your choice is to do nothing and hope he wakes up—only to die soon. Or do the surgery now. It may kill him, but it may give him back his life. At least with surgery he has a chance."

Albert cleared his throat. "Knowing you'd be his wife if circumstances were different, we wanted to ask your opinion, Hannah. Can you help us decide what Thom would want?"

The door cracked open, and Roberta cautiously entered. She went to Hannah and turned her into her embrace. Oh, it felt good and warm. She snuggled close, loving her mother now more than she ever had. "What is going on?"

"We're deciding whether the doctors should try to remove the bullet from Thom's skull." The horrible words slid out of Hannah's mouth, almost making her retch. "Either way, he's at death's very door."

Roberta gently set Hannah away and looked into her face. "And what do you think? Would Thom want another chance at life?"

Hannah nodded. "I know he would."

"Then say so. Take charge. That is why the Irish bloke loves you so much, my dear."

Hannah wiped her eyes with the back of her hand and looked at Dr. Stockbridge. "You're right, Mother. Thom deserves this. He served eight years for a crime he never committed. He deserves a little happiness coming his way."

"Good. I think it's a wise choice," Dr. Stockbridge said. "Now, if you two will please wait outside with the rest of the townsfolk."

Hannah stood her ground.

Her mother tugged the sleeve of her dress. "Come on, Hannah, we need to let the doctors get to work."

This is it. The last time I might see—No! She couldn't think like that. She stepped to the table and carefully buried her face in Thom's neck, breathing in his masculine scent. Oh, how she wished she could crawl onto the table and hold him close. Instead, she whispered into his ear, "Come back to me, Thomas Donovan! Do you hear me? Live! Live so we can be a family. I love you. I love you so much it hurts. Don't you dare die on me now, do you hear? Fight for your life!"

"Hannah." Her mother was waiting for her at the door.

"This will take several hours," Dr. Thorn said. "You're tired. It might be best for you to go on home, get some rest. You'll be the first—"

"I'll be right outside, Doctor."

CHAPTER FORTY-FOUR

*E*verything hurt. From the bottom of his feet to the top of his head. A dull, ripping pain slipped up Thom's body and then dribbled back down, sizzling as it went. Woozy spins kept him confused.

If only he could get that annoying mosquito out of his face. Murmured voices wafted across the room. If he weren't so blasted bone-weary spent, he'd ask whoever it was chattering in the corner to come kill it. Lifting his arm seemed as difficult as lifting a team of draft horses. He struggled to open his eyes, but as with his arm, both lids felt like sheets of lead.

Where was he? What was that strange aroma? Someone was definitely here with him, he was sure; unless the ringing in his head was more misperception and he was hearing it as voices. Voices all around. But not a chance of making out any of the words.

Thom felt someone's presence next to him. He fought to open his eyes.

"Thom, can you hear me?"

A man. He'd heard the voice before but couldn't place it. "Thom, try to say something. Squeeze my fingers." Warm fingers slipped into his palm.

Thom squeezed; at least he thought he did. Panic surged into his throat. Nothing happened. Again he told his hand to crush the fingers he felt wiggling in his palm. "Come on, Thom. By now, you should have some strength back. Give it another try."

My God!

The bullet. It had moved.

The nightmare had come to pass.

Nooooo, his mind screamed. He wanted to shriek for life's injustice. He searched his mind. Tried to find the last thing he remembered. When? How? Nothing. His life was now a black, mysterious void. Everything gone.

No. Wait. If everything was gone, he wouldn't remember the bullet. It took so much energy just trying to remember. *Oh, Lord, help me* was his last thought before drifting off…

The familiar female humming slowly came into his awareness, and again Thom wondered who it was. A thump and then a scraping noise sounded to his right.

"I'm only going to leave this window open a moment, Thom. Just enough to freshen up the room. The cold air will do you good."

Snow!

Cold, crisp, clean.

"No back talk," the person said and then chuckled. His shoulders were lifted. Warm liquid placed in his mouth. Reflex made him swallow. The spoon was back, and he swallowed again. Several more times. A sound reached his ears, and he realized it was his own groan. "Only three more and I'll let you lay back." A towel at his chin wiped away a bit of liquid that had escaped over his lip.

"Good boy. I think you're getting stronger. Now, lay back and relax, it's time for a bath."

His covers came off with a whoosh, and the air swirled up his body, causing gooseflesh.

He liked it. Something different. He heard a bang. Wondered what it was.

"Mother, I'm home," a distant voice called.

Hannah!

"I'll be down in a moment, dear. I've just finished giving Mr. Donovan's limbs a good stretching, and now he's having a bath and shave. Getting all spruced up for Thanksgiving. You stay downstairs."

My God.

Roberta.

Taking care of him as if he were a baby.

November crept by, followed by December. Hannah hurried around the parlor, preparing for the company she expected to knock at any time. Every few minutes she stopped to gaze at the striking Christmas tree the Logans had dropped off yesterday. It was lofty, almost ten feet tall. When Uncle Frank helped Markus place the star tonight, it might even touch the ceiling.

She tossed a misplaced pillow onto the sofa and found a forgotten sock underneath. Straightening a tintype of Caleb on the mantel made her think of Dwight and how he'd been cleared of any suspicion of being in league with the rustlers. Last month he'd left for New Meringue, where he planned to open a saloon.

"It's beautiful," her mother said, coming into the room. She glided over and slid her arm around Hannah's waist. They stood in silence for a few moments looking at the tree.

"Everything is ready, and the table is set. It's going to be a lovely Christmas Eve," Roberta said softly.

Hannah nodded and smiled. She didn't want to put a damper on the party. The months since Thom's operation had drawn by slowly. She wanted him back.

"Susanna is bringing the plum pudding," Hannah replied. Her mother already knew that, but it was the only thing she could think of to say.

Roberta touched her head to Hannah's. "Stop worrying so much," she whispered. "He's getting stronger all the time." She gave a sad little chuckle. "More often than not, he resists my efforts. You know, those arm and leg stretches Dr. Thorn insisted were to be done twice a day." She gently took Hannah's chin, making her daughter look at her. "I always said he was a fighter, and it's true. He's fighting back now—and that's good."

Laughter and a loud knock on the door drew them apart.

"Markus," Hannah called. "Company's here!" Rapid-fire boot heels descended the stairs, echoing through the room.

Hannah looked at her mother. "Still running."

Roberta responded, with a melancholy smile, "I'm just glad he's able to."

Two hours later, with a delicious dinner finished and the tree almost decorated, Hannah tousled Markus's hair. "It's lovely, son. Should Uncle Frank help you set the star?"

Before the child answered, another knock rattled the front door.

"I wonder who that could be," Frank said, striding to the entry. He opened to a bluster of wind and snowflakes. A group stood outside, wrapped in big coats, scarves, and hats. Hannah, and the rest, gathered around the door.

"It came upon a midnight clear,
That glorious song of old,
From angels bending near the earth,
To touch their harps of gold..."

Hannah couldn't sing. Her heart shuddered with sadness and felt as if it would shatter into a million pieces. All her friends were here. The Logans and Gabe. Brenna and her brood. Win. Nell and her brother, Seth. Reverend Wilbrand. Dr. Thorn. Even Violet and Maude seemed to have made peace, at least for tonight. Lorna

Brinkley and her husband waved from the side, a beautiful skirt made from expensive fabric hanging below her coat. A couple stood far in the back, and Hannah had to strain to see Jake with his arm around Daisy.

Hannah willed a smile onto her face and happiness into her heart. These were wonderful friends. Good people. Oh, how she wished she felt their joy.

The song ended. Markus ran out and took Sarah's hand, pulling her into the room.

Roberta clapped her hands. "My brilliant grandson, that's a wonderful idea. Please, everyone come in and get warm. We have hot apple cider and lots of dessert!"

"We can't," Maude called out. "We have several more houses to visit. But thank you all—"

"Do you have time for one more carol?" Hannah asked, finding her voice around her sorrow.

"Of course!" Win's smile lit up the night.

She opened the door wider. "In here. Upstairs for Thom."

Everyone looked around. "We're pretty wet, Hannah," Dr. Thorn said.

"We don't mind, do we, Mother?"

Roberta hurried to take Win's arm. "Of course not. Please come in."

Jessie came in first. "That's a fine idea. Everyone be sure to wipe on the rug as you enter."

It took a few minutes for the group to crowd into Thom's bedroom and circle his bed. Ivan got up from where he slept and moved closer to the bed. Markus squirmed in close and took Thom's hand into his small one and stroked it, as he did often.

"What shall we sing fer our sweet Thom?" Violet's voice faltered. Her loving gaze almost did Hannah in.

Hannah thought a moment. "I think he'd like 'Silent Night.'"

Reverend Wilbrand hummed one long note so everyone could hear. The group started very softly at first. Again, it was impossible for Hannah to sing. Her throat burned as she held back her tears.

When they started the second verse, Hannah glanced up at the singers. Chase's lips wobbled uncontrollably as he gazed at Thom's face. Win had stopped singing completely. His eyes were clenched tight and tears trickled silently down his cheeks. Daisy had turned toward Jake's shoulder, hiding her face. Hannah needed to get the group back out into the cold before they were all overcome with grief. This was Christmas Eve. A night of miracles, not sadness. As soon as they were finished, she would see them out.

Opposite Markus, Hannah took Thom's other hand and kissed the back of it. "Merry Christmas, darling," she whispered. "Come back to me. I love you." Unable to stop the tears a moment longer, she shut her eyes, offering up a silent prayer.

"Look!" Markus yelled, his shrill alarm startling them all. He pointed straight at Thom's face.

Everyone stopped singing.

Thom's eyes fluttered once. Twice. Then opened completely. He took in the sight for a few moments, then the corners of his lips slowly tipped up. Ivan woofed and wagged his tail.

Hannah dropped to her knees and buried her face against Thom's chest, breathing in his scent. His arm moved over her. He was as weak as a newborn, but he was finally coming around.

Chase and Jessie stepped back, letting Dr. Thorn get to the side of the bed. He felt Thom's pulse and looked into his eyes. "Can you speak? Can you tell me your name?"

Thom stroked the back of Hannah's hair. She felt a rumble in his chest before the words came out of his mouth.

"Yes. I. Can. Doc." His voice was soft. Raspy.

Everyone gasped. Then cheered.

"Thomas Winslow Donovan. Irish, twenty-three years old, deputy sheriff of Logan Meadows, in love with my soon-to-be wife, Hannah May Hoskins, and father to my soon-to-be son, Markus Hoskins." He took a deep breath. "My dog is named Ivan. And you, Win, were singing out of—"

"Praise God!" Reverend Wilbrand exclaimed. The smile on Dr. Thorn's face said it all.

Hannah gazed into Thom's face. Held his cheek in her palm. He reached up and brushed away her tears with his thumb. All the nights she'd sat by his bedside or crawled into bed next to him, praying, begging God to bring him back. This was the most wonderful Christmas present she'd ever received.

"I love you," she whispered. "I have since forever. Nothing, and no one, not even a million years will ever change that. In *sickness* and in health," she stressed. "Good times *and* in bad."

His lips trembled as he said hoarsely, "I was a senseless fool to think a piece of metal could keep us apart. It's you who makes me whole, Hannah, you and Markus. And whether it's trouble or just my own fears, I promise you, I'll never run away again."

Don't miss more heartfelt romance by Caroline Fyffe!
Three days are all she asks of him. Three days to ignite a love
neither of them ever imagined possible…

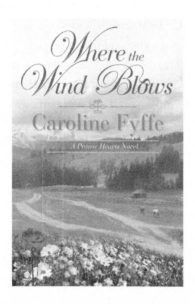

"A sweet Americana western…Here is the type of story readers
reach for when they need to be uplifted."—*Romantic Times*

Available now on Amazon.com

ACKNOWLEDGMENTS

*F*irst, a huge debt of gratitude goes to my phenomenal editor, Caitlin Alexander, for her countless wonderful suggestions, gentle nudges, and encouraging me always onward. Working with her was a joy from beginning to end and I feel so blessed to have had the opportunity.

To Gene Harm, for the crackling fires, gallons of savory coffee, and plethora of uniquely creative ideas.

To Pam Berehulke, Leslie Lynch, Sandy Loyd, and Lisa Tapp, for your time and talent.

Never to forget my wonderful readers! Thank you from the bottom of my heart!

And as always, much love and gratitude go to my husband, Michael, and sons, Matthew and Adam, for their support and encouragement.

ABOUT THE AUTHOR

Photo by The Family Gallery, 2007

*C*aroline Fyffe was born in Waco, Texas, the first of many towns she would call home during her father's career with the US Air Force. A horse aficionado from an early age, she earned a Bachelor of Arts in communications from California State University–Chico before launching what would become a twenty-year career as an equine photographer. She began writing fiction to pass the time during long days in the show arena, channeling her love of horses and the Old West into a series of Western historicals. Her debut novel, *Where the Wind Blows*, won the Romance Writers of America's prestigious Golden Heart Award as well as the Wisconsin RWA's Write Touch Readers' Award. She and her husband have two grown sons and live in Kentucky.

Made in the USA
Coppell, TX
28 November 2022

87311875R00173